SPEAK NO EVIL

OTHER BOOKS BY LIANA GARDNER

7th Grade Revolution
The Journal of Angela Ashby

AWARDS

Speak No Evil
Finalist in Young Adult Fiction
2019 International Book Awards

7th Grade Revolution
Silver Medal in Middle Grade Fiction
2018 Nautilus Book Awards

Winner in Best Use of Social Media in a Book
2018 Digital Book World Awards

Winner in Pre-Teen Fiction (Ages 10-12)
2018 American Fiction Awards

Finalist in Juvenile Fiction
2018 Silver Falchion Awards

Finalist in Best Book (Children's)
2018 Digital Book World Awards

Finalist in Children's Fiction
2018 International Book Awards

Honorable Mention in Children's Fiction
2018 Hollywood Book Festival

The Journal of Angela Ashby
Finalist in Juvenile / Young Adult
2019 Silver Falchion Awards

Honorable Mention in Children's Fiction
2018 Hollywood Book Festival

Early Praise
Nautilus Book Awards Winning Author

"... suspense and intrigue ... Melody's story is grim, but hope is weaved in throughout ... highly emotional." *~School Library Journal*

"Gardner tackles difficult topics, including bullying and abuse of all types, in a way that is both artistic, respectful … [and] masterfully written." *~BookTrib*

"… a touching tribute to the power of love, faith and steadfast, patient kindness to heal the damage done by human cruelty and thoughtlessness." *~IndieReader*

"… a very powerful novel that depicts the cruelty and injustice of the world while also highlighting the ever-present beauty that few see when struggling with dark issues. The book displays the power that love and music have even in the darkest of times. Gardner does an excellent job of portraying a teenage worldview while focusing on adult concepts." *~ US Review of Books*

"There are too many Melody Fisher's in our homes and schools who lock themselves away in a world where they are both desperate to be heard and afraid to speak up … *Speak No Evil* is their story. A brilliant and novel approach to addressing important social issues." **~Viga Boland, Author of *No Tears for my Father***

"… alternately beautiful and troubling—and a totally compelling read … Gardner's characters are finely drawn and credible, and her plot is so relevant considering the thousands of children lost in the foster care system and at the mercy of those charged to care for them." **~Jack Magnus, *Readers' Favorite***

"… Melody's silence signifies the way some women feel about sharing their stories with other people, and how difficult it is to overcome the desire to retreat. I urge others to read it; the story of Melody and her bravery will speak to you and stay with you for quite some time." **~Tracy Young, Bulgarian Review**

"Any victim of abuse, or those who blame themselves for events out of their control, needs to read this novel … This book should be in every school library and youth centre. I cannot recommend it highly enough." **~Lesley Jones, UK author**

"WOW! Just WOW! Gardner is a great author telling a story of death, sorrow, and so much more. You will fall in love with Melody … You will feel her sorrow … You will feel her shame … you will feel everything with this character. A MUST read that will make you sit and think well after you turned the last page." **~Bookworm Tri-Cities, Bookstore**

Recommended for the INDIE NEXT LIST
IndieReader Approved

SPEAK NO EVIL

LIANA GARDNER

Original Song Lyrics: Lucas Astor

Speak No Evil

Original cover art by Marcela Bolívar
http://www.marcelabolivar.com/about/
Title treatment and cover design by Michael J. Canales
http://www.MJCImageworks.com

Public Domain works included in *Speak No Evil*:
Do Not Stand At My Grave And Weep—Mary Frye (1922)
"Amazing Grace"—John Newton (1779)
"His Eye is on the Sparrow"— Civilla D. Martin (1905)

ISBN: 978-1-944109-36-3

Published by Vesuvian Books
www.vesuvianbooks.com

Printed in the United States of America
10 9 8 7 6 5 4 3 2 1

To all those like Melody who need time to find their voice.
And to those who believe in them and don't give up.

TRUTH IS THE HARBINGER OF HELL.

Sixteen is a pivotal age, stranded in the badlands somewhere between the dreams of childhood and the realities of adulthood. At sixteen, the proclaimed worst moment of your life might be superficial, like not being asked to the prom by the right person, or something much darker, which causes your soul to scream in anguish. Your emotions range from ecstasy to despair, hitting every note in between along the way.

At sixteen, some still wear the mask of innocence, while others toss off the mask to glare at the world through experience-weary eyes.

~ Melody Fisher, Valedictorian, Laurel High

CHAPTER ONE

December 22, 2014 – Melody, age 15

The door swung open and a broad-shouldered officer pulled a skinny woman toward the front desk by her bony elbow. The officer jerked his thumb toward Melody. "Why isn't she in a holding cell?"

The cop behind the desk looked up from the document he'd been flipping through. "Her social worker is on the way and said she'd raise holy hell if we put her in a holding cell with adults since she's a minor."

The uniformed cop's belt creaked as he shifted his weight. "She stabbed Troy Alexander, for chrissake. Doesn't stabbing a classmate make her a danger to society?"

As if on command, the TV in the lobby switched to breaking news. The reporter stood outside Mercy Hospital.

"Turn it up, I wanna hear this." The officer smoothed the sides of his nearly shaved head. "My little brother played a year or two with Troy, and he said he was one of the best players he's ever known."

The reporter stared at the camera with a subdued expression. "We have received the following update on good authority. Troy Alexander will be released from the hospital shortly. And your best local news team is on the spot ready to bring you up-to-the-minute information."

The TV cut away to a commercial. The woman at the counter cracked her gum. "Really? Some kid getting released from the hospital is breaking news?"

The officer squared his shoulders. "That shows how much you know." He sneered at her. "Troy Alexander is the hottest prospect coming out of

Asheville in years. All the college coaches across the nation are drooling over the chance to get him to play for them."

She shrugged. "It's just a game."

The cop's face turned red. "Just a game! I'll have you know…" He pointed a stubby finger at Melody. "… if she'd hurt him any worse, we'd have to put on extra officers, and take her into protective custody because there'd be a lynch mob forming outside the station."

The news came back on and Troy exited through the double doors. "The doc says I should rehab for a week, but I'll be ready to play in the big game two weeks from now."

Melody turned away and her body shook. She plugged her ears and rocked.

The uniformed officer put his hand on the wall behind Melody and lowered his face to hers. "You're lucky, kid. If his football career had been ruined, the folks around here would want your head on a platter. No amount of whining about being an orphan and the hard life you've had would matter for spit."

The doors swung open again.

"Officer, I believe you should take a step or two back." Miss Prescott hauled her purse to her shoulder. "You wouldn't want to deal with a misconduct charge for intimidation of a minor."

She went straight up to the desk. "You have a room where I can speak with Melody in private?"

The desk cop pulled out a set of keys. "Marv, can you please take them to room six? Although, I don't know what good it'll do. She hasn't made a sound since we brought her in."

Miss Prescott ignored him. "Melody, come on. We have some things to discuss."

Melody followed Miss Prescott and the uniformed cop down the hallway. He opened a door to a small room containing nothing but a table and a couple of chairs inside.

Miss Prescott put her oversized purse on the table with a thunk. She arched a brow over her hazel eyes. "You can close the door on your way out, Officer." She pulled back a chair and sat.

She patted the table. "Come on, Melody. Take a seat. We have a few things to cover." Brushing her red hair out of her eyes with one hand, she rummaged in her purse and pulled out a file folder with the other.

Melody sat and buried her face in her hands.

Miss Prescott reached across the table, touched Melody's arm, and her voice softened. "Don't worry, honey. I've known you for nearly half your life at this point. And I know you would have had a good reason for what you did."

Melody raised her eyes to stare into Miss Prescott's.

"I'm telling you the truth. With all you've gone through in your life with the stoicism of a rock, it breaks my heart to know you had to go through something so awful, you snapped." She opened the folder and pinched the bridge of her nose. "I'm sorry it took me so long to get here, but I had to get as much done as I could during business hours." She flipped through the top few pages. "It took some fast talking, but I convinced the judge juvenile hall or a jail cell would be the worst place for you."

Melody straightened.

"He wouldn't agree to your continuing in the public school system, so you'll have to be homeschooled." She blew a pesky strand of hair out of the way. It floated up and settled back in the same place. "The next hurdle was your current foster placement. As soon as they heard the news, they contacted me to say they would no longer have you stay under their roof."

Melody stared past Miss Prescott's shoulder at the patch on the wall where the paint had peeled. The paint had faded so much, the missing strip barely showed.

"Because they refused to have you come back to their home, I picked up your things. I have them in the car." Her face flushed. "I am very sorry to say several people I contacted had heard the news and flat out refused to take you in. But I did find a temporary placement for you."

Melody rolled her eyes.

Miss Prescott held up her hand. "I know, I know. I've said those words too many times to you. I'm not going to lie … this time the temporary placement may be long-term. At least until we get this situation straightened out."

She reached across the table again and held Melody's hand. "You haven't said a word for almost two years. Not even in therapy."

Melody's hand trembled.

"Honey, if ever there was a time to talk, now is it."

Melody pulled her hand back from Miss Prescott's grasp and tucked it under her arm to hide the shakes she couldn't control.

"Oh, sweetie." A tear rolled down Miss Prescott's cheek. "We're going to get this taken care of, and I'll be here the whole way for you."

CHAPTER TWO

February 23, 2008 – Melody, age 9

Daddy stopped and raised his hand in the air as the sun crested the peak on Grandfather Mountain. The signal for me to follow silently at a distance. He stepped forward through the frosted brush underfoot, making no noise, while I shivered in the early morning chill. My breath made puffy clouds as I exhaled.

A small creek lay ahead on the Nuwati Trail. Daddy said the Nuwati was our best bet because the piles of rocks and fallen tree limbs off the trail were used for shelter. Before he got too far in front of me, I took a step. Dead leaves crunched under my boot.

Daddy's head snapped in my direction and he raised a forefinger to his lips.

My shoulders slumped. I had forgotten to look for leaves. I'd never be able to walk as quietly as he could, no matter how hard I tried. 'Specially in boots.

My first hunt and already I'd messed up. I'd begged him to take me and had to promise to be quiet when we got close.

For one scary moment, I'd thought Mama wasn't gonna let me go. She hadn't been sure she wanted her *little* girl to go out on a hunt. I'd reminded her I wasn't little. At nine, I was nearly in double digits. But she insisted I'd always be her little Melody.

I concentrated on walking silently, following the steps Daddy had taught me.

Crouch.

Check for leaves.

Sweep any twigs to the side.

Heel first then roll to the toe.

Shift weight forward and repeat.

Looking up, I had to bite my tongue to keep from calling out. I couldn't move fast and quiet at the same time. In a few steps, the brush would swallow Daddy and I wouldn't know where he'd gone.

Wait, Daddy. I'm not with you.

How could he move so fast and so quietly at the same time, especially carrying the heavy diesel tank on his back? I had an empty can and I made a lot more noise.

Fortunately, before he disappeared, he stopped and checked over his shoulder. He waited for me to catch up and I remembered to keep my pace slow so I wouldn't make noise. When I got to within ten paces of him, he moved forward again.

As Daddy rounded a curve, he stopped and held out his hand, palm facing me. The signal for me to stop and wait. I placed the empty can on the ground and gently lowered the handle so it didn't clank against the side. The breeze blew a loose strand of black hair across my cheek. I tucked it behind my ear as I straightened.

Inhaling the musty scent of the fallen leaves, I wanted to remember everything about this day. The way the sunlight shone through naked branches and remaining leaves on the trees. The toasty feeling of huddling inside my coat with a beanie keeping my head and ears warm. Even my frozen fingers and nose.

Daddy reached behind his back for the wand and pointed it toward a black hole in the rocks. He flipped the switch on the tank and pulled the trigger. The liquid sprayed all over the ground and rocks before Daddy stuck the nozzle into the hole. Diesel fumes smothered the woodsy scent in the air.

Snake after snake slithered out of the opening. My eyes opened wide. I'd never seen so many in one place. Some snakes were a grayish-brown with black jagged bands—canebrake rattlers. Others were tan or orangish with pinkish-tan bands edged in dark brown—copperheads. One copperhead, so big it filled the entire opening, stopped halfway out and tested the air with its tongue. The canebrakes were longer, but the copperhead dwarfed them. Once outside, the snakes weren't sure where to go. Their heads swiveled from one side to the other and their tongues licked the diesel-filled air.

"Melody!"

I took off for the creek as Daddy had made me promise. Twigs snapped and cracked as I raced toward the water's edge. Dead leaves rustled and rattles sounded behind me. Panting, I reached the bank and turned to look.

Less confused, the snakes were slithering away from Daddy. He had a big canebrake caught in the snake-stick.

"Get in the water."

I shook my head. "But they don't scare me."

"Melody." Daddy's tone told me not to argue. He put the snake in the can I had carried.

A canebrake and a copperhead reached the bank as I backed into the water. The grayish-brown canebrake rattler on the left curled and rose into striking position. It swayed with its head almost as high as my chin. I stared into its yellow eyes. Was I in striking distance?

Before the sliver of fear could grow, I opened my mouth and sang.

Rattlesnake, rattlesnake, I fear you none
Crawling beneath, the moon and sun
Show me no harm, under the sky
I will show no fear, though afraid to die

The rattle vibrated against the ground. Staying as still as possible, I sang the words as they came from my heart.

On your belly, slither on by
Rattlesnake don't bite, don't make me cry
The hills are full, in the green green grass

Please leave me be, let me pass

The copperhead slowed its approach then stopped at the water's edge. The snake poised to strike, swayed with the music and lowered to the ground. Its rattle stilled as I sang on.

Snakes slithering away from Daddy changed course and came toward the two in front of me. I wanted to laugh. I'd never given a concert to snakes before. They kept coming until the entire nest curled together in front of me.

Rattlesnake, rattlesnake, I fear you none
Crawling beneath, the moon and sun
Show me no harm, under the sky
I will show no fear, though afraid to die

Daddy walked silently behind the snakes. "Be still, baby. I'll get them as quickly as I can."

I didn't want him to hurt them. And they wouldn't do anything as long as I sang to them. So I sang to Daddy. "*I'm fine. They're not going to hurt me. They like my song.*"

He nodded then circled past the large nest of pit vipers in front of me and entered the stream.

The ground is yours, you own the dirt
Your poison, your venom, I know would hurt
So with you in mind, at night I pray
Rattlesnake grant me, another day

"Keep singing and wait for me to come behind you." Daddy's words were soft but clipped, like when he got upset.

I didn't know why. It's not like I hadn't been around snakes from the time I was a baby. He and Mama handled them every week at church.

As I repeated the chorus, he glided through the creek toward me. Slowly. He might spook the snakes if he moved too fast. But they had all calmed down. They wouldn't hurt me.

From behind, he lifted me straight out of the water and strode down the center of the creek.

After moving ten feet from where we had been, I twisted toward him and he hugged me tight.

"Stop singing or they might follow." His breath caught in his throat and he squished me tighter. "I've never seen anything like that in my life."

"Daddy, I can't breathe."

"I'm sorry, honey." His grip loosened and he gave a weak chuckle. "I'm so glad you're safe."

I put my hands on his cheeks and gazed into his dark eyes. "I was always safe, Daddy. They wouldn't hurt me. They came for the concert."

He made a sound between a cough and a laugh. "Well, my crooner, I think it's best to keep the snake concert between you and me, or your mother won't allow you to come on a hunt ever again." He hugged me tighter. "Where did you learn the song?"

"I didn't learn it, I just sang it." I nestled my cheek against his. "I remembered the story you told me about when Chief Yellow Snake died and the words came out."

Daddy carried me out of the creek, set me down, and took my hand.

I kicked my boot through the leaves. "Can I ask you a question?"

"Sure, honey. You can always ask me anything."

How should I ask so he wouldn't get upset? "Why does Mama not want me to touch snakes when she handles them every time we go to church?"

Daddy's cheeks puffed out as he exhaled. "That's quite a question, Melody. And it's not an easy one to answer."

Great. *Not easy to answer* meant I wouldn't be getting one. I scuffed the toe of my boot in the dirt and waited for him to tell me he'd answer it when I was older. The way he usually did when I asked a hard question.

He took off his hat and ran a hand through his shoulder-length black hair before settling the hat on his head again. "But my little girl is growing up and you're getting old enough to need some answers."

My heart stilled for a moment. Would he tell me the truth? Or would he tell me a Cherokee fable instead?

"Your mama has a strong faith in God."

I nodded. "It's why we go to church every Sunday and Wednesday night."

He took my hand again with a smile. "Your mama and Uncle Harlan were raised to believe they have to do certain things to show God they believe in Him." He nodded toward the nest we had chased the snakes from. "Let's go get our catch, then we'll head back on the trail."

Thank goodness we didn't have to be quiet anymore. My boots crunched across the twigs and fallen leaves.

"And while your mama will pick up snakes to confirm her faith in God, she's frightened of them."

Why would she be afraid of snakes? The snakes wouldn't hurt anyone unless they had reason to. I struggled to keep my tongue still. With Daddy, it was sometimes best to keep my questions to myself and let him tell me in his own way.

Daddy looked to the sky for a few moments before continuing. "When she was about your age, at church one Sunday, the preacher picked out a big canebrake rattler during his sermon and he held it above his head and swung it around for everyone in the congregation to see."

Pastor Wolfson showed the congregation snakes all the time.

"And it twisted and bit him in the face."

Ugh. I'd never forget the time Sister Wolfson, Pastor Wolfson's wife, had been bit. She had come to the front to handle the snakes and started doing this weird dance. Most folks who handled danced with the snakes, but this was different. Instead of dancing to the music, she'd stared down the snake, holding it with one hand. She used her other arm like a serpent, wiggling it all around the snake's head. And she shouted words, but not in a language I had ever heard before.

The snake had watched her for a few moments, as if in a trance, but when she'd made a striking motion, it had struck back getting her hand. The blood seeped out of the puncture wound and it trickled down her arm.

She'd raised the snake over her head and screamed she had been blessed by the Lord. He would show the congregation His strength by healing her.

Afterward, Pastor Wolfson said she had been filled with the spirit of the Lord and had been speaking in tongues.

I wasn't afraid of the snake as much as I was afraid of Sister Wolfson.

"The preacher dropped the snake as he fell to the ground and it slithered to the front row and rose to a striking stance. Well, your mama sat front row center with a snake staring her in the face, ready to strike again."

Kinda like the one by the bank. Except I hadn't seen someone bitten in the face. I shivered as the wind whipped through. "Oh my gosh. What happened?"

Daddy frowned at me.

Whoops. "I meant, oh my goodness …"

If Mama had heard me, I'd be in trouble. Kids at school said *gosh* all the time and nobody said a thing.

He raised one eyebrow and grunted. "One of the elders grabbed it and put it in the serpent cage before it lashed out. But your mama had nightmares about the snake biting the preacher and staring her down for years."

Kree-eee-ar.

The cry startled me. Tilting my head back, I scanned the sky until I spotted the red-tailed hawk gliding in front of the clouds.

"And Harlan used to tease her with them. He'd chase her around with a milk snake trying to get it to snap at her."

How mean. Uncle Harlan, always so straight-laced and strict, it was hard to picture him as a boy pulling nasty pranks. But my cousins, Jeb and Samuel, were always nasty to me, so maybe they took after their dad.

We reached the can and Daddy grabbed it. The rattle vibrated against the metal.

Daddy cleared his throat. "The preacher didn't survive the bite which made it worse for your mama."

He died? No wonder Mama didn't like snakes.

"And she loves you so much. She doesn't want you to ever be hurt. She wants you to share her faith in God, but doesn't want to see you handle." He rested his hand on my head. "And before you start objecting about how you're getting older and are big enough, I know you are good with animals. And have always been good with snakes. But you're our only daughter, and you're not going to overcome your mother's fears easily."

Mama was too overprotective. But it's not like I wanted to jump around in church with a snake in my hands anyway. I didn't want to hurt them, and I didn't think they'd find all the bouncing much fun. If some giant came along and held me in his hand and jumped around, I think my stomach would hurt.

But I didn't understand. "If Mama is so afraid, then why do we keep the snakes? And why do you go hunting for them?"

He peered at the sky, tracking the flight of the hawk. "The Cherokee believe rattlesnakes are sacred and are not to be killed unless absolutely necessary. And the snakes used in the church services get sick. So I told your mama I'd go to church with her, as long as I could do my part to keep the snakes healthy."

Would the snakes die if Daddy didn't take care of them?

"When I notice a snake getting sick, it's time to find a replacement. Then we nurse it back to health and release it back to the wild." He patted my shoulder. "It's the right thing to do. The snake should not die as a declaration of faith to God. The same god we worship created all the earth's creatures, and we must show our respect for the gifts God has given us."

He dropped to one knee next to me and pointed at the hawk. "Watch."

The red-tailed hawk tilted its wings and zoomed downward. My heart pounded as it plummeted. Was it going to crash?

It skimmed the ground, then pulled up and soared into the blue sky, something dangling from its claws.

"Nature is raw and violent. Don't ever forget, Melody. The hawk is a hunter—it sets its sights on its prey, waits for its opportunity, then strikes. All animals act according to their nature. Some are the hunter and others are the hunted."

He hugged me and whispered, "People put on masks to hide their nature, so you must learn how to look behind the mask for your own protection. You have many gifts. Follow your passion and soar like the hawk."

CHAPTER THREE

Spring 2015 – Melody, age 16

"This one here never says a peep."

Mrs. Langdon gripped Melody's shoulder and propelled her over the threshold. Melody clutched her MP3 player tight and tucked her chin to her chest. Her long, black hair fell forward and curtained her face. With a light shove, Mrs. Langdon let go. Melody rolled her shoulder to ease the discomfort.

"She won't write nothin' down, neither. So good luck to ya in tryin' to figure out how to talk to her."

Melody shot a glance through the fringe of her bangs at Mrs. Langdon.

The doctor continued to make notes. "I take it this is Melody Fisher."

Mrs. Langdon slung her purse back on her shoulder. "An' you can't tell what she's thinkin'."

Melody unwound the headphones, which had been tightly wrapped around the player, and used the controls to select a song.

Mrs. Langdon's glare caught her halfway to putting the buds in her ears, and her arms dropped to her sides.

"'Course, with some of the chatterboxes I've fostered, having someone who ain't whining all day long is nice." She moved the long, frizzy lock which covered her eye and stumped forward a couple of steps. "So how does this work? I leave her here and come back in an hour?"

"Two." Dr. Kane laid his pencil on the desk.

"What's that?" She gripped the back of the chair, then leaned forward and held out one hand. "Name's Doris Langdon, by the way, but you can call me Dory. Everybody does."

He pumped her hand once and released it. "Please give me two hours before you return, Mrs. Langdon." He pushed his glasses into place and smiled at her. "Melody and I will need the time to get to know each other."

"Well, like I said, she never makes a sound, unless you do this." Mrs. Langdon whipped around and ripped the music player from Melody's grasp.

Immediately, Melody dropped her mouth open, arms rigid at her sides, and high-pitched shrieks penetrated the air. Short blasts of ear-piercing sound at regular intervals reverberated throughout the room.

Mrs. Langdon stretched over the desk, boobs jumbling the papers on top, and yelled to be heard. "She'll go on like this for hours. Won't stop until she gets the music player back. I know 'cause I took it away and wasn't gonna give it back until she spoke. She kept on like this until she was hoarse and even then wouldn't stop."

Holding the MP3 player in front of her, Mrs. Langdon heaved herself upright. "Watch this." She thrust the player back into Melody's hands.

The shrieks stopped and silence assaulted the senses.

Melody gripped the music player tighter than before and scuttled out of Mrs. Langdon's reach.

"Thank you, Mrs. Langdon. I'll take it from here." Dr. Kane rose from behind the desk and straightened the lapel on his navy suit coat.

Mrs. Langdon settled a fist on her hip. "Well, if yer sure." She lumbered toward the door then turned and pointed at Melody. "You listen to the doc and do what he says. I'll be back for ya in a couple hours."

The door closed with a bang. Dr. Kane sank into his chair and busied himself with straightening the disarranged papers on his desk. After a few moments, he peered over his glasses. "Take a seat, Melody, and relax. I'll be with you in a moment." He waved toward a couch and chairs grouped around a coffee table with a box of tissue on the top. "I won't take your music from you."

She shuffled to the couch and sat at the farthest point from the doctor, clutched her stomach, leaned forward, and gently rocked.

He tapped the papers on the desk, grabbed a leather binder, then joined her in the alcove. "Do you mind?" He slipped off his suit jacket to reveal a crisp white shirt, folded the jacket, and draped it over the arm of the vacant chair.

He sat in the plump leather chair opposite the couch, smoothed his burgundy tie, and crossed his legs. He slid the pen from the holder of his leather binder and jotted something on top of the yellow notepad inside.

Setting the pen down, he looked directly at her. "We'll start with introductions. I'm Roger, or you can call me Doctor Kane."

A squirrel scampered up the tree outside the window.

"I like having the bay window on the green. Gives me a chance to pretend I'm outside and communing with nature when I spend most of my day cooped up in this office." A wistful smile crossed his face. "But back to the reason we're here. The letter from the court states we're to have daily sessions until you are able to share your side of the story with the court."

Melody rocked faster.

"We're not going to delve into what happened right this minute."

Dr. Kane had altered his tone to the same kind used to calm a flighty horse.

"The first thing we need to do is establish an environment where you feel safe enough to talk. You *can* talk … our job is to allow you to be heard."

Her agitation decreased, but she stared at the blue and burgundy braided throw rug beneath her feet.

"We're going to take our time and figure out what is so frightening about speaking and give you the tools to help you overcome your fears. Why do you think you stopped speaking?"

Melody pressed the buttons on her music player to change the song.

Dr. Kane allowed the silence to stretch for a few minutes before continuing. "Your case file arrived this morning, so I haven't had much of an opportunity to review it before you came in. I know you're in foster care and you've bounced around from place to place. Do you want to tell me about it?"

She changed her song selection.

The rays of afternoon sun filtered through the trees, turning the grass into a dancing patchwork of light and dark. A light breeze rustled the leaves and made the petals of the early blooming irises, spring beauties, and yellow violets, flutter. The fox squirrel raced down the tree trunk and over to the flower beds. He reared to full standing height and checked for predators. A small cone clamped in his jaws, he used his paws to furiously dig a hole next to a purple iris.

Dirt flew up in spurts with periodic pauses while the squirrel checked the depth. Once satisfied, he dropped the cone into the hole and covered it.

"I wonder whether he'll remember where he buried his treasure come winter or whether another tree will take root."

Melody jumped at the sound of Dr. Kane's voice.

"Half the time, they forget and the gardener winds up weeding out the sprouting trees from the flower beds. Seems a waste after all the effort." He scribbled on his notepad.

The squirrel darted back up the tree.

He shuffled the papers in his lap. "You were first placed in foster care when you were nine?"

Melody looked away.

The silence between them grew, marred only by the ticking of the doctor's big, gold wristwatch, and the occasional *whish* as he flipped through the pages.

After ten minutes, he glanced at his watch then at her. "Do you like my watch? It was my grandfather's and he gave it to me when I opened my practice." He ran a thumb along the band. "Grandpa kept this watch in tiptop working condition. I wasn't allowed to touch it when I was a kid. His company gave it to him as a token of appreciation when he retired."

He raised his right eyebrow and quirked the corner of his mouth. "You're good, kid. Not even an eye roll to show me how sappy my story is." Dr. Kane tapped the end of the pen on his pad. "You know I have thousands of lame stories to regale you with, and will … until you start talking and telling me your stories."

She navigated the menu on her music player.

"Another thing I'll do is read aloud. You'll find I delight in lamentable fiction." He pointed to the bookcase next to the bay window.

A wide wooden bookshelf overflowed with paperback books. The top had paperbacks held upright between two agate bookends. Agatha Christie, Dick Francis, and Barbara Cartland graced the top and the first shelf and were stacked three deep. James Patterson and Tom Clancy peppered the lower shelves, while the classics populated the middle.

Shadows crept across the grass outside the window. Flashes of light reflected off the ripples on the pond, barely visible from the window. Almost like the pond wanted to take part in the conversation through some variation of Morse code.

Melody held an earbud between her fingers. An inch at a time, she raised the bud to her ear and shoved it in.

Dr. Kane shook his head. "I don't have many rules for our sessions, but one non-negotiable rule is you can't deliberately block me out."

She yanked the headphone out of her ear.

He ran his forefinger along the stubble on his tanned jaw. "Tell you what. Tomorrow we'll hook your player to speakers and you can share your music with me."

She stared into his blue eyes.

"I know you probably think the time we've spent together so far has been a complete waste, but I assure you—"

The door flew open and banged against the wall.

Melody jumped.

"Well, get a move on girl. I got things to do that don't revolve around you."

Mrs. Langdon didn't make it five steps into the office before Dr. Kane leaped to his feet. His receptionist trailed behind Mrs. Langdon, her face flushed.

"Lily, please escort Mrs. Langdon back into the waiting room. Melody and I are not quite finished."

"I'm so sorry, Doctor. She didn't stop at the desk, but barreled right past."

Mrs. Langdon's mouth popped open like a fish about to take the bait.

Dr. Kane held up his hand. "We still have time left in our session and Melody and I are not finished discussing what we need to. I cannot have you bursting through the door in the middle of our sessions, Mrs. Langdon. Our discussions are confidential."

She snorted. "Got her talkin' already, Doctor? An' I told you, you can call me Dory."

Dr. Kane strode to where Mrs. Langdon stood and placed the palm of his hand flat against her upper back. "You must respect Melody's time with me. Melody will be out when we have finished. I will not tolerate any further interruptions to our sessions." By the time he finished speaking, he had ushered her through the door and closed it behind her. Then he turned the lock.

"I'm sorry, Melody. The disruption never should have happened." He ran a hand through his loose, curly brown hair. "And we'll make sure it never happens again." Rubbing his forehead, he sat in his chair and picked up the leather binder. "Now, where were we?" He glanced at his notes. "Right. I was getting ready to explain to you what I've observed while we have had this time together."

Melody stiffened and fidgeted with the charm hanging from the end of her silver necklace.

"Now, don't get all riled. You were calm before we were rudely interrupted. There's nothing bad or upsetting about what I'm going to say." He set the binder to the side and laced his fingers over his knee. "Based on your reaction to having the music player taken from you and the pendant you're wearing, music is important to you. So, starting tomorrow, you'll share it with me." He grinned. "It'll help pass the time."

She plucked at her shirt, straightening the wrinkles.

"And you have an affinity for nature. Watching the squirrel, the shadows and light through the trees, the flowers bending in the breeze helped you relax." He smiled. "Which is a good thing. I want you to feel comfortable here. Comfortable with me. We're going to join forces and help you conquer your issues. I'm on your side." He rose. "Session over for today. I think we did well."

Melody walked to the door and he opened it for her.

Mrs. Langdon struggled to rise from the couch. "'Bout time. Let's go, Melody." She rummaged in the bottom of her purse for the keys. "I don't know about your doctor's bedside manner, but he certainly is a good-looker."

Melody cast a glance over her shoulder at the doctor as he closed the door with a smirk on his face.

CHAPTER FOUR

Spring 2015 – Melody, age 16

Mrs. Langdon stumped into the office while Melody hung back in the reception room. "What're you waiting for? The doc doesn't have all day for you to decide whether yer gonna walk in."

Dr. Kane came to the door, shoved his hands in his jean pockets and cocked his head, inviting her in.

Melody shuffled forward, pulling her arms in front of her to keep from brushing against Mrs. Langdon as she passed.

Mrs. Langdon eyed Dr. Kane from head to toe. "You sure changed from yesterday, Doc."

The corners of his mouth turned down as he glanced at his tennis shoes. He shrugged. "Yesterday I had a speaking engagement. Today I normally don't see patients, but Melody requires daily weekday treatment, so I came as is." He tugged the collar of his form-fitting polo shirt. "You don't like?"

Mrs. Langdon sputtered. "Jeans don't look professional."

He cut his eyes toward Melody. "I don't think my patient minds whether I am professional looking." He winked. "You're lucky I wasn't changing the oil in my car or working on my bike. I might have arrived covered in grease and wearing grungy clothes." He held his arm out toward the door. "We'll see you in two hours, Mrs. Langdon."

"Dory."

He continued to hold out his arm, showing her the way.

"Humph. Well, I'll say you haven't made much progress so far. She didn't say a single word last night."

Dr. Kane lowered his arm and peered through his glasses. "Mrs. Langdon, you haven't tried to get Melody to talk, have you?"

She drew herself up to full height. "I thought that was the whole purpose of her comin' here. To make her talk."

He took a deep breath. "Mrs. Langdon, I'm going to say this one time and one time only. You are not to interfere with our work here by attempting to get her to speak at home."

Mrs. Langdon tilted her head and narrowed her eyes as if trying to understand another language.

"The sessions I have with Melody are for the two of us to work through the issues."

She opened her mouth, but Dr. Kane cut her off.

"When Melody is ready to speak, she will. Until such time, you are to perform your duties, which do not include *making* her talk."

She tossed her head back. "Don't get huffy with me. I was tryin' to help you."

The dents around his nostrils turned white. "While I appreciate your motives, unless I expressly request you to do something as a part of Melody's treatment, I must insist you do nothing to *help*. How can I explain it to you?" He ran his hands over his head, ruffling the brown curls. "Trying to help when you don't know what you're doing is the same as loosening the lug nuts on your tires before taking it to the shop to have them rotated." He glanced at the ceiling. "You're doing something *you think* will be helpful, but halfway to the shop the tires will come off and you'll cause more damage than existed in the first place."

"I certainly don't mean ta cause damage."

"Like Michael Dooley said, 'Great intentions become tragic actions when delivered without careful thought.'" He put a hand on her shoulder and escorted her to the door. "Let me deal with Melody. It's my job and one I'm well-equipped to perform."

Dr. Kane closed the door and locked it before turning to face Melody. "I'd tell you to call me if she starts interfering again, but I guess my phone will stay as silent as you." He gave her a crooked grin. "Let's get started, shall we?"

He led the way to the furniture filled alcove by the big bay window. On the coffee table in front of the couch stood a set of speakers with a docking station for the music player.

He hadn't forgotten.

Melody perched in the same spot on the couch as she had the day before.

The leather seat sighed as Dr. Kane sat. "Give me a moment to regroup." He pressed his palms and fingers together, almost in an attitude of prayer, and bowed his forehead against his fingers. He inhaled deeply through his nose and exhaled through his mouth after holding his breath for a few moments. Raising his head, he took another deep breath. "There. Now we can start."

Melody's knee bounced rapidly.

"Remember, you don't need to be nervous. We're going to sit here, watch nature, listen to some music, and I'm going to ramble on about anything crossing my mind. You're going to work on relaxing and being comfortable." He held out his hand. "May I see your music player? I'd like to see what kind of music you like."

She hesitated.

"I won't do anything except look at song titles. And I already promised I'd never take it away from you. If I did, I'd destroy the very thing I'm trying to establish—trust."

She gripped the player tight and bit her lower lip, moving the player farther away from the doctor.

His arm stayed stretched toward her for a few more moments.

"Too much too fast?"

Melody's knee resumed its staccato bounce.

"I can't say I'm surprised. You understand I had to ask." He leaned forward and clapped his hands together. "Well then, you go ahead and pick something for us to listen to."

She concealed the player in her hands and rocked.

"Hey … hey. No pressure." The doctor's voice lowered to soothing tones. "If you're not ready to pick out a song, we'll wait."

The rocking slowed and she lowered her fist. She opened her hand and stared at the music player, the quiet measured by the ticking of the doctor's gold watch. The seconds melded into minutes, and the minutes marched past the quarter hour and headed toward the half.

As she clutched the player, she raked a long, black lock of her hair fiercely behind her ear. Then she turned her head away from the doctor and, with a tremor, held the player out.

"Thank you, Melody."

She faced him.

His hand closed over the player and he blinked twice before gazing into her eyes. "I know how hard that was for you to do. I'm touched."

Dr. Kane cleared his throat and pressed the navigation button. He scrolled through the music with his thumb. Stroking the player, he raised his eyebrows and his eyes widened. "You have a ton of music on this thing. Do you listen to it all?" He shot a glance her direction. "And all types. This is amazing." He kept scrolling through the selections. "You've been collecting music for a while. Picking something to listen to is going to be tough."

As he continued to scroll through the music, a squirrel ran down the tree and sped toward the flower beds under the windows. A high-pitched chattering sounded as chunks of dirt flew into the air.

"Ah, why don't we start with some classical? What do you say to a little of Vivaldi's *Four Seasons*?"

He connected the player to the speakers and pressed play. Orchestral music filled the room.

Dr. Kane closed his eyes, leaned back in the chair, and listened to the music. A smile slowly crossed his lips. He inhaled deeply then exhaled and opened his eyes. "The tension is flowing out of me. How about you?"

Melody had stopped rocking and her knee had gone still.

"I enjoy listening to music patterned after nature. I bet if we watch what's happening outside, the leaves will dance and the grass will bow and bend to the music."

Melody leaned back against the couch. The breeze rustled through the leaves.

"This part of the *Spring* concerto makes me think of water rushing past rocks in a creek."

As Melody relaxed, the music changed from *Spring* to *Summer*. The squirrel stopped digging in the flower bed and ran through the grass. He made a zigzagging pattern as he raced through the green, tail bouncing with each leap forward, perfectly in time with the music.

"Do I see a smile?"

Melody's face went blank.

"You have a beautiful smile. And there is no need to hide your enjoyment of listening to music and watching our squirrel's antics."

A crow landed on the grass and pecked at a cone on the ground. The squirrel scampered over, sputtering and swishing its tail. It made darting motions toward the crow as if trying to scare it off. It jumped forward and back, chattering away as the crow surveyed it.

When the squirrel jumped a little too close, the crow spread its wings and cawed, hopping toward the rodent. The squirrel froze, then scurried back as the crow flapped its wings. From a distance, it kept up its excited chatter.

"I think our friend may have met his match. He won't want to anger the crow too much. Crows hold a grudge, you know."

Melody turned her gaze on Dr. Kane.

"What?" His glasses slid down his nose as he peered over the top. "I've been watching the wildlife outside my windows for a few years. So, through the power of observation and Google, I've learned about our friends."

He pushed his wire-rimmed glasses back into place. "For example, I can tell you the crow is an American crow and not a fish crow, and it's definitely not a raven."

He turned sideways in his chair, put a hand on his cheek, and raised the pitch of his voice. "Really, Dr. Kane? That is so fascinating. But how can you tell?"

He swiveled to the other side of the chair, lowered his hand, and resumed his normal speaking voice. "I'm glad you asked, Melody. Our crow is bigger than a fish crow, and it has a more rounded tail, where the raven's is more diamond-shaped. But there are two things making this the American crow versus anything else."

He turned in the chair again and raised his voice. "I can't believe you know all this. Tell me more."

He straightened. "When he opened his wings, he had five feather fingers, not four, and he cawed instead of giving the harsher sound of the raven, or the nasally sound of the fish crow."

Melody remained still, her gaze unwavering.

Dr. Kane shook his head. "Man, you are a tough nut. My performance should have warranted a huffy arm crossing at the very least." He sighed. "We may have to bring in the fox squirrel to crack you."

Melody whirled her head away.

"Ah, I'm starting to get to you. It's my charm, isn't it? Mother always said I could talk an Eskimo into a big scoop of ice cream in the wintertime."

Melody refused to look at him.

"All right, be that way. I'm going to enjoy your music and pretend you didn't just hand me the biggest snub of my career." He sniffed.

Halfway through *Autumn*, Melody snuck a peek at Dr. Kane. Legs crossed, head thrown back, he conducted the recording with his index finger. She allowed the corners of her lips to curve up and relaxed against the couch back.

The music swelled as the sun waned, and together, the trees, wind, and rays of sun combined to create shadows dancing across the green. The crow spread his wings and took flight, soaring to the treetops. As soon as the crow took wing, the squirrel dashed in to pick up whatever the crow had left behind.

The squirrel turned right and left, searching for a place to hide its treasure, while the crow cawed as if in victory over the squirrel's quandary. The squirrel took off, running as if banshees were chasing it, leaping through the tall grass until it reached the base of a tree nearer the pond. It quickly buried the future meal and checked for predators.

The crow gave a mighty caw and swooped from the top of the tree, dive bombing the squirrel as it raced over the grass.

Dr. Kane chuckled as the crow passed right over the squirrel with barely an inch to spare. "I knew the squirrel took things too far." He checked his watch. "Mrs. Langdon will be here soon. And since I'd rather not have her break the door down when she finds it has been locked, we should probably finish." He switched off the music player, disconnected it from the speakers, and held it out to her.

Melody took it and closed it in her fist.

"Thank you for sharing your music with me. I think we took a big step here today, and I'm pleased with our progress. You should be, too." He stood. "I look forward to our session tomorrow."

He crossed to the door and opened it. "Ah, Mrs. Langdon. Right on time. Will you join us for a moment?"

Mrs. Langdon bustled in, her lips pursed.

"Melody and I had a good session today. And I want to reiterate what we discussed this afternoon. You are not to ask her any questions about our time here together. Nor should you try to make her speak."

Mrs. Langdon frowned. "I don't know what good it's gonna do if we don't make her talk when that's what she's supposed ta be doin'."

"Mrs. Langdon—"

"Call me Dory."

He blew past her as if she hadn't uttered a word. "When you dropped her off, we covered your interference and how it can be detrimental."

Mrs. Langdon threw up a hand. "While you were here doing who knows what, *not* makin' her talk, I went to the library to read up on kids who don't talk."

Dr. Kane's head snapped back.

"The librarian was most helpful. She showed me how to look things up online."

"Mrs. Langdon, please …"

"You were right in one thing you said this afternoon, Doc. I hadn't read up on the subject and might do some harm. I figured I'd do a little reading, so I'd know best how to help."

Dr. Kane ruffled his curly locks. "I have made it a point to study human behavior for years, and you simply cannot discover the necessary information to properly treat a patient in an hour and a half Google search."

Mrs. Langdon rested her fists on her ample hips. "I don't know about that, Doc. I read how most kids who have trouble talkin' have a lot of anxiety and when you reduce their anxiety, they start talkin' again."

Red spots appeared on his cheeks. "Did you happen to come across this little nugget? Trying to force someone to talk is the worst possible thing you can do."

She nodded. "I believe I did read that in one article."

"Good." He pressed his lips into a thin line and inhaled deeply. "Let me be clear, then. Should you attempt in any way to force Melody to talk, I will contact social services and advise them the placement is not working out and they must remove her from your *care* immediately. Do you understand?"

Mrs. Langdon's eyebrows rose. "I will remind you, Dr. Kane, I am only trying to help. You'd think you'd be grateful I took the time to read up on the subject."

He sighed. "While I appreciate your interest, you must not attempt to try any methods you read about at home. Melody's case is unique and what you read on the internet may cause more problems than you'd think." He stroked his stubble. "It'd be like putting diesel in an engine made to run on gasoline. You're giving it fuel, but it's gumming up the works." He opened the door. "Can you give me a few more moments with Melody? I'll send her out as soon as we're done."

"But you said you were finished." At his look, she waved her hands in the air. "All right, I'll go back out to the waiting room."

When she closed the door behind her with a bang, Dr. Kane faced Melody.

"I want you to know I'm available to you any time, day or night." He moved to his desk and grabbed a business card and a pen. "I'm writing my cell number on the back of the card so you can reach me." The right corner of his mouth curved up. "I'd have you call the number on the front because, after hours, it goes to my answering service who will then contact me, but they won't call me when no one speaks on the other end." He held out the card. "If your foster mother attempts to make you talk or pesters you, I want you to call me. Don't worry about saying anything. Play the Vivaldi and I'll know who and what the problem is." His blue eyes bore into hers. "Deal?"

She took the card and gave a barely perceptible nod.

His smile broadened. "We took a lot of strides forward today and we'll continue tomorrow."

Melody stepped through the doorway to join Mrs. Langdon.

"All set this time? That doctor of yours does change his mind." She struggled to her feet and hoisted the purse to her shoulder. "An' he talks about cars a lot. Mebbe he has a lot of mechanical problems. I'll have to ask him tomorrow."

Mrs. Langdon pushed open the exterior office door and led the way, talking the whole time.

CHAPTER FIVE

May 27, 2006 – Melody, age 7

Wild strands of hair whipped across my face. Mama had braided it, but the wind had loosened the weave. I skipped ahead of Daddy on the path of the Tanawha Trail. We hiked the trail past Raven's Rock to look at the rhododendron and mountain laurels. School had let out and Daddy and I were starting our annual hikes through the mountains. It was our special time together every week.

He wanted to share his love of the mountain and the land with me and teach me the Cherokee beliefs through nature.

"Daddy, look at the pretty flowers. They look like tiny umbrellas."

The inside of the flower had spines attached to the petal. And the buds on the bushes looked like closed umbrellas.

"Can we pick some to bring back to Mama?"

Daddy shook his head. "We'll leave these here for other hikers to enjoy."

I pouted. "But Mama would really like these. And she doesn't get to come hiking with us very often."

Daddy put his hands on his hips and paced, studying the bush. "Well, we can stop by the nursery and get some laurel for planting at home."

"Yay." I clapped my hands.

"We can plant it along the side of the house, so it gets the morning sun." He gave me a mock stern look. "But I'd better have help in digging the holes."

"I promise, Daddy." I reached out and touched a petal.

"And you have to promise not to ever eat it. The mountain laurel is poisonous."

I wrinkled my nose. "I don't eat plants."

Daddy's eyebrows rose while the corners of his mouth turned down. "Really? You eat vegetables."

"That's not what I meant."

"And I recall you plucking some sour grass along one of our walks and eating it."

Oh yeah. He was right. "I promise I won't eat the tiny umbrellas. They're too pretty to eat, anyway."

We had been alone all morning on the path, but footsteps approached as we continued past the mountain laurels. I liked our hikes best when Daddy and I were alone because then I could pretend the mountain belonged to us.

Elder Lowrey of the Ani'-Wah' Ya clan climbed through the brush to the path. Daddy, being a part of the clan, stopped to talk with him.

I pretended the flowers on the bush were bells and played a song and made the ding-dong sounds. After I finished, I glanced at Daddy. He had his arms crossed and nodded at whatever Elder Lowrey said.

Someone walked through the brush and stood behind Elder Lowrey wearing weird clothes and a wolf hat.

Who was that?

I covered my mouth to hide my snickers. Not a cap with the picture of a wolf, but an actual wolf skin with the nose acting as the brim and the paws hanging down the front like a shawl.

His clothes were like those I had seen at the museum. Deerskin shirt and pants, rawhide boots, and he wore paint on the lower half of his face. Daddy always talked to the tribe members, but Daddy ignored him. *Strange.*

I moved on to the next bush because it had brighter flowers.

"Melody, don't get too far ahead. You need to stay in eyesight."

Whenever Daddy got to talking with Elder Lowrey, he always took FOR-ever. Something rustled under a bush on the other side of the path.

I squatted to peer through the leaves.

Awww. A baby fawn. It was so cute. I moved toward it slowly, not wanting to scare the poor thing. What was it doing out here all alone?

Its nose twitched as I got close. Dropping to the ground, I crawled the last couple feet. Poor fawn. Its heart beat so fast its sides heaved with each thump.

"It's all right, little fawn. I won't hurt you." Moving the leaves aside, I crawled in the bush cave with the fawn. I hummed and held my hand out so it could get my scent.

Gently, I laid my hand on its back. Then moved it up to the head and scratched it between the ears. My humming made it go calm. I wished I could take it home, but it would miss its mama.

The fawn's nose twitched, and its ears wriggled.

Yip. Yip. Yip.

The sound came from the right side. The fawn trembled again. I hugged it and leaned forward to peek through the leaves.

The sound changed from yips to a whooping noise with laughter in between.

In the gap between the ground and the bottom of the bush, four furry legs came into view. Like a big dog. Yipping, it angled toward the bush, one paw at a time.

The fawn bleated. I moved closer to try and see a little better. The dog dropped its head and growled, baring its teeth.

I scuttled back next to the fawn. It wasn't a dog. It was a coyote. I needed something to scare it off.

The fawn bleated again. I hushed it and searched for a stick or a rock. Anything I could throw.

The growl, low and threatening, came closer.

I found two stones. They weren't big, but maybe they would scare off the coyote. I didn't want it to attack the fawn. The baby was too small to defend itself against such a big bully. I had to save it.

I crawled closer to the edge, then hunched over and hurled a stone sidearm as hard as I could through the gap.

The rock hit the coyote's back leg and he retreated a few paces.

If I sneaked out from the bush, I might be able to hit the wild dog on the nose. The pain should chase it away.

"You wait right here, little fawn."

On hands and knees, I inched out of the fawn's hiding place. Peering around the bush, I looked at the coyote, which had closed in again. It was huge.

Before throwing the rock, I checked for more ammunition. The broken tree branch a few feet away would be good. Small enough for me to throw or use like a bat, but big enough to hurt. My fist tightened over the rock.

Now or never, Melody.

I hurled it as hard as I could and hit the coyote smack on the nose.

It threw its head back and howled.

"Melody, where are you?" Daddy sounded a little panicky.

I grabbed the tree branch and yelled at the wild dog. "Get out of here."

The coyote lowered its head and bared its fangs. He stalked toward me, growling.

I raised the branch as Daddy came around the bend and stopped. He scooped up a rock and let it fly at the coyote, hitting its left flank. The rock didn't faze it. The coyote slunk closer, keeping me in its sights.

When it leaned back on its haunches, I swung the branch like a bat and screamed. I hit it along the side. It staggered back, then came at me again.

Daddy didn't have a chance to reach me before I swung the branch. Direct hit on the coyote's head. He turned tail and ran off as Daddy scooped me up.

"What have I taught you about confronting a coyote?" Daddy hugged me tightly, but his tone was stern. "You don't. You stay still or make loud noises to scare it off."

"But Daddy ..."

"No." He set me on the ground and knelt in front of me. "You listen to me, Melody Rose. Coyotes are predators and they can be nasty, so you don't confront them. Especially if they are traveling in a pack."

Tears filled my eyes. "But Daddy, I had to."

"No. The coyote attacked you." Daddy's frown lines deepened. "You have to respect nature, and if you can't listen to what I'm teaching you and remember it, then we won't be able to come on our hikes."

A big, fat tear slid down my cheek. "But I had to protect the fawn. The coyote was going to eat it."

The grooves between his eyes softened. "The fawn?"

I moved the branches aside and crept back into the bush cave. "The coyote would have killed it." I scratched between the fawn's ears to calm it. "I couldn't stand by and watch the coyote tear it apart. It's only a baby."

Daddy reached into the hiding place and patted my back. "You did the right thing protecting the fawn, Melody. But if it happens again, I want you to yell for me as loud as you can."

"But, what if you're not with me? I have to be able to take care of myself. Aren't you teaching me about life on the mountain so I can?"

Daddy shook his head. "How did I get such a smart girl?" He backed out of the bush. "We should get on with our hike."

My heart lurched. "But what about the fawn? We can't leave it here or the coyote might come back." I had to make Daddy understand. We couldn't leave the fawn unprotected. "What happened to its mama?"

Daddy stood and shoved a hand in his front pocket. Then he paced next to the bush. I giggled because all I could see from inside was his boots stomping back and forth.

His footsteps stopped. "Melody, come out here." He whispered. "Be quiet. And listen."

I gave the fawn another pat and listened as hard as I could. I heard a funny buzzing noise.

The fawn shook its head and bleated.

"Come on, honey. Don't wait."

I crawled out from the bush ready to convince Daddy we needed to stay but closed my mouth once I poked my head out. A doe stood no more than twenty feet away across the path. She made the buzzing noise again and the fawn bleated in response.

Daddy held his hand out to help me up. "Move slowly. We don't want to spook her." He kept his voice soft and low.

I'd never been closer to a doe in my life. It was taller than me. Daddy squeezed my hand and took a step back. We backed one step at a time into the thicket behind us. When we reached the trees, the doe raced to the fawn and nuzzled it through the bush.

We stayed half hidden as the fawn rose on unsteady legs and followed its mama off into the brush.

"Bye-bye, little fawn." I hoped its mama would take better care of it so it wouldn't be eaten by a coyote.

CHAPTER SIX

Spring 2015 – Melody, age 16

When the receptionist, Lily, told them they could go in, Melody opened the door, strode through, and turned to face Mrs. Langdon before she crossed the threshold.

"Thank you, Mrs. Langdon." Dr. Kane barely looked up from the paperwork on his desk.

"You listen to the doc, Melody." She shot a glance at Dr. Kane. "This one can't wait to get here these days. Not like when she first started with you. Must be a charmer, you are."

The corners of Melody's mouth twitched as she slowly closed the door in her foster mother's face. Then she turned the lock, walked to the couch, and took her seat.

In a few moments, Dr. Kane joined her. She held out her music player, but he shook his head.

"I think today is the big day when you share a song with me."

The beginning of her smile faded as she pulled the player back. Tension spread through her shoulders and her stomach twisted. Her forehead wrinkled, shoulders hunched, and she rocked.

Dr. Kane leaned forward and propped his elbows on his knees. "You don't need to worry. All you're going to do is pick one song and we'll put it on speaker. The same thing we've been doing for a week and a half, but this time instead of my song choice, it'll be yours." He leaned back. "Take your time. We're not in a rush. Take a few deep breaths."

She closed her eyes.

"That's right. Relax. No pressure."

Melody bit the inside of her lip and tried to take a calming breath. She clamped her hand over the music player so tightly it bit into her palm.

After a few moments, Dr. Kane broke through her pensiveness. "I've been choosing songs relating to nature, but you don't have to. Pick what you want. It can be something about how you feel, or a song to make you smile, or something silly. It's up to you."

Time slowly ticked by.

Melody stared out the window, watching for the squirrel. When she saw his tail flitting through the leaves, she leaned against the couch back. She uncurled her fingers from the music player. Frowning, she touched the button to bring up the menu.

She scrolled through a few songs, then stopped. She shook her head and continued scrolling. The tension crept back into her shoulders as she rejected song after song. Her knee bounced. Faster and faster she went through the songs.

She stopped. Her hand moved to her silver necklace as she stared at the song title. The touch of the heart-shaped treble and bass clef charm comforted. She ran her thumb over the smooth bevels, following the curves, repeatedly. Chewing her lower lip, she connected the player to the speakers and pressed play.

Dr. Kane immediately sat up and leaned forward. He opened his mouth as if to say something, but then pressed a finger against his lips.

Music filled the office—an acoustic guitar and single vocalist through the first verse. With the addition of the second verse, a piano joined. Once the music ended, Melody lunged forward and pressed the stop button.

Tears stood in her eyes and her throat closed as she swallowed her emotion. She turned away from Dr. Kane.

"Thank you for sharing with me. What an interesting arrangement of 'Amazing Grace'. I don't think I've heard that version before."

The leather squeaked as he shifted in the chair.

Several minutes later, Melody slumped against the couch back and stared out the window.

Dr. Kane leaned forward and stretched his hand toward the player. "You obviously have a deep connection with the song. Do you mind if I play it again?"

He waited, hand hovering over the play button.

Melody took a deep breath. She touched the silver charm, then let her hand fall to her lap. She met his eyes and gave a nod.

He pressed play and the guitar chords filled the room, followed by the voice of a child.

CHAPTER SEVEN

April 11, 2004 – Melody, age 5

The gravel path to the blue-faced church building had been smoothed, and the edges where the new grass made its way toward the early morning sun had been trimmed. My shoes sparkled in the sunshine as I walked up the path with Mama and Daddy on either side. I didn't want to get a speck of dirt on my brand new shoes on this special day.

Mama had bought me a new spring dress and pulled my hair back from my face with a matching bow. She put a hand on my shoulder and crouched to look me in the eye. "Before we go in, I have a present for you." She pulled a small wrapped package out of her purse.

With a huge grin, I clapped my hands. "Is it for Easter?"

Mama held the package out to me. "It's for your first solo."

After ripping off the paper, I opened a small box. Inside laid a silver charm attached to a silver chain. It looked like a heart, but crooked.

Mama pulled the necklace out of the box and held it in front of me. "These are two musical symbols put together to make a heart." She touched the curly upside-down 'S' part. "This is a treble clef for the higher notes." She moved her finger to the part like an ear. "And this is the bass clef for the low notes." The silver charm sparkled in the sun. "Together, they show your love of music—just like your name."

Mama unclasped the necklace and reached the ends around my neck to hook it together. As soon as it dropped against my chest, I snatched it up to watch it twinkle as the sun rays caught it.

Mama stood and held out her hand. "Are you ready to go in?"

I gripped her hand and grinned. A splinter of nervousness pricked my tummy, but excitement drowned it out. Easter was always a special day, but this Easter was even more special than all the others. I wanted to skip ahead, but then remembered about keeping my shoes clean. At least until after the service.

An occasional rattle came from the snake case Daddy carried. Today he had his hands full because he had his guitar case in his other hand.

Pastor Wolfson waited at the door for us. "Good morning, Fisher family. Are you ready for your part of the worship service this morning?"

Mama ran a hand down my hair. "Melody is so excited, I'm not sure she slept last night."

"It's not every five-year-old who gets this opportunity." The pastor reached for the snake case. His middle finger had turned black from the knuckle to the tip. It looked creepy.

"I'll take the serpents from you, Will." He moved to the side. "Come on in and get settled."

I stepped through the door and turned to wait for Daddy and Mama. Daddy always said Mama looked like an angel. The sunlight shone on Mama and made her look angelic; the rays hit her reddish-gold hair and lit it like a halo.

Daddy loved Mama's hair. He said she got it from her Scottish mother along with her fair skin. When I asked why Mama and Uncle Harlan didn't look much alike, Daddy told me it was because Uncle Harlan took after their black father while Mama had more traits from her mother. Then he told me not to ask about it around Uncle Harlan because he had never forgiven Mama for having lighter skin.

Skin color seemed a funny thing not to forgive. But Uncle Harlan was always grumpy about something. And Mama's skin got darker during the summer.

When Mama joined me, she took my hand. "Come on. I want you to go to the bathroom before the service starts."

We walked down the aisle. Each of the pews had bows on them. "Why is Pastor Wolfson's finger black, Mama?"

"That's not something you should ask, Melody."

"But—"

She squeezed my hand. "I don't know. And it would be impolite to ask. Maybe Pastor Wolfson doesn't want to talk about what happened."

How could you not want to talk about what turned your finger black? Mama's face paled like it did when something upset her. I bet she guessed what had happened to Pastor Wolfson.

I stopped and gripped the end of the last pew. "My skin won't turn black if he touches me, will it?"

"Oh, Melody." Mama's tone was the one she used when I said something wrong and she pulled me forward.

I didn't want him to touch me with a finger that looked like it had been burned.

Mama squeezed my hand. "You're not going to be hurt by his finger. Now hush."

When I went into the cold metal stall, the tiny butterflies in my stomach started flying around. "Mama?"

"Yes, baby."

"Are you sure people are gonna want to hear me?" What if they didn't like me?

"Do you remember the other day when we talked about what a calling is?"

I kicked my feet back and forth, watching the sparkles blur with the motion. "Yeah. You said it was something God gave you a talent for because he wanted you to share it."

"The first time I held you in my arms, you were the joyous song in my heart—my little Melody. God's spirit told me then you were special and had a gift. It's time for you to share it with more than Daddy and me."

I smiled. I liked it when Mama told me stories about when I was born and how I made the family complete.

"Don't dawdle, Melody. You don't want to be late."

Oh yeah. I finished and stood on tiptoes to get a squirt of liquid soap for my hands. After I washed my hands in the cold water, Mama and I went back into the church.

Daddy motioned us to the front row. "When it's time, the pastor will call us to join him." He pulled me on to his lap. "Are you ready?"

I snuggled against his chest and nodded.

"You're going to do fine."

"I'm not scared, Daddy." *Well* ... I held my thumb and forefinger together so they almost touched. "Only this little."

He hugged me and whispered in my ear. "They'll think an angel has come down from heaven to sing for them."

The church filled behind us and Pastor Wolfson stood in front to start the service. I couldn't pay attention to the sermon because I was listening for him to call us up to sing. And every time he waved his hand through the air, I watched his black finger. The pastor read the passage from the Bible about Jesus rising from the dead.

"This concludes our scripture reading for today. Now it's time for us to be blessed by the musical ministry of the Fisher family."

I squeaked as I hopped off Daddy's lap and hurried to stand next to Pastor Wolfson. Daddy pulled out his guitar and put the strap over his head. Mama sat behind the keyboard.

I faced the congregation. The church was full, and a few folks stood in the back because there weren't any more seats. I shot a frightened glance at Daddy and he smiled at me.

Something about Daddy's smile always made me feel like nothing could go wrong. He was there with me and nothing bad could happen. When I woke in the middle of the night with a nightmare, Mama would soothe me, but one smile from Daddy and all the monsters disappeared.

He raised his eyebrows and I nodded. Pastor Wolfson switched on the microphone and handed it to me. I took it carefully, making sure not to let my fingers brush his.

Daddy strummed the opening notes. I took a deep breath, closed my eyes, and sang.

Amazing grace. How sweet the sound

That saved a wretch like me.
I once was lost, but now am found,
Was blind, but now I see.

When I opened my eyes, Uncle Harlan sat in the second row with his arms crossed and a frown on his face. Was I singing bad? My breath hitched in my throat.

'Twas grace that taught my heart to fear,
And grace my fears relieved.
How precious did that grace appear
The hour I first believed.

"Amen." A lady at the back of the church stood and raised her arms in the air. "Praise Jesus."

She smiled at me and I felt better.

Through many dangers, toils and snares
I have already come;
'Tis grace hath brought me safe thus far
And grace will lead me home.

During the musical interlude, Mama played on the piano, Brother Ferrell ran to the serpent cases, opened one, and pulled out a rattler. He held it with two hands over his head and bounced with the beat of the music.

The Lord has promised good to me
His word my hope secures;
He will my shield and portion be,
As long as life endures.

Several other members of the congregation hurried to the front and took up serpents. Brother Ferrell put his snake on the ground and danced before it. Pastor Wolfson swayed through those who were handling, waving his hands in the air.

I couldn't help watching his hands.

His black finger broke off and sailed through the air. Pastor Wolfson's mouth popped open and he half dove toward it but couldn't catch it.

It hit the floor and rolled toward me.

My heart pounded. The black finger touched my sparkly white shoe, but I had to keep singing.

Yea, when this flesh and heart shall fail,
and mortal life shall cease,
I shall possess within the veil,
A life of joy and peace.

Before I could kick it away, Sister Wolfson stormed the stage and slid on her knees scrabbling at the floor, searching for the finger. The snake on the ground slithered toward Sister Wolfson. She crawled to me, racing against the snake.

Mama stood and knocked her chair over.

Sister Wolfson reached the finger first and snatched it up. After standing, she held it over her head and yelled, "*Praise Jesus,*" over and over. Brother Ferrell chased the serpent and took it up again and twirled off.

The notes from the piano and guitar died away and I shot a quick look at Mama. Pale, she nodded.

I closed my eyes and sang the last verse *a cappella* … slower and higher than the other verses—like we practiced.

When we've been there ten thousand years
Bright shining as the sun,
We've no less days to sing God's praise
Than when we've first begun.

When I opened my eyes, everyone stood and clapped, except Uncle Harlan, who remained in his seat, arms still folded.

Handing the microphone to Pastor Wolfson, I wanted to run back to Daddy and Mama, but the pastor put his hand on my shoulder.

The hand with the missing finger part. I held my breath—I didn't want the stubby finger touching me. He held his other hand in the air until the clapping stopped and the congregation reseated themselves.

"We have been blessed. Thank you, Melody, for sharing your gift with us. The Lord has spoken to our hearts through you. Will you share with us again?"

Eyes wide, I looked at Mama. I didn't expect them to ask me to sing again. She nodded.

"Yes, Pastor Wolfson. Thank you." But I didn't want him to touch me with his stub again.

He let go of my shoulder and I scurried across the front to where Daddy knelt next to his guitar case, threw my arms around his neck, and hugged him tightly. He stood while I still clung to him and carried me back to our seats.

"You did a wonderful job, baby. I'm proud of you."

The whispered words tickled my ear and I tightened my hug.

When the service was over, we stood on the path and I held Daddy's hand tight as people came to thank us for the music. Uncle Harlan paced on the grass, head down and arms tightly crossed against his chest. Aunt Ruth had to jump out of his way because he nearly ran into her. My cousins stood next to the trees lining the parking area.

Pastor Wolfson joined us and thanked us again for providing the music for the service.

"Did you see what I rescued?" Sister Wolfson joined him and held up the black finger.

Pastor Wolfson winced. "Why don't you throw the dead finger out, sweetheart?"

She shook her head. "I want to keep it."

"Now, why would you want to keep a thing like that?" Pastor Wolfson's brow furrowed.

Her eyes gleamed. "So when you die, I can still have a piece of you."

A dead piece of him. I'd never forget the crusty black thing touching my shoe.

After everyone else had moved on to the parking area, Brother Hill held his hand out to Daddy. "Can't tell you how much I enjoyed the music, Will. Your little girl has some pipes."

Pipes? I didn't have any pipes.

Daddy shook his hand. "Thank you, Thomas. She's been singing like a songbird from the time she could talk. We thought we should share."

"I turned my old shed into a recording studio. How about putting together a track of Melody singing?"

I rocked on my heels and twisted back and forth to create a swirly hole in the path. Mama put her arm on my shoulder and pulled me to her side.

"Sounds like a great idea."

Brother Hill pulled a card out of his wallet and handed it to Daddy. "Give me a call next week and we'll get something set up."

As Brother Hill walked away, Uncle Harlan stormed toward Mama with a huge frown. "What is the meaning of this travesty, Allison?"

Mama pulled me closer to her. "What travesty, Harlan? We had an uplifting Easter service. Nothing wrong happened."

Nothing happened, except the pastor's finger flying across the stage in the middle of our song. But I didn't say anything because Mama already looked upset.

Uncle Harlan's face turned dark red as a turkey wattle and a big vein stood out on his forehead. "'Thou shalt have no other gods before me. Thou shalt not make unto thee any graven image, or any likeness *of any thing* that *is* in heaven above, or that *is* in the earth beneath, or that *is* in the water under the earth.'"

Mama's nails bit into my shoulder and I wriggled to loosen her grip.

"And what does the passage from Exodus have to do with today?"

Uncle Harlan leaned closer to Mama. Face-to-face, they looked more like complete opposites than brother and sister. He was as dark as coal and she as light as the sun. Not only in looks but the way they behaved, too. Mama was always happy at home. Uncle Harlan rarely cracked a smile outside of church.

He shook as he spoke. "I will not allow my sister to whore out her daughter in the name of the Lord."

Daddy put his arm between Mama and Uncle Harlan and grabbed Uncle Harlan's shoulder. "Melody, go stand by your cousins."

As I raced off, Daddy told Uncle Harlan he had crossed the line. *Ooh,* "crossed the line" meant Daddy didn't like what Uncle Harlan said.

When I reached Aunt Ruth, Jeb sneered at me and Samuel stuck out his tongue. I showed him my tongue back and turned to watch Daddy and Mama.

Daddy had marched Uncle Harlan back a few steps and stood between him and Mama. He kept his hand on Uncle Harlan's shoulder. I couldn't hear what Daddy was saying, but he didn't look happy.

A butterfly flew past and landed on a flower between the trees. I put my arms out to the side to be wings. What would it feel like to be a butterfly? I couldn't fly, but I could twirl. I spun and my skirt flew out. I spun faster, watching my skirt swirl. I twirled so fast my hair flew like my skirt.

"Melody Rose." Mama's tone was sharp, so I stopped spinning.

"Coming, Mama." I took a step, but the world kept spinning and I nearly fell over. I took a couple of steps before Mama picked me up and carried me to the car.

She had mad lines on her forehead.

"Did I do something wrong, Mama?"

She kissed me on the cheek and put me down. "No. You did a beautiful job singing, Melody. I'm upset with Uncle Harlan."

She opened the back door and I crawled into my booster seat and buckled in.

Daddy put his guitar in the trunk then started the car. He looked past me as he reversed, faced front, and pulled out of the parking lot with a spurt of dirt billowing behind us.

"Mama and I decided we'd stay home for Easter dinner today instead of going to Uncle Harlan's and Aunt Ruth's like we usually do."

Good. I didn't want to see my stinky cousins anyway. All they did was pick on me when everyone's back was turned.

"What do you say to peanut butter sandwiches and lemonade out on the porch?"

"Yay. Peanut butter is my favorite."

Mama sniffed and put her hand against her cheek while her shoulders shook.

She was crying? I leaned forward and stretched my fingers as far as I could to touch her shoulder. "Don't cry, Mama. We don't have to have peanut butter."

She turned and touched my hand, her hand wet with tears. "I'm not crying about peanut butter. Mama's upset right now. I'll be better in a few moments."

As soon as we reached home, Mama hurried into the house and disappeared into her and Daddy's room. Daddy took me into the kitchen and pulled the step stool out.

"How'd you like to help me make the sandwiches?"

I climbed the steps and leaned against the counter. "Is Mama gonna be okay?"

He smoothed my hair. "She'll be fine. She just needs a little time away from Uncle Harlan."

I grabbed the butter knife and pulled a glob of peanut butter out of the jar. "Why didn't Uncle Harlan like my song?"

His cheeks puffed out as he exhaled. "Uncle Harlan has some different ideas about how to give glory to God. But no matter what Uncle Harlan says, God was very happy with the way you sang for Him today."

I spread the peanut butter on a slice of bread. "It was fun. I liked singing for everybody. It made me bubbly."

Daddy made tickle hands. "Did it tickle you inside?"

I shrieked and hopped off the stool. I ran straight into Mama as she walked into the kitchen.

"Whoa." She hugged me and removed the peanut butter knife from my hand. "What's going on here? I thought you were making sandwiches."

"Daddy turned into the tickle monster."

She lifted an eyebrow. "Will, how many times have I told you? The tickle monster doesn't belong in the kitchen."

Daddy grabbed Mama's waist and spun her around. "The tickle monster doesn't follow rules." He tickled Mama.

"Will." Mama laughed.

He spun her to face him and kissed her. "Do you know how much I love you?"

She smiled.

"My love for you is bigger than the oceans, longer than the life of the trees, higher than the eagle soars. I love you to the stars and back and will carry my love for you beyond death. I love you more than life itself."

CHAPTER EIGHT

Spring 2015 – Melody, age 16

Melody crossed her legs and leaned back in the chair. Sitting next to her, Mrs. Langdon rummaged through her purse. "I could have sworn I put those pamphlets in here." She glanced at Melody. "You know. The ones I showed you on new ways to make kids talk. I thought your doc might be interested."

Melody bit her lip. Her gaze met Lily's, who made a big show of crossing her eyes.

Mrs. Langdon pulled out a package of cough drops, a miniature umbrella, and a pair of wooly socks. "Now how did these get in here? I've been lookin' all over the place for them." She patted Melody on the arm. "I use them to keep my feet warm at night. You'll know what I mean when you get to be my age."

Melody edged her arm away.

Lily caught her attention and cocked her head toward Dr. Kane's office door.

She popped out of her chair and had her hand on the handle before Mrs. Langdon looked up and saw she had moved.

"The doctor will see you now, Melody." Lily failed to keep a straight face.

Mrs. Langdon stood and scooped everything back into her purse, but before she could take a step toward the door, Melody closed it with a smile.

After locking the door, she pulled the music player out of her pocket and went to sit on the couch. Dr. Kane tapped away on his laptop, brow furrowed as he peered through his glasses. The keys clacked in rapid-fire succession as his fingers flew over the surface. He clicked the mouse, closed the laptop lid, and stood.

He pulled his glasses off and tucked them into the pocket of his royal-blue collared shirt. His sleeves were rolled up to the elbows and showed off the beginning of a tan. The color of his shirt brought out the color of his eyes. His windswept brown hair curled at the collar and a three-day stubble framed his cute smile.

Melody turned the player on and scrolled through the songs.

When he sat, he tapped the end of the pen against his notepad in a staccato beat. "I think it's time we change things up a bit." He stroked his stubble. "We've been listening to music and while I think we've made some progress, it's time to take things up a notch."

Melody's knee bounced rapidly and she twisted her fingers together.

"Don't get all uptight. I haven't led you astray yet, have I?"

Taking a deep breath, her agitation slowed.

"Better. We're not going to do anything difficult. I think it's time for us to talk about things from your past. I'll talk and you correct me if I get anything wrong." He pulled her file from the side table onto his lap and opened it. "For instance, I see here you were born January 17, 1999, to Will and Allison Fisher."

He glanced at her. "See? Nothing to be afraid of."

Melody pressed the navigation menu on the player.

He flipped the page. "You grew up in the mountains. No wonder you like nature so much."

She scrolled to another song while he scribbled a note.

"Your father was a member of the wolf clan and involved in the Cherokee community."

After hitting stop, Melody selected another song.

"Ah, here is an interesting tidbit. You attended a snake-handling church with your parents before—"

She stiffened and backed out to the upper-level menu to select a different category.

"You keep fiddling with your music player. Are you still agitated? Why don't you put your current song on the speakers, lean back, close your eyes, and listen?"

Her fingers froze and she shot him a look. Her knee resumed its agitated bouncing. The click sounded extra loud as she connected the speaker cable to the player. Finger trembling as it hovered over the button, she pressed play with a deep breath.

The intro filled the room as she wilted against the couch back and closed her eyes.

God bless and protect
For these days will not last
They're all I have
And they grow up fast
I need You with them
Both day and night
When they're alone in the dark
God show them light

I'll pray on my knees
Till bruised and blue
For all I have
Is my faith in You
My children are
Blessings from above
God show them light
Show them Your love

They're not always with me
I'm not always with them
So in Your Name
I pray Amen
If You hold my children

In the palm of Your hand
They'll see the light
Footprints in the sand

As the last notes hung in the air, Melody opened her eyes and switched off the player.

Dr. Kane sat with forefingers steepled against his lower lip, his blue eyes clouded in thought. Giving his head a shake, he leaned back in the leather chair. "What a tender and loving song. I don't think I've ever heard it before." He nodded toward the speakers. "Play it again."

CHAPTER NINE

February 23, 2008 – Melody, age 9

Daddy and I tromped across the twigs, leaves, and rocks on our way back to the truck. We had parked outside the lot in a place Daddy knew about. He said some people didn't understand about the snakes, so it was better not to advertise what we were after. If they saw the snake stick, they'd be suspicious and might follow us.

I held his hand and thought about what happened back at the creek. How had I known what to sing to calm the snakes? The words and tune had just come out of me. I hadn't had to think about it.

"Daddy, why do you think the snakes all came to listen to my song?"

His jaw pulsed like it always did when I asked something he didn't want to answer. "I wish I knew, Melody. I'm still trying to figure how they heard you because they don't have ears."

I never thought about that. *Hmm.* They did hear me, though. Otherwise, they would have slithered away from Daddy into the woods instead of coming toward the creek. Rattlesnakes and copperheads don't like water so they wouldn't come in.

"Do you think …?"

Daddy squeezed my hand. "Not now, sweetheart. I need to block the image of all those sidewinders heading toward my baby."

I gripped his hand back. "I'm not a baby anymore, Daddy."

He smiled at me. "You'll always be my baby girl."

"Oh, Daddy." I huffed.

Funny how snakes had always liked me. Even though I never handled them in church, I wasn't afraid of them. An old memory popped into my head.

"Have I ever sung to snakes before?"

Daddy peered at the sky and angled our path to the left before answering. "When you were about three. Hush, now. We don't want anyone to hear us."

Since we were too far from the trails to be heard, his words were nothing more than an excuse not to talk about it. But I remembered …

Laying down the yellow crayon, I smiled at the picture I'd colored. The sun shined on our house, and the flowers sprouted in the garden. Mama would like the happy picture. She'd think the pink, purple, and green with orange polka-dot flowers were beautiful.

I got up to take the picture into the kitchen but remembered she'd asked me to play in the family room while she finished baking. My lower lip slid out. She said the oven would be too hot and I might get burned. So she'd brought out the tub of crayons and a stack of drawing paper and put them on my pink plastic table.

When I'd asked what I should do when I was done coloring, she'd said I could read my books or play with puzzles. Most times I had to ask to get the puzzles out. Mama didn't like it when the pieces got scattered.

I moved the finished picture to the top of the table and grabbed another piece of paper. But I didn't feel like coloring anymore. I wanted Mama to see the one I already drawed. I held each crayon over my head and dropped them into the crayon tub. The breeze through the open front door lifted the corner of my picture. I squealed and put the crayon tub on the picture so it wouldn't blow away.

Now what? I could read. *Raksha!* I hurried to the bedroom. Mama didn't want me to leave the family room, but I'd forgotten Raksha Waya. I dove onto the bed and grabbed the stuffed wolf that had slipped down behind my pillow.

"Poor Raksha." I kissed his nose. "How could I forget you?" Hugging him to my chest, I ran back to the family room. "I'm gonna read you a story, Raksha."

I stroked his soft fur while searching the bookshelf. "What do you want me to read? You should pick it since you were left alone."

I held Raksha toward the bookshelf. His nose touched a book.

"Good choice, Raksha. *One fish two fish red fish blue fish.* I can read you the whole thing by myself."

We walked to the reading corner and I settled against my special reading pillow and tucked Raksha Waya on my lap. Holding the book out, I opened to the first page. "Can you see the pictures?"

Reading all the words on the page, I pointed to the pictures so Raksha could learn his colors. He told me he didn't know colors too good, so I had to teach him like Mama had taught me.

When would Daddy be back?

He was getting the wood for the fireplace ready. He said winter would come soon enough and we needed to be prepared. He wouldn't let me come with him because Mama said I had a cold.

I did a big sniff. My nose was snuffy but I didn't feel bad. But Mama said the wind outside was too cold for me.

I wanted Mama to finish her baking so she could read me a story with Raksha. Snuggling with Mama was one of my favorite things. I turned the page.

The screen-door opened a crack. I finished reading the page before something dragged across the floor. Why did I hear a rattle?

"Jus' a minute, Raksha." I put the book down next to me and looked toward the sounds.

A big snake moved slowly across the floor toward us. Its tongue flicked out like it tasted the air. I stuck my tongue out. Mama's baking smelled good, but I couldn't taste it. The snake had squiggly bands on it.

When it got close to my feet, the snake stopped. It pulled its head back and wiggled its rattle. I cuddled Raksha Waya in my arms. The snake might be afraid Raksha would attack, so I sang to the snake. Raksha always liked my singing, so the snake might, too.

Daddy came to the door and grabbed the handle, then stopped. "Melody, be very still, honey."

What was wrong with Daddy? His eyes looked funny.

"Is that you, Will?" Mama's footsteps came toward the family room.

The snake flicked its tongue against the bottom of my slippers.

Ew. Who wants to lick the bottom of feet?

Daddy moved toward the entry and put his arm out to stop Mama.

"Melody?" Mama, her voice high and weak, struggled against Daddy's arm. "I have to get my baby."

The snake curled around my feet and moved its head next to my ankle.

"I singin' the snake a song."

Daddy nodded. "Keep singing, baby girl."

The snake hissed and wiggled the rattle. Once I started singing again, it stopped making noise and moved a little closer.

Mama looked upset. "Will, do something."

"Stay calm, Allie. I'm going to get the snake stick and case. Make sure Melody keeps singing because it seems to soothe it."

The snake slithered along my leg and it tickled. When it reached the pillow, it turned and circled by my knee.

Mama gripped Daddy's arm and stopped him from leaving. "Will? Help her."

The snake laid its head across my ankles and closed its eyes. I switched to singing the lullaby Mama sang to me each night. *God Show Them Light.*

Daddy took Mama's hand off his arm. "It's going to sleep. Stay here. I'll be right back." Daddy moved silently out the door.

Mama's eyes were big and worried. Maybe she needed the lullaby, too.

"Sing with me, Mama."

When I spoke, the snake lifted its head, so I sang more. Mama joined me, but her voice shook.

Daddy came back with the snake stick and took one step at a time across the family room. He opened the jaw of the stick and slowly lowered it over the snake's neck.

The jaw whispered across my leg as he closed it and picked up the snake. As Daddy put the snake in the case, Mama ran to me and scooped me up.

"Mama, don't hug me so tight."

She stroked my hair and put my head on her shoulder.

"Mama, Raksha is getting squished."

She pulled her head back and kissed my cheeks. "I was so worried about you, baby."

"Don't cry, Mama. Raksha Waya protects me."

Daddy took the snake out to the shed and came back and hugged Mama and me. Why was everyone so upset?

"Did I do sumpthin' bad?"

"No, Melody. Mama is happy you're okay." She showered me with kisses.

Daddy kissed my cheek. "You were such a brave girl."

Brave? I wrinkled my nose. "But I didn't have to be brave. Raksha Waya was with me, an' he always protects me from bad things. He scared away the monsters in the closet and under the bed."

Daddy touched my face and his dark eyes stared into mine. "Melody, snakes have poison and can hurt you."

I shook my head. "He came in to see what Mama was baking and wanted to take a nap." Remembering my picture, I squirmed. "Mama, let me down. I want to show you sumpthin'."

She set me down and I grabbed my picture. "Look. I drawed our house."

Mama took the picture and smiled through her tears. "It's beautiful, Melody. I'll put it on the refrigerator so I can see it every day."

We reached the truck. Daddy unlocked it and put the snake behind the seat. It had been a long time since I had thought about when the snake came into the house.

Mama still sang the lullaby to me.

CHAPTER TEN

Spring 2015 – Melody, age 16

Melody flipped down the visor to block the sun and opened the mirror cover. She fluffed her bangs and ruffled her hair behind her ears so it cascaded in waves down her back. Her finger brushed her lips, then she pulled a tube of gloss out of her purse.

Mrs. Langdon stopped the car at a red light. "You know you ain't got no chance with that doc of yours." She met Melody's eyes in the rearview mirror. "He's probably got at least one girlfriend and isn't gonna be interested in a schoolgirl like you."

Melody's cheeks burned. She focused on the visor mirror and raised the gloss wand to her lips.

"'Sides, he won't want someone who don't talk. Man'd get tired of doing all the conversatin', so don't go gettin' yer hopes up."

With deliberation, Melody smoothed the gloss over her lips, plunged the wand back in the tube, and snapped it in her purse.

The light changed and Mrs. Langdon pulled away.

After another look in the mirror, Melody rubbed her lips together to spread the gloss evenly, then flipped the visor back into place.

"I don' know what the two of you do for two hours every day, anyway. Sit there an' stare at each other?"

Melody rolled her eyes and turned to watch the passing blocks through the window.

Mrs. Langdon pulled into the parking lot. "I'm not sure he's doin' a good job. It's been a couple weeks and you still ain't made a peep."

When the car came to a stop in the parking spot, Melody hopped out before Mrs. Langdon shut off the engine. She shut the door, waved goodbye with a smile, and hurried up the walk to the office.

Lily looked up when she opened the door. "Go on in. He's ready for you."

Dr. Kane closed his laptop and stood when she entered.

He waited for her to close and lock the door then swept his arm toward the alcove. "You look nice."

She grinned as she passed, then plopped in her spot at the end of the couch and crossed her legs.

"I've not seen you carry a purse before." He sat and cocked his head. "Practical, yet stylish. Nice choice."

Melody ducked her head and turned from his gaze.

He flipped open his notebook. "I've been thinking about the lullaby you shared with me last session. It may be time to talk about what happened to your mother."

Her smile disappeared and a block of ice formed in her stomach.

"Remember, I'm here to help you work through these issues. Nothing can ever compare to the loss of your mother, especially at such a young age."

She couldn't meet his eyes, so she focused on his mouth instead.

"Death of a loved one is difficult. We'll go slow. Nothing I can say will change what happened in the past. I'm so sorry for your loss."

Tears burned but didn't fall.

"Try closing your eyes. Lean your head back. Take a few deep breaths."

Melody followed his directions.

"I want you to focus on a good moment at your mother's funeral. It doesn't have to be a big moment, just something you remember. Something comforting."

Melody clutched her music player and opened her eyes a slit to see the navigation menu.

"If you're going to pick songs, I want to hear them."

She connected the player to the speakers and pressed play. Leaning back, she listened as "His Eye is on the Sparrow" filled the room.

After the song completed, Dr. Kane tapped the end of his pen against his lips. "I asked you to think about a comforting moment at your mother's funeral and you picked a song where the refrain talks about being happy and free. Did you feel that way or is it your mother who is happy and free?" He raised his eyebrows and waited a moment. "Still not talking, huh? That's okay, you shared a memory through music and we just took a step closer to having a conversation."

He scribbled something on his notepad, then placed the pen at the top. "What I'm going to ask you to do next might be a little harder. I want you to think about how you felt at the funeral."

Her thumb twitched and she picked up the music player, focused on finding a song.

"Don't forget to put it on speaker when you push play."

Melody snapped her head up and gave him a long look. She fumbled with the speaker cable as she pulled it out and pushed the cable back in again. She set down the player, hid her eyes with her fists, and rocked.

"Take your time. We're not in a hurry."

His voice helped soothe her. She stopped rocking and took a few breaths. With a trembling finger, she pressed play. The bluesy notes flowed out of the speakers.

You may be gone
And free to fly
But with you gone
I will always cry
For all I love
Has disappeared
Whispers from lips
Are all I hear.

The ignorance of man
Angers me so
Mouths move without thinking
When only God could know
If it was His will
For all I know to be gone
It doesn't help
When what I feel is wrong.

Tears silently rolled down her face unchecked. Dr. Kane leaned forward, yanked a tissue out of a box, and handed it to her.

I am too young
To feel this way
Forever eclipsed
By a darkened day
The sun doesn't shine
On me anymore
Afraid of not knowing
What I have to live for.

With no idea
Why do mouths speak
Not knowing themselves
What it is they seek
When passing judgment leaves
God's eyes on fire
Mouths that move
Make man the liar.

The end result
Is still the same
I am alone
Still in pain

I will stand
At your grave and weep
Without you
No peace
No sleep

The chorus repeated and her shoulders shook as she sobbed.

CHAPTER ELEVEN

February 27, 2008 – Melody, age 9

Standing on the gravel path leading to the blue-fronted church, I clutched Raksha Waya to my chest. I hid him in the car on our way over because Uncle Harlan would've had a fit, and I couldn't face today without him. His worn, matted fur helped me feel like I might get through the day.

I swallowed hard. Dressed in an unfamiliar, slightly too large, black dress, I scuffed my toe in the gravel. The last thing I wanted to do was enter the door and join the service. If I didn't go in soon, my uncle would send Aunt Ruth to fetch me. Or worse, Uncle Harlan would come get me himself.

He couldn't yell at me in front of the whole congregation for bringing Raksha, could he? Jeb and Samuel had already gone inside. They had to wear a tie with a stark white shirt and black pants for the occasion. Nobody argued with Uncle Harlan about what they wore. He had been in such a bad mood.

Mine wasn't any better.

Taking a deep breath, I forced my feet to shuffle toward the door. Pastor Wolfson stood inside, beckoning me. As I reached the doorsill, he leaned forward and grasped my hand between his, the hand with the stubby finger on top.

"I'm so sorry for your loss, Melody. Sister Harper wants you to know she'll sing her best to honor your mother."

Uncle Harlan stormed up behind Pastor Wolfson. "Don't worry

about her feelings, Pastor. She chose to disrespect her mother's memory."

My jaw went slack. I would *never* disrespect Mama's memory.

Pastor Wolfson straightened. "Brother Ramsey, I don't quite follow your logic. What on Earth could this blessed child have done?"

I squeezed Rakkie tighter afraid of what Uncle Harlan would say.

"It's not what she's done, but what she *isn't* doing. You gave her the opportunity to sing for her mother." His nostrils turned white at the corners. "But instead of giving her mother one last gift, she chose to be selfish and refused to sing."

What? I hadn't refused. How could I sing for Mama with a throat so tight I could hardly breathe?

Pastor Wolfson held up his hands. "No, you misunderstood, Brother Ramsey. I only asked Melody if she *wanted* to sing because if it would help her deal with the situation, I wanted her to know she could."

Uncle Harlan opened his mouth to respond, but his gaze dropped to Raksha Waya. He spluttered and his face darkened. "You're not bringing that filthy thing inside." The vein along his forehead popped.

My head drooped. I couldn't do this without Raksha.

Pastor Wolfson put his hand on my shoulder. "Brother Ramsey, I think it's fine. A time like this a girl needs a friend." He smiled at me. "I'm sure her friend won't make any disturbance."

Uncle Harlan frowned and anger lines ran from his nose to his chin. "All right. Go sit with your cousins."

I hurried down the aisle as people whispered behind me.

Poor girl.

Such a sad thing to happen.

So lucky to have such a devout uncle like Brother Ramsey to take her in.

I nearly choked. How could *anyone* call me lucky? My heart and spirit were broken and I was lost and alone. Swallowing hard, I forced back the tears. Uncle Harlan had already told me fifty times tears weren't going to change anything, and I dishonored God's will by being sad.

God's will? Every time he said it, anger flamed through me. This wasn't

God's will … it couldn't be. Or God was a terrible and mean God, who wanted to hurt his children.

I sat at the front next to Samuel, pressing my arms to my sides so I wouldn't touch him and give him any reason to pester me. Uncle Harlan would blame me, and he'd probably blow up if anything happened during the service.

Settling Rakkie on my lap, I raised my head. My eyes filled with tears. *Mama's casket.* Plain with clear-varnished wood and brass fittings, it gleamed in the dim light. A cross of white roses and lilies lay across the casket lid. Uncle Harlan and Aunt Ruth wouldn't listen when I told them Mama would want pink mountain laurel. They were her favorite after Daddy and I planted them next to the house.

My heart hitched. Daddy. Where was he? When was he coming back? He wouldn't leave me forever … would he? I needed him. Fear twisted my stomach. He'd move heaven and earth to be here for me today, unless … I swallowed a sob.

The whispered hush quieted when Pastor Wolfson stood in front of the pulpit and held up his hand. He wore the deep blue vest Mama had always liked over his light-blue, long-sleeved shirt.

"Friends, neighbors, and family of Allison Ramsey Fisher, we gather today to honor her memory and say our goodbyes."

A tear rolled down my cheek and dropped on Rakkie's back.

"Sister Fisher was a beloved member of this church and community, and we shall all feel the loss since she is no longer here to walk among us." He gripped the sides of the pulpit and stared at the ground for a moment before continuing. "She had the most special smile of anyone I have had the privilege of knowing. It came from her pure heart."

And I'd never see Mama's smile again.

"I'd like to open Allison's memorial service with these words from Mary Frye—words I had the pleasure of discussing with Allison one morning after a church service."

A pew creaked, marring the moment of silence.

"Her heart had been heavy about the loss of one of our members, and she shared these words with me as having helped her deal with her grief."

He shuffled papers, then closed his eyes for a moment before reciting the words.

Do not stand at my grave and cry,
I am not there, I did not die,
I am the thousand winds that blow,
I am the diamond glint on snow,
When you awaken in the morning hush,
I am the swift uplifting rush,
Of quiet birds in circled flight,
I am bright stars that shine at night,
I am the sunlight on ripened grain,
I am the gentle autumn rain.
Do not stand at my grave and weep,
I am not there, I do not sleep.

My heart felt so heavy I couldn't listen to Pastor Wolfson anymore. The words bounced off me. I could do nothing more than stare at the casket. Mama was locked inside ... in the dark.

Was she with God? Did she go into the light? Or was her spirit still here, watching us as we prayed for her soul?

Sister Harper joined Pastor Wolfson at the front. Mama used to say that Sister Harper's smile could light the way in a coal mine. But today she didn't smile at all. Before she sang, she looked directly into my eyes and the warmth of her heart comforted mine.

I couldn't understand why Uncle Harlan got mad when I told Pastor Wolfson no ... he never wanted me to sing in church. He thought I sang for my own glory. But Mama always said my voice was a gift and by singing I brought glory to God.

Singing for Mama would have been too hard. Not here. Not now. I'd sing for her but would do it alone. Where it would be a song just for her and me. And I'd sing one for Daddy, too ... wherever he was.

After Sister Harper's solo, Pastor Wolfson laid his hand on her arm. "Let's let one of Sister Fisher's favorite hymns, 'His Eye is on the Sparrow', speak to our hearts."

Why should I feel discouraged,
why should the shadows come,
Why should my heart be lonely,
and long for heav'n and home,
When Jesus is my portion? My constant Friend is He:
His eye is on the sparrow, and I know He watches me;
His eye is on the sparrow, and I know He watches me.

I sing because I'm happy, I sing because I'm free,
For His eye is on the sparrow, and I know He watches me.

"Let not your heart be troubled,"
His tender word I hear,
And resting on His goodness, I lose my doubts and fears;
Though by the path He leadeth, but one step I may see;
His eye is on the sparrow, and I know He watches me;
His eye is on the sparrow, and I know He watches me.

The congregation went into the chorus again. Mama had sung the song around the house while cleaning or cooking. She used to rock me to sleep and would sing it like a lullaby.

Mama loved the mountain and hearing the birds in the trees, the way the breeze bent the grasses down by the creek. How would I make it through without hearing her voice ever again? All I wanted to do was curl up on the floor and cry my heart out. I hugged Raksha Waya closer. He'd have to be my family from now on.

When the service finished and the bearers had carried Mama's casket out, Pastor Wolfson came over and put his hand with the stubby finger on my shoulder.

"I want you to know how much your mother will be missed, Melody. She's with God now. And if you ever need to talk, I'll be here to listen."

He tried to be kind, but I didn't want Mama to be with God. I still needed her. How could she leave me?

We drove to the cemetery and Pastor Wolfson read verses over the grave about there being a time for everything. It wasn't Mama's time to die. *It wasn't.*

She still had stuff to do on earth. I prayed as hard as I could for God to send Mama back to me. He could do miracles, right? If Jesus rose from the dead, then why couldn't God do the same for Mama?

Maybe He'd do it at Easter. That's when Jesus had come back. Mama would have to wait a little longer to rise from the dead than Jesus had, but if I prayed hard every night and Raksha Waya prayed with me, God would answer my prayers.

When they lowered the casket into the ground, I gripped Rakkie tight. I didn't want to say goodbye. Would she be able to get out if they put dirt on top of her? Jesus had to move a big stone out of the way, so Mama should be able to dig her way out. She liked digging in the garden.

How many days would it be until Easter? It had to be coming soon because we had already done the ceremony with the ashes. I'd have to ask Pastor Wolfson. He'd know. Then I could put it on my calendar and mark off each day. And each day marked off would remind me to pray to tell God I wanted him to give me Mama back. And Daddy.

The service finally finished. Aunt Ruth put her hand on my back and led me toward the car.

"Wait, Aunt Ruth." I ran to Pastor Wolfson.

He grabbed my hand in both of his. "I'm so sorry for your loss, Melody."

"I have a question."

He smiled. "How may I help you?"

I felt Uncle Harlan staring at my back but didn't want to turn around and make eye contact. I had to get an answer first. Then I could go back to his house.

"What day is Easter this year?"

Pastor Wolfson's eyebrows rose. "That's not the question I expected, but Easter Sunday is March twenty-third."

With two days left in February, that meant I only had to wait twenty-five more days. I'd better start praying to God and letting him know all the reasons I needed Mama back.

I climbed into the car next to the boys and didn't even care when Samuel pinched me. I had a plan.

CHAPTER TWELVE

Spring, 2015 – Melody, age 16

Melody gripped the crumpled tissue and balled it in her fist. Her tears no longer flowed, but they were still close to the surface.

Dr. Kane handed her a bottle of cold water. "Take a sip and you'll feel better. It's hard to face the memories of a life-changing loss, so take a moment and collect yourself."

The ice-cold of the bottle seeped into her hand. The cap made a snapping sound as she twisted it off. She took a long drink and her throat relaxed, but the cold water made her teeth ache.

Dr. Kane ran both hands through his hair as he leaned back in his chair. "Are you doing better?"

She nodded.

He flicked his wrist and checked his watch. "Believe it or not, we still have a lot of time left in our session. Thank you for sharing something you felt so deeply. It was a powerful and emotional song." He gave a quick frown and settled his glasses more firmly in place. "But I think you need a break from thinking about the funeral." He flipped through the pages in her folder.

"You spent about a week with your uncle after your mother's death before going into foster care?" He made a notation on his pad. "It's not unheard of, but it is unusual. Let me see ..."

He reached over his chair and hefted an accordion file onto his lap. He dug through the contents. "Usually you would stay with family unless there was a reason you shouldn't. Why would you be removed from your uncle's house after a week?"

Melody twiddled with the navigation menu.

Dr. Kane raised a finger in the air. "Uh-uh."

She connected the player to the speakers and fast-forwarded on the song. When it reached the right place, she hit play.

The end result
Is still the same
I am alone
Still in pain
I will stand
At your grave and weep
Without you
No peace
No sleep

She pressed pause.

Dr. Kane narrowed his eyes. "Same song, but only the tail end of the second verse. And I get it … you feel alone and in pain with the loss of your mother and disappearance of your father." He ran his fingers along the scruff on his jaw and stared off into space for a moment.

"I wonder how you felt about living with your uncle and his family." His words were spoken more to himself than to her.

She hit the reverse button on the player and after spot-checking a couple of times, pressed play.

The ignorance of man
Angers me so
Mouths move without thinking
When only God could know
If it was His will
For all I know to be gone
It doesn't help
When what I feel is wrong.

Melody jabbed the pause button again.

His blue eyes pierced through her.

After staring, Dr. Kane shook his head and went back to digging through the accordion file. "For a second it felt almost like we were having a conversation. Sounds as if you didn't like your uncle much." He yanked up the corner of a paper and peered at it before shoving it back in the file. "I'm trying to find the initial report filed by your caseworker, Rebecca Prescott, on why you were placed into foster care. It has to be in here somewhere. I imagine it was a rough day for you. No matter the reason."

Melody bit her lower lip, then took a deep breath and pressed play.

I am too young
To feel this way
Forever eclipsed
By a darkened day
The sun doesn't shine
On me anymore
Afraid of not knowing
What I have to live for.

"Aha!"

Melody jumped as she switched the player into pause mode.

Dr. Kane whisked out a few stapled pages from the accordion file. "Found it." He put the file back on the floor and put the papers on his notepad. "Give me a moment while I read through. My interest is piqued." He grabbed the remote from the side table and switched on the floor lamp.

The wind tore at the leaves in the tree. The squirrel had been absent all afternoon with the storm blowing in. Ominous clouds rolled across the sky and swallowed the waning afternoon light.

Dr. Kane ran his finger along the page as he read. "Ms. Prescott says the teacher uncovered the problem after you fell asleep during class. Were you having trouble sleeping? It'd be understandable, if so."

Melody fiddled with the music player, but this time when she hit play, a lone voice came out of the speakers, singing *a cappella.*

Rattlesnake, rattlesnake, I fear you none
Crawling beneath, the moon and sun
Show me no harm, under the sky
I will show no fear, though afraid to die

Dr. Kane dropped his mouth open and his finger froze on the page. He looked from Miss Prescott's report to Melody and back again.

CHAPTER THIRTEEN

March 2, 2008 – Melody, age 9

One lone dress hung in the closet. The detested black dress I'd worn for Mama's funeral. With a sigh, I pulled it off the hanger and slipped it over my head. The rough material rubbed uncomfortably against my skin. Uncle Harlan and Aunt Ruth still hadn't taken me back home to get my clothes. If they didn't take me soon, I'd go get them myself.

Uncle Harlan glanced through the open door as he passed in the hall. "Good. You're almost ready."

I pulled on the sleeve of the dress. "What happened to the other dresses Aunt Ruth gave me?"

He frowned. "I had her take them away. Black is fitting for mourning." He checked his watch, then continued down the hall.

But I didn't want to wear black. Mama always liked me in colorful clothes. I flopped onto the bed and pulled Rakkie on my lap. When he came to pick me up, Uncle Harlan wouldn't let me bring anything but essentials—hairbrush, toothbrush, and I had to fight to bring Raksha Waya. He didn't even mention Mama.

No. I won't think about what happened.

I had Aunt Ruth to thank for having Raksha Waya with me. Uncle Harlan said stuffed toys were for babies. He didn't understand Rakkie was part of the family—not a toy.

Jeb poked his head in the door. "Dad says get your half-breed butt in the car, now."

Gritting my teeth, I slipped Rakkie under my pillow until I returned.

Jeb never lost a chance to make fun of me because Daddy was Cherokee. *Stupid, Jeb. It wasn't like he didn't have different kinds of blood in him, too. Just not Cherokee.* He might be in high school but from what I could tell, he hated everyone and everything. It must hurt to carry hate around all the time.

After glancing over his shoulder to make sure I followed, Jeb strode toward the car. Things had been so hard over the past few days, I didn't need him to make fun of me for being different. I didn't want to go to church today. Except, God would be there and He might listen to me when I prayed in church more than He did at Uncle Harlan's house.

I used to ask Mama how she knew God was with us. She said we could always feel God through love and would know He was with us then. At home, I felt love everywhere, in every corner. At Uncle Harlan's house, I couldn't find love at all.

Maybe it was hard for love to grow when everyone had so many different feelings. Uncle Harlan was filled with anger, Jeb with hate, Aunt Ruth with dread and doubt, and Samuel with spitefulness. How could love live with all those bad emotions?

As I slid across the vinyl backseat, a drop of fear tried to grow. If God stayed away from Uncle Harlan's house because of all the bad stuff, how would He hear me and Raksha praying for Him to bring Mama back to me? I'd have to ask God in church. I didn't worry about reaching him there because God had to go to church, just like I did. It was His job to be there.

When we entered the church, Brother Ferrell walked in carrying a snake case. As he passed me, the snake inside hissed and shook its rattle. A picture of an attacking snake flashed in my head and I whimpered and backed into the pew.

Uncle Harlan grabbed my arm, yanked it, and dragged me back outside.

"We're going to nip this in the bud right now. I will not tolerate any fear of snakes. You disrespect God's house and God's word when you show fear of His creature."

What was wrong with me? The rattle made me feel all shaky inside.

I'd never felt nervous around them before.

He leaned over, put his face right in mine, and shook me. "Do you understand me?"

I nodded.

He dropped my arm and straightened. "Then we'll go back inside, and you'll prove your faith to God by taking up a snake during the service. You're old enough to start handling."

What? Mama and Daddy had said I was way too young to start handling yet. They said kids weren't allowed to handle because of the danger involved. "But Uncle Harlan …"

"No buts, Melody. You either come with me into the service and be prepared to take up a snake to prove your faith and show your respect to the Lord, our God …" His frown deepened. "Or you can go sit in the car during the service and I'll deal with you later."

I didn't know whether I could do it. Mama hadn't wanted me to. It was too soon after her death. But if it meant God might listen to my prayer, I had to try.

Sitting in the pew next to Aunt Ruth, I couldn't stop my knee from bouncing. Why had Uncle Harlan insisted on my handling? Jeb didn't handle yet, and he was a lot older than me. And Samuel didn't handle, either. So it wasn't fair for him to force me to do it. Maybe Uncle Harlan wanted me to prove something to *him*—not God.

During the music ministry when others ran to the front to pick up snakes, Uncle Harlan glared at me. The knots in my stomach tightened. Rising to my feet, my knees shook, but I pushed on out of the pew. Taking a step toward the front, sweat broke out on my forehead and I got dizzy.

Step. I shook uncontrollably. I had to do this to bring Mama back.

Step. Folks in the pews nudged one another and pointed in my direction. Eyes forward, I focused on those dancing with the snakes. Brother Farrell's snake stared right at me. My breath caught in my throat and the edges of my vision turned dark.

I couldn't do it.

My heels clicked against the floor as I ran down the aisle and out the door. My feet flew along the path to the parking area. I yanked open the car door and sat in the back. I buried my face in my hands. Would God hate me for running out? I hadn't had a chance to ask Him my questions yet.

Shivering, I rubbed my arms. The cold morning cut through my dress and I didn't have a coat. I stared at the trees. The wind ruffled the new leaves trying to grow. Daddy used to tell me God was everywhere we looked. He was in the trees and the brooks; He filled the sky and was the rock on which we stand. Maybe God would hear me here. I tried to remember the verse Mama had taught me about the lilies of the field.

She'd said it meant we're not supposed to worry about things we don't have. God will take care of us if we have faith in Him. I did remember one verse because Mama sang it to me.

But seek ye first the kingdom of God, and His righteousness; and all these things shall be added unto you.

I only needed two things—Daddy to come home and Mama to come back to life.

Uncle Harlan didn't say a word to me as he drove us back to his house. When the car stopped, I ran in and grabbed Raksha.

Uncle Harlan slammed my bedroom door open. "You're going to learn to show the Lord respect, girl." He grabbed my neck and forced me to walk in front of him.

My neck hurt where he dug his fingers in.

He took me outside and shoved me toward the shed. He slipped the key in the lock and removed it from the hasp. The door creaked as it opened and then he thrust me through.

"I'm not going to allow you to follow your mother's footsteps. You'll learn to make peace with snakes and not show them any fear. Or else."

He grabbed a snake case from the shelf, put it on the ground, and opened it. He stepped backward out of the shed and swung the door shut. The latch clicked. Uncle Harlan on one side of the door, and the snake and me locked inside.

"I'll come get you in time for school in the morning."

His footsteps receded.

Light filtered through the cracks in the shed slats. In the dim light, the snake coiled in the corner, its tongue flicking out periodically. I slowly lowered to the ground and hugged Raksha Waya tight.

The inside of the shed was slightly warmer than outside. Staying warm might be a bigger problem than keeping the snake calm. It ignored me and remained coiled, but the cold seeped into my bones. I scanned the shelves. There had to be something in here I could use to help keep warm.

A tarp sat on a shelf on the opposite side of the shed from the snake. But I might not be tall enough to pull it down. Standing on tiptoes, I grabbed a corner and tugged. My fingers slipped. I set Rakkie on a lower shelf, then reached with both hands and tugged.

The weight of the tarp almost knocked me over as I caught it.

Making sure to keep my movements small so I didn't threaten the snake, I unfolded the tarp and spread it out. Then I grabbed Rakkie and carefully crawled under a corner. Once settled with Rakkie on my lap, I pulled it over us and tucked it under my chin.

The hours passed as the light changed and moved through the shed. My tailbone ached and my back hurt from sitting still for so long. Twilight came. Surely Uncle Harlan didn't really mean to leave me here with the snake all night.

When the darkness was complete and I could no longer see my hand in front of my face, I faced the hard truth—Uncle Harlan meant it. I'd spend the night locked in a small space with a pit viper.

While my toes still felt frozen, the rest of me was warmer with the tarp. My eyes drooped and closed. Then I heard it.

Hiss. Rattle. The whisper of something dragging across the floorboards.

The snake was on the move. The slight rattle as it slithered through the shed made my heart pound. I froze. I had no idea where it was and whether it was close to me. Would it sense my fear?

Trying not to freak out, I took a deep breath and sang my rattlesnake song.

Rattlesnake, rattlesnake, I fear you none
Crawling beneath, the moon and sun
Show me no harm, under the sky
I will show no fear, though afraid to die

The big body slithered over part of the tarp. I wanted to whimper, but I didn't want it to attack. Its head poked underneath the tarp and it slid through the gap. If the snake bit me, I would probably die. Even if someone knew I'd been bitten, they'd pray, but they wouldn't take me to the doctor. Whether I lived or died would be according to God's will.

On your belly, slither on by
Rattlesnake don't bite, don't make me cry
The hills are full, in the green green grass
Please leave me be, let me pass

The snake curled against my leg. I finally understood. It was cold and needed a source of warmth. I relaxed against the shed wall. I wouldn't be able to sleep, but Mama must be watching and taking care of me from heaven. She wouldn't let the snake hurt me.

Gray fingers of light crept across the shed floor. The night had passed, and the snake remained snuggled against my leg. How long before Uncle Harlan came to release me? My bones had turned into rock and I wasn't sure I'd be able to move.

I wanted to stretch and loosen up but didn't want to disturb the rattler. My tummy twisted at the thought of what might happen when Uncle Harlan came to get me. I couldn't move because of the snake and Uncle Harlan would get cranky. What if he ripped the tarp off and the snake attacked?

When I thought he might have forgotten me, the key scraped against the lock. The door swung outward and Uncle Harlan stepped through the doorway.

"Don't just sit there. You have to get washed up, changed, and ready for school."

The rattlesnake stirred against my leg. My throat went dry making it hard to speak.

"Shhh—"

He cut me off. "Don't hush me, girl." He turned his head from one side to the other, checking the inside of the shed. "Where is the snake?"

Its rattle vibrated against my leg.

"Under the tarp." I said the words as quietly as I could.

"Don't be ridiculous." He strode forward and yanked the tarp off.

Rakkie tumbled off my lap to the ground. The snake hissed, coiled, and raised its head, ready to strike. It threatened Uncle Harlan, but I didn't want to move for fear of attracting its attention.

Sweat broke out on Uncle Harlan's brow. How could he be sweating in the early morning chill? The snake continued to shake its rattle, its mouth open. I had to calm it. Even though I didn't like Uncle Harlan much, I didn't want him to get bitten by the snake.

The ground is yours, you own the dirt
Your poison, your venom, I know would hurt
So with you in mind, at night I pray
Rattlesnake grant me, another day

I sang as softly as I could. The rattle stilled, so I hummed the chorus.

Uncle Harlan took a step backward and the snake rattled loudly, then sprang forward. It landed with a *thump* inches from Uncle Harlan's foot, but instead of biting him, slithered through the open door as quickly as it could.

Uncle Harlan's jaw had dropped, and the snake was out the door before he closed his mouth again. His face reddened and he pointed at the door. "Go get ready for school. We'll talk about you hiding the snake later."

Hiding the snake? I wanted to cry. Why did Uncle Harlan hate me so much?

Ms. Tucker called the class to attention after morning recess and pointed to our next assignment written on the board. Read the next chapter in our history book. I pulled out the book, opened it to the right page, and stifled a yawn. I'd never been this tired in my life.

While reading the first paragraph, I closed my eyes for a moment. Someone drummed a pencil on their desk and my eyes flew open again. I reread the first paragraph and forced myself to read the next one. My head bobbed.

Shaking my head, I put my finger on the page to help my eyes focus and I propped my cheek on my hand so my head couldn't bob. My eyes closed. I needed a moment of rest.

"Melody."

Ms. Tucker called me softly and laid her hand on my shoulder. "Are you okay?"

Oh, no. I had fallen asleep. How much trouble would I be in for falling asleep during class?

I rubbed my face and nodded. Ignoring the snickering from my classmates, I followed Ms. Tucker into the hall.

Ms. Tucker crouched so we were face-to-face. "Are you sure you're okay? You don't feel sick?"

I shook my head. "I'm just tired. I didn't sleep last night."

Ms. Tucker's eyes saddened. "I'm sorry you're having trouble sleeping, Melody. Sometimes after someone we love passes on, we can't quiet our mind."

She looked so sympathetic I couldn't stop the words from tumbling out. "But that's not why I'm tired. I didn't sleep last night because Uncle Harlan locked me in a shed with a big rattlesnake."

Shock lines wrinkled Ms. Tucker's forehead. "He … he locked you in the shed? With a rattlesnake?" Her voice rose to a squeak. "All night?"

"Please don't keep me after school for falling asleep. I'll try really hard to stay awake for the rest of the day. And I don't want to get in any more trouble with Uncle Harlan."

She blinked a few times. "Melody, you aren't in any trouble for falling asleep. I was concerned about your welfare." She stood. "I'm going to send you to the office so you can lie down and get some sleep. But first, give me a few moments to write a note to take with you."

"But I thought you said I wasn't in trouble."

"You're not. You need sleep, but you can't in class. The office has a cot you can lie on and be more comfortable."

I followed her back into the classroom and waited for her to write the note. She called the office to let them know I was coming and needed to sleep.

As soon as I walked into the office, I handed over the note and they led me into a room with a cot and covered me with a blanket. I don't think my eyes stayed open for more than two minutes.

When I woke, social services had arrived. They took me to my house to pick up my clothes and told me they were working on a placement for me. They asked me to tell them what I had told Ms. Tucker. I did. And my life changed forever.

CHAPTER FOURTEEN

Spring 2015, Melody, age 16

Dr. Kane jumped to his feet and paced, talking to himself. "Coincidence?" He ran a hand through his brown curls. "No. It can't be." He reached the bay window and stood next to the lamp, hands on hips, staring out.

The afternoon light had been devoured by the gloom from the storm clouds. The day had changed from bright sunlight to darkest night. The grooves of his furrowed brow were clear in the window's reflection as he stood lost in thought.

The couch squeaked as Melody shifted her position and the muscles in her throat tightened.

Dr. Kane turned toward the squeak. "I'm sorry, Melody, but the most incredible thought occurred to me, and I needed a moment to wrap my head around it." He completed a couple more pacing circuits before settling in his chair.

He seesawed his pen between thumb and forefinger drumming it against the notepad. "What do you think those clouds are going to do? Will we only get rain or a thunderstorm?"

Melody queued up Toto's "Africa" performed by the *a cappella* group, Perpetuum Jazzile, on the music player and glanced at Dr. Kane, who frowned as he flipped through his notes. She turned the speaker volume to the highest level and pressed play.

The sound of forty to fifty people rubbing their hands together came out of the speakers, followed by fingers snapping to mimic raindrops.

Dr. Kane's head popped up and he stared at the music player as the raindrops turned into a cloudburst. His eyes widened when the rain gave way to the rumble of thunder.

Melody stopped the music after the third thunderclap. She tried to keep her fingers from trembling as she folded her hands.

He pointed the pen at the player. "That wasn't a coincidence." He shifted his gaze to her, his jaw slack. "You directly answered my question." A grin lit his face. "We just had a conversation! With music. I thought it was fantastic when you used the music to convey your emotions, but this? This is amazing."

Melody buried her face in her hands and swallowed the bile trying to force its way up her esophagus. She rocked back and forth as her anxiety threatened to spiral out of control.

"No, no, no. This is a good thing. You don't have anything to fear, Melody."

She peeked through her fingers as he leaned back in his chair. Her hands slid onto her lap.

"We had a significant breakthrough. Unexpected, but wonderful." He stroked his stubble. "I am so proud of you for sharing your response. You were brave."

Lightning flashed outside and the thunderclap shook the windows. Dr. Kane jumped in his seat as rain poured down. "And you were right … thunderstorm it is."

He stood and paced the room again. "I have an idea I'd like to try during the last part of our session today." He checked his watch. "I'm going to ask some questions, and you'll use your music selections to answer."

A shiver ran down Melody's spine.

"Let's start with something relatively calm. Before your mother died, but on the same day, share a happy moment with me."

Melody searched her player for the right selection. She hit the forward button, then stopped. Flute music floated from the speakers before she hit forward again. Next stop a clarinet note escaped before she continued searching for the section she wanted. French horns sounded next. Then, finally, she had it queued to the right spot. She flicked her eyes toward Dr. Kane and he nodded.

She pressed play and the lively music of a string section filled the room.

Dr. Kane nodded in time to the music. "Prokofiev's *Peter and the Wolf.* Nice selection. Give me a moment." He grabbed the file folder and scanned a couple of pages. "Got it. You went hunting with your father on the morning of your mother's death."

Melody gave a brief nod.

"Fantastic." He clapped his hands together. "Now I'm going to ask something more difficult from you." He sat in his chair and leaned forward, peering earnestly through his glasses. "I want you to share with me how you felt when your mother died. Will you do that for me?"

Taking a deep breath, she queued another song.

You may be gone
And free to fly
But with you gone
I will always cry
For all I love
Has disappeared
Whispers from lips
Are all I hear.

She hit fast forward to the chorus.

I am too young
To feel this way
Forever eclipsed
By a darkened day
The sun doesn't shine
On me anymore
Afraid of not knowing
What I have to live for.

Dr. Kane whipped a couple of tissues out of the box and handed them to her. "You're doing great. How did she die?"

Melody returned to the *a cappella* song she had played earlier.

The ground is yours, you own the dirt
Your poison, your venom, I know would hurt
So with you in mind, at night I pray
Rattlesnake grant me, another day

Thunder rattled the windows.

CHAPTER FIFTEEN

February 23, 2008 – Melody, age 9

Daddy pulled the truck to a stop. I hopped out while he pulled the snake canister out from behind the seat.

"Go tell your mother we're home. She'll be worried about you and will want to see with her own eyes you're okay."

Mama worried too much. I'd been with Daddy. Nothing bad was going to happen.

I ran into the house. "Mama?" She wasn't in the kitchen or on the service porch. "Mama, we're home." Nothing but silence.

Maybe she went down by the brook. She liked to walk along the water and, as she told me, *commune with nature*. Daddy said nature spoke to her in a special way and I'd know what he meant in a few years because I took after my mama.

Daddy was the only one who told me I took after Mama. Everyone said how much I looked like Daddy and thought my love of the outdoors came from him. But Daddy said I related with nature more like Mama.

I ran down the hill, using the smooth sections to slide, and filled my lungs with the clean air, tinged lightly with smoke. Joy filled my heart. I reached the brook and the bubbling sound of the water rushing over the rocks and roots matched the way I felt inside.

Which way would Mama go on her walk? I looked both ways along the water and didn't see her. I'd follow the slope down a ways toward where the brook met up with the river. I had to remember not to go too far or Daddy would miss me. Tugging the beanie over my ears to fight the cutting breeze, I trotted along the water's edge.

After going around the bend, I saw Mama in the distance rounding a curve. I ran to catch up. I took in a deep breath to yell to her when I reached the curve Mama had disappeared around.

I held my breath.

She strolled with a man at her side and he had his arm around her shoulders. A funny feeling erupted in my stomach. Who was the man? And why was he dressed weird?

The woman was definitely Mama. Her red-gold hair hung down her back and she wasn't wearing a hat. I'd have to tease her. She never let me leave the house without something to keep my head warm during the cold weather months.

The man wore a long duster coat. It looked more like a preacher's robe than anything. But it wasn't Pastor Wolfson, and he didn't wear robes usually anyway—only for what he called the holy days. Why did the man have his arm across Mama's shoulders?

I opened my mouth to shout and let her know Daddy and I were home but stopped again. The funny feeling grew. I didn't want that man to see me. It felt wrong. Like something really bad would happen. Like the sunshine in my day had been hidden by a storm cloud.

I turned around and ran back to the house. Daddy was still in the snake shed, so I went into the house and sat on my bed. My feelings were all confused and I didn't know why.

"Melody?"

Mama called to me from outside. Would the strange man still be with her?

"Coming, Mama." I hopped off the bed and went out the front door.

Mama smiled when she saw me, and I ran to give her a big hug. No sign of the strange man.

"Did you have a good time?"

"Yes. I always have a good time on the mountain with Daddy."

Mama squeezed me against her side as we walked toward the snake shed. "And did you mind your daddy?"

"As soon as he gave me the signals to slow and stop, I did." Should I mention going to stand in the creek? "I only made one mistake and stepped on some dead leaves and they made noise."

"Sounds like you had a good first hunt."

We stopped at the door to the snake shed. Mama didn't often go inside. Since Daddy had told me the story about Mama and the snake, I knew why.

"Hey, Allie. I'd give you a kiss, but my hands are full at the moment."

Daddy had the snake we had captured in his hands. He raised an eyebrow at me. "Why did it take you so long to find your mother, miss?"

Mama stroked my hair. "You were looking for me? Did you think I was hiding in your bedroom?"

Daddy took a couple of steps closer. "She was supposed to be. What's up, baby girl? Where were you, Allie?"

I couldn't meet Daddy's gaze.

"I went for a walk by the brook."

Why didn't Mama say who walked beside her?

"Melody, do you want to explain why you didn't go look for your Mama like I asked you to?" Daddy's voice was stern.

"I did." The funny feeling was back in my tummy.

"You were in the house when I got back from my walk." Mama cupped my face and looked into my eyes. "Were you too tired after the hunt to look outside?"

"No. I did go down to the brook and I found you." Oops. I hadn't meant to say that. Why did I feel so weird?

"But honey, why didn't you let me know you were home if you found me?"

I bit my lower lip.

Daddy took another step toward us. "Melody, answer your mother."

"Because I didn't know who the strange man was, and I didn't want to disturb you if it was important." I said the words as fast as I could just to get them out.

"What man?"

Mama looked confused. "I don't know what she's talking about."

Daddy's frown deepened.

"The man with the duster coat who put his arm across your shoulders."

Daddy's hands tightened on the snake. It bared its fangs and struck.

It bit Mama in the face. She screamed and it struck again and hit her neck.

"Allie!" Daddy dropped the snake to catch Mama as she crumpled to the ground.

The snake slithered away.

Blood oozed from the bites on Mama's cheek and neck and mingled with the urine-colored venom. Daddy held her in his arms and lowered her to the ground where he cradled her.

I couldn't catch my breath. What was going to happen to Mama? Tears filled my eyes.

Daddy grabbed my wrist, his eyes full of tears. "Melody, sing your song."

What?

He tugged on my arm. "Sing the snake song. Ask the snake spirits to spare her. You have to sing and heal her bites."

The tears rolled from my eyes. "I can't remember the words, Daddy."

He pulled me down to the ground. "You have to, baby girl. You're special. The snakes will listen to you, like in the story about Chief Yellow Snake."

Sobbing, I tried to remember the words that had come out of my mouth in the creek.

Rattlesnake, rattlesnake, I fear you none

Mama was afraid of snakes and the thing she feared had happened. My voice broke off.

"Keep singing, Melody." Daddy smoothed Mama's hair. "Allie, you're going to be okay. I'm going to call for help. Melody will stay with you and will sing you a song to heal you."

Crawling beneath, the moon and sun

"I can't feel your touch, Will." Mama's mouth barely moved and her voice was weak. "And we're not supposed to get a doctor."

Daddy gently laid Mama's head on the ground. "I have to, Allie. Stay with her, Melody, and don't stop singing."

Show me no harm, under the sky

My voice shook as I sang. I'd never seen Daddy scared like this. And Mama was hurt so bad … I couldn't stop my tears.

Daddy came back faster than I expected.

"Will, I'm having trouble breathing. I'm scared." Mama barely whispered the words. "I love you."

I will show no fear, though afraid to die

Daddy scooped her up in his arms. Her last breath sent a shudder through her body. Wailing, Daddy rocked back and forth holding Mama close.

Sirens sounded in the distance. Too late … for Mama … for Daddy … for me.

Rakkie gripped tight in my hands, I sat on my bed, waiting. For what, I didn't know. I was numb. If I closed my eyes, I saw the snake with its jaw wide open. I couldn't believe Mama was dead. She couldn't be. I loved her too much for her to be gone. What would Daddy and I do without her?

Daddy came in and knelt in front of me. He put his hand along the side of my face and wiped the tears away with his thumb. Tears ran freely down his cheeks, too.

"Melody, I want you to remember you will always be my baby girl."

I sniffed.

"Mama's spirit has called me, and I have to go. I want you to go stay with Uncle Harlan until I return." He choked back his tears. "I don't know how long I'll be gone. Just remember who you are and how special you are."

"Can't I go with you?" I didn't want him to leave me. And Uncle Harlan didn't like me and never had.

He pulled me into his arms and hugged me. "I wish I could bring you, but I must do this alone." Daddy picked up Rakkie from the bed. "Raksha Waya will watch over you for me and protect you, as he always has. I love you, baby."

He put me back on the bed and strode out of the room before I could say another word.

CHAPTER SIXTEEN

Spring 2015 – Melody, age 16

Dr. Kane jumped to his feet and grabbed his tablet from the desk. "After our last session, I'm excited to dig in and see how much further we can go." He settled into his chair and opened the cover on his tablet.

Melody arched her eyebrow as she glanced at the electronic device.

He gave her a cockeyed grin. "After yesterday, I want a faster method to capture information than the old school yellow pad."

She turned the lock after she closed the door. Her hand dropped to her side, where she tapped her fingers against her leg in a fit of nervous energy.

Dr. Kane waved her to the alcove. "You had my mind revving all night thinking about music and how you answered my questions yesterday."

Melody sat on the couch and folded her hands in her lap. Her knuckles turned white from the firmness of her grip.

"So where do we start?"

She wouldn't—couldn't meet his gaze. As much as she tried to control it, her knee went into rapid bounce mode.

"Whoa, Melody." Dr. Kane immediately soothed her. "Remember, I'm here to help you get through this thing. I didn't mean to make you nervous with my excitement." The leather squeaked as he shifted his weight. "I'm excited because we had such a huge breakthrough yesterday. And I understand why it makes you nervous to know I will understand some of your answers to my questions."

The ticking of his watch measured off the moments.

"It's scary when you haven't communicated with anyone for almost two years, to open up and let people know your thoughts."

A huge lump of ice formed in her stomach.

"As I told you when we started these sessions, there are reasons you stopped talking. My job is to help you deal with those reasons and make you feel comfortable sharing what's going on inside your head." The tablet screen clicked as it was unlocked. "So, I want you to relax, breathe deeply, while I find something for us to talk about today."

The sunlight sparkled on the leaves of the tree as it beamed down, yesterday's thunderstorm a thing of the past. Trees, grass, and flowers were fresh and clean, the soot deposits from the city hadn't yet tarnished them. Her fingers relaxed, allowing the circulation to be restored. Fingertips prickling as normal color returned, her bouncing knee slowed.

"Good. You're relaxing. It is easier to communicate when you're relaxed."

Dr. Kane waited while Melody released the tension from her body.

Finally, her back touched the couch and she sank against the cushion.

Dr. Kane flashed a smile, showing off his straight, white teeth. "Let's start with your foster placements. Except for your first placement, you've bounced around in the system."

Melody reached for the music player, but her fingers froze. She couldn't bring up the menu.

"Don't hold back now. How do you feel about having moved around so much?"

She stared into his blue eyes for a long moment before picking up the music player. Once the song had been selected, she pushed play and turned her head away.

Dr. Kane raised his voice to be heard over the intro. "Excellent choice. 'In Control of Me' captures the longing perfectly."

Keeping her body faced away, she craned her head around to peek over her shoulder. Dr. Kane had his eyes closed, mouthing the words, and used his index fingers to play the air drums.

Am I not human
Kicked to the ground
Covered in mud
Am I forever bound
I pray for strength
To break out of jail
Yearn to be free
God post my bail
Never fitting in
Held back by chains
Alone in hell
Where the devil reigns
I want to move on
I want to be free
I want to be
In control of me

After the chorus, Melody hit pause.

His eyes shot open. "Hey. You cut me off before my drum solo."

She stifled a grin.

He pointed his finger and wagged it. "Don't think I don't see you trying to hide that smug smile from me. I happen to *rock* the drum solo." He tossed his head as if offended.

Melody giggled. Then her hands flew to her mouth and she froze. Her stomach twisted in knots.

Dr. Kane jumped from his chair, arms raised to signal a touchdown. "Finally. I can't believe I got you to laugh. I should be doing an end zone dance or a victory lap." He pretended to wipe sweat off his brow. "You had me worried. I thought I might have lost my touch … or worse, that I have never been funny in the first place. My pride has taken a beating, session after session."

He stopped clowning around and grew serious for a moment. "Laughter is good for you, Melody. Nothing horrible is going to happen because you think something is funny and show it."

The knots in her stomach relaxed.

The corner of his mouth twitched. "Besides, you made my week. I'm going to bask in the glory of the moment all day." He sat, put his hands behind his head, and leaned back. "I can see it now … front page news … adoring fans … autograph requests. All over the world, I'll be known as the guy who made Melody Fisher laugh." He leaned forward and rubbed his hands together. "We should get back to work. After all, you'll need to be able to talk to confirm my moment of awesomeness."

Melody shook her head.

He curled his lip. "So, you think I'm delusional? I'll show you." He grinned. "But we really should get back to it." He checked his tablet. "You stayed with the Jacksons for only a short period of time before moving on. What did you feel about your life with them?"

Without changing the song to a different one, she hit play. The heavy, driving beat resumed.

So damn angry
And I know why
Breaking my heart
Making me cry
Life shouldn't be
What my eyes see
I want to be
In control of me

She hit pause and bit her lower lip before raising her eyes to meet his.

CHAPTER SEVENTEEN

December 22, 2011 – Melody, age 12

Two brown paper bags full of my belongings sat on the floor between my feet. As dusk fell, I didn't move from the back seat of the car. I glanced apprehensively at the house. The memory of Quatie Raincrow strapped to a gurney being wheeled out to the ambulance flashed in my mind. She had looked so weak and pale. We belonged together. What would I do without her?

Miss Prescott opened the door. "Come on, Melody. The Jacksons are waiting for you."

But I didn't want anyone to be waiting for me. I wanted to go home.

Peering over the window into the car, Miss Prescott made a sad face. "Honey, I know this is hard on you. I love Quatie, too, and she told me she loves fostering you, but the best thing you can do for her is to stay with someone until she is better."

She stood to the side to allow me room to get out and peered at the sky. "Don't worry about your stuff. The rain will hold off for a little longer. We can bring your things in later. Let's meet the family first."

At least Miss Prescott didn't call them my *new* family. I slid across the cloth seat, swung my legs out the door, and stood. The pavement was wet from the earlier cloudburst, and trees and bushes still dripped. I didn't want to meet these people. I had my family in Quatie Raincrow. She had to get better. Then I could go home.

Miss Prescott shivered while she waited for me to walk up the path. The Christmas lights on the other houses on the street blinked on. The houses were closer together than I was used to, but still not as close as the middle of town. Land separated each house, but the Jacksons' house stood out like a gaping hole in the bright, cheerful lights. My gut twisted. Why did the lack of decorations make me so uneasy? I'd never celebrated the commercial aspects of Christmas.

With Mama and Daddy, we'd never put up lights on the house. We'd always have a tree inside because Mama liked the way it made the house smell. And Quatie had a tree in her yard she called her Christmas tree. I'd gather boughs of spruce and decorate her mantle because the smell always made me think of Mama. We'd string seeds and berries into garlands to decorate the tree because Quatie said the birds and squirrels would call it their Christmas feast—a symbolic celebration of the birth of Christ through feeding the cycle of life.

Two years ago, I had asked to put lights on the tree, but Quatie said there was no need ... God had provided. That night she'd brought me out on the porch and the moon lit the tree and the stars twinkled in the background. As we sat muffled up, sipping hot cocoa and rocking on the swing, no store-bought string of multicolored lights could possibly compare with the grandeur of what God had provided.

Quatie and I made presents for each other every year because Quatie always wanted something from my heart and not the store. The thought of the muff I had knitted for her, hiding in the closet, waiting to be wrapped brought a tear to my eye. Would I be able to give it to her and explain it was for keeping her hands warm as she rocked back and forth on the porch swing watching the sunset?

Mama and Daddy hadn't been big on store-bought gifts either.

Although Rakkie had been a Christmas present when I was little. I didn't remember ever not having him. I wished I'd grabbed him out of the bag instead of leaving him in the car. I didn't care whether it made me look like a little kid. Raksha Waya would always be my protector. And I needed him.

When I joined Miss Prescott on the porch, she smiled. Probably trying to tell me everything would be okay. But it wouldn't. Not in a strange place with strange people. She knocked on the door.

After a few moments, shuffling footsteps came from the other side. Two locks snicked back and someone fumbled with a third before the door creaked open. A woman poked her head through the opening and pulled her thin beige sweater tight. Her light-brown hair, pulled back into a loose ponytail, escaped its binding and fell forward across her face. "Yes?"

Miss Prescott held out her hand. "Mrs. Jackson, I'm Rebecca Prescott. I spoke with you earlier about bringing Melody by."

Mrs. Jackson scraped her limp, thin hair behind her ear and shook Miss Prescott's hand briefly. "Come in." She stepped back and allowed us to pass.

Her face, oval and smooth, had the skin tone of a china doll, her creamy white complexion marred only by a sprinkle of freckles across her cheeks.

"Grady and Boyd are in the family room." Mrs. Jackson led the way.

The hall walls were painted a grayish white and didn't have any pictures or paintings. They were stark and without decoration of any kind. When we entered the family room, the walls were the same. Painted, no decorations. The wood flooring had a braided oval rug of blue and gray—the only decorative thing in the room.

A boy sat on the floor assembling something with wooden dowels and boards. His dark hair hid his eyes and he didn't look up when we entered the room. A man had paper spread over the coffee table and held a piece of wood in one hand and a knife in the other. Wood curls scattered across the paper. A glass with brown, pulpy looking juice sat on a coaster.

"Grady, this is Miss Prescott from child services. She brought Melody to us."

The man grabbed the glass and spat brown liquid into it before rising. His lower lip puffed out from the chew tucked inside.

Gross.

The man held out his hand to Miss Prescott. "Thank you for bringing her by. We'll do our duty by her."

Duty? So far no one had said anything to me. I didn't want to be the thing to fulfill someone's sense of duty. This wasn't how it was supposed to be.

Miss Prescott shook his hand briefly, then released it and put her hand on my shoulder. "We should probably bring Melody's things in and get her settled."

I didn't want to stay with this family, but I didn't have a choice. No one ever asked me what I wanted. Child services worried about who would take me on short notice, but that was all. Once Miss Prescott left, they'd forget all about me. All I wanted was to know what was going on with Quatie. And every time I said something about this being temporary, they said we'd have to see. Those words held no reassurance or comfort. The only reason I'd come with Miss Prescott was because Quatie needed to rest and get better. But as soon as she was better, I wanted to go home.

Light sprinkles fell as we pulled my belongings out of the car. The sick feeling in the pit of my stomach grew. Why did I feel abandoned?

At the door, Miss Prescott stopped. "Don't worry so much, Melody. The Jacksons are good people."

How could she say that? They hadn't looked at me yet.

When we reentered the family room, the boy had almost finished putting his wood pieces together. My stomach lurched even more. He had made a working guillotine and inserted the blade. What was he going to do with it?

The bag ripped as I clutched it tighter.

Mrs. Jackson led Miss Prescott and me down the hall and opened the door to a room containing a bare bed and a dresser. Nothing but gray-white paint covered the walls.

"I'll go get some bedding and a pillow. This will be Melody's room."

They hadn't bothered to prepare a room for me. How much could they really want me here? Although, they hadn't had much notice. No one had. Neither had Quatie, but she had made me feel welcome.

Miss Prescott put the bag she carried on the dresser. "We didn't have a chance to get all your things. I'll pick up the rest tomorrow and bring them over."

I didn't want all my things here. "Leave them. Quatie Raincrow will get well soon and I'll be back home."

Miss Prescott frowned, and her eyes saddened. "As much as I want Quatie Raincrow to get better, I still have to do my job, which includes making sure you're taken care of."

I wished she wouldn't look at me that way.

Mrs. Jackson hurried in and placed a blanket, pillow, and a set of sheets on the bed. She pulled her sweater tight around her again. "Why don't you get your things put away and then join us?"

The blade of the guillotine slid down the rails and thunked into the base. Boyd picked up something from the back and flicked the release handle.

Mrs. Jackson jumped when the blade hit. "What are you doing, Boyd?"

"Cutting earthworms in half."

Mr. Jackson's head wrenched up and he shook his knife at Boyd. "Boy, you'd best not be getting anything on your mother's floor or I'll whoop your ass."

"Naw, Dad. I ain't getting nuthin' on the floor." He flipped his head to the side to get his bangs out of his face. "I got trays."

Mrs. Jackson's forehead wrinkled. "Is it a school project? I didn't think you had any homework over the break."

Boyd curled his lip. "I don't have school work. I heard that if you cut a worm in half, it don't die." He sniffed and rubbed his nose. "I wanna see if it's true."

What a horrible thing to do. Didn't he think about whether it would hurt the worm?

CHAPTER EIGHTEEN

Spring 2015 – Melody, age 16

Melody struggled against Mrs. Langdon's grip as she pulled her into the waiting room.

Lily's head popped up when Mrs. Langdon pushed past the reception counter, Melody's upper arm still firmly in her grasp.

Melody dug in her heels, but scooched forward, feet sliding over the floor. Her arm hurt from the vise-like hold.

Mrs. Langdon shoved the door open to Dr. Kane's office before Lily could get up from behind her desk. Melody held back a smile when the door bounced off the wall and hit Mrs. Langdon broadside.

Dr. Kane immediately rose. "Why are you bursting into my office unannounced?"

Lily brushed against Melody's back. "She barreled through reception without stopping, Dr. Kane."

Mrs. Langdon gulped as her breath came in short, stertorous bursts. "You're askin' me?" Her face turned red and she trembled.

Melody ripped her arm from Mrs. Langdon's grip and rubbed it.

"She's the one you should be askin'." Mrs. Langdon pointed at Melody. Her frown caused deep grooves to run from the corners of her nose down to the edge of her chin.

Dr. Kane's eyebrows rose. "Lily, can you please close the door on your way out?" He moved from behind the desk. "What has you so upset, Mrs. Langdon?"

"Dory. Why don't you ever call me Dory?" She folded her arms. "I'll tell ya what has me upset." She glared at Melody. "She's been pullin' the wool over all of us. That's what."

Melody's throat constricted. She moved to the couch to get away from the daggers in Mrs. Langdon's eyes.

"All this time she's been pretendin' she can't talk, but she's been laughin' behind our backs."

Dr. Kane cleared his throat. "Exactly why would you say she's been pretending?"

Plop. The chair groaned as Mrs. Langdon sat.

"Because I had to go to the pharmacy to pick up my allergy meds, you know how slow they can be sometimes … well for once they were quick an' I come back to the house an' open the door, an' what do I hear but this one singing a song all by her lonesome."

Melody craned her neck to peek at Dr. Kane. He didn't look surprised.

"And because you heard her singing you believe since she won't talk it's all a sham?"

"Of course, it has been a sham. She can talk if she can sing."

To stop a crick in her neck, Melody moved to the chair next to the couch.

"Those two things are completely unrelated. If Melody sings to herself, it does not mean she can speak to others." Dr. Kane stood in front of Mrs. Langdon, offered his arm, and kept talking as she took hold. "She has always had the ability to make sound; the problem is her ability to speak to others. Which is what we are working on in these sessions."

He hefted Mrs. Langdon out of the chair and escorted her to the door. "I must remind you not to meddle in Melody's therapy. I consider it a positive sign you found her singing. You either calm down before returning for Melody, or I will have social services remove her from your placement."

Mrs. Langdon bridled. "Again with the threats, Roger?"

He pinched the bridge of his nose. "You will address me as either Doctor or Dr. Kane. This is my office, I have earned the degrees hanging on the wall, and you will give me the respect I deserve. As for the rest, I did not make a threat, but advised you what my course of action will be should you choose to badger Melody about speaking." His jaw pulsed. "I thought we had already settled this when I began seeing her. Melody will speak when she is ready to and not a moment before."

"You don't have to get so huffy. You'd a thought I'd've committed a crime by tellin' ya she was singin' around the house." Mrs. Langdon hefted her purse on her shoulder. "Here I thought you'd want to know things like that."

He flexed his fingers. "Sharing information is fine. Storming into my office practically breathing fire is not." He checked his watch. "And I'd like to get my session with Melody started. We're now late."

Mrs. Langdon turned on her heel and her purse thunked against the door as she blundered out of the office.

Dr. Kane closed and locked the door behind her, then rested his hand against the door for a moment.

Melody moved back to the couch and pulled out the music player.

When Dr. Kane took his seat, he contemplated her for a few moments. "I don't think I need to tell you how maddening your foster mother is. Her behavior is beyond outrageous and continues to get worse." He opened her file, flipped through to the page at the back and ran his finger down it. He peeled the cover back on his tablet and swiped across the surface.

"I'm making a note to call your caseworker. I think it's high time we had a conversation." He tapped the screen and focused on the entry in the folder while typing the information into the tablet.

As he finished, Melody turned to stare out the windows. The squirrel's antics were always good for a tension break. There he was, scampering across branches in the tree. She smiled.

Dr. Kane placed her folder on the side table, crossed his legs, and rested the tablet on his knee. "Let's get started. We've been enough delayed as it is."

The squirrel's tail bobbed as it clawed at the bark on the trunk of the tree. He finally managed to pull off a section of bark, then grabbed something and stuffed it in his mouth.

"Melody?"

She slumped against the couch and took a deep breath. A comfortable silence grew between them as she connected the music player to the speakers.

"According to your file, your longest foster placement was with a woman named Quatie Raincrow out on the reservation." Dr. Kane slid his finger across his screen. "I'd like us to talk about that placement today—why you had to leave, and how you felt about it."

Melody stiffened. She scrolled through the list of songs, looking for one in particular. When she found it, she pressed play.

Dr. Kane held up his hand when the first note pierced the air. "Wait."

She pressed stop.

"I'm going to ask you to be brave and do something for me. If you can't yet, I'll live with it, but I think this should be our next step."

Melody dipped her chin and blinked.

"I'd like you to sing along with whatever song you have selected."

The chirps from the birds in the trees filtered through the glass. Melody buried her face in her hands and attempted to clear her throat without making a sound. Her breathing sped up and became shallow.

After rocking for a moment, Melody took a deep breath and gave a nod. She pressed play and opened her mouth, but no sound came out. She punched the stop button, then rewound to the beginning.

"You're doing great, Melody."

She shook her head and frowned. Curling the fingers of one hand into a fist, she took another deep breath, pressed play, and scatted through the opening notes of the upbeat gospel tune.

Dr. Kane's jaw dropped open.

She smiled at his astonishment, then launched into the lyrics for *The Promised Land.*

My time has come
To say goodbye
Worry none

Please do not cry
To the land of peace
I'm on my way
Glory hallelujah
I feel alive today

Melody closed her eyes and allowed the music to flow through her.

Your expression says
There's no time left
You see as I see
The angel of death
Celebrate now
As you hold my hand
I'm on my way to Heaven
To the Promised Land

By the end of the chorus, she had her hands raised in the air and swayed to the beat.

Upon my head
The touch of death
The stealing of
My final breath
To fly with angels
My destiny
Now that I'm free
Don't fear for me

Quatie Raincrow always felt close when she sang this song. Melody allowed herself to become lost in the moment.

Your expression says
There's no time left
You see as I see

The angel of death
Celebrate now
As you hold my hand
I'm on my way to Heaven
To the Promised Land

Clapping her hands, she continued to belt out the song. The office melted away and she sang with abandon.

My eyes are closed
It must be done
I see the light
I see the Son
He welcomes me
With a smile on His face
Glory hallelujah
Amazing grace

As the music faded, she gazed into Dr. Kane's stunned eyes. For a few moments, she had forgotten her life.

He closed his mouth. "Where on earth did you learn to sing like that?"

The reality of what she'd had and lost crashed down.

CHAPTER NINETEEN

January 17, 2012 – Melody, age 13

The gray light filtered through the curtains. I flicked them aside. Raining. Perfect. The weather suited my mood. Today I turned thirteen and no one cared but me. Quatie Raincrow and I had talked about how to make this day special for months.

Quatie wanted to make a big deal out of me becoming a teenager. She said it only happened once in a girl's life, and it was important to celebrate it the right way. On my way to adulthood.

But they wouldn't let me go back and live with Quatie. I'd been praying every night for her to get better so I could go home and take care of her. But with each day, keeping my hope alive got harder. The Jacksons wouldn't let me call to check on her anymore. And Miss Prescott told me she'd let me know when and if the situation changed.

Didn't they know how much I loved Quatie Raincrow? Didn't they know how much we belonged together? How could I sit here with the Jacksons, who were not nice people, and not worry about how Quatie was doing?

I refused to let her think I had forgotten her. My mind was made up. The Jacksons wouldn't celebrate my birthday … heck, they wouldn't mention it. So my first step on my way to adulthood would be finding Quatie Raincrow and visiting her. She should be in the nursing home next to the hospital closest to her house. I knew where it was … all I had to do was figure out how to get there. I'd pretend to get ready for school and instead I'd visit Quatie.

Having made up my mind, I jumped out of bed, got ready as fast as I could, hurried through breakfast, and left the house. Leaving early meant I didn't have to walk with the detestable Boyd.

Money I had saved jingled in my pocket. Maybe I could catch a bus. But I didn't want anyone to know where I was going, and the bus driver might ask why I wasn't in school.

The rain had stopped, but the trees still dripped moisture as I walked under them. Someone had left their bicycle out in the rain. If I borrowed it, I'd be able to get to the hospital faster. I wouldn't be *stealing* the bike. Just borrowing it for a time.

I looked to make sure no one was around. Holding my breath, I tiptoed to the bike and quietly raised the kickstand. Wheeling the bike down the grass to the sidewalk, I kept expecting someone to yell at me any minute. Once on the sidewalk, I threw my leg over the bar and started riding.

Getting to the nursing home took much longer than I expected. By the time I arrived, my legs were tired from all the pedaling. I jammed the bike into the stand and rushed through the doors. Inside, I halted. What now? I didn't know what room Quatie Raincrow was in.

The person at the information desk wore her glasses low on her nose and frowned at the papers she shuffled. I forced myself to take step after step to the desk.

"Yes?" The woman peered over her glasses at me.

My heart beat faster. "Um, I'm here to see Quatie Raincrow."

"Raincrow." She punched the name into the computer. "Room 232. Up one level and to the left."

That was it? I tried not to show how relieved I was and measured my steps so I didn't run up the stairs.

When I reached the closed green painted door with the number 232 on it, I hesitated. What if she was sleeping? Or worse, what if she wouldn't wake? What if they had lied to me about her condition?

I closed my eyes and the astringent smell of cleaning supplies mingled with the aroma from the kitchen. I took a deep breath, fueled by the thought of the words Quatie said all the time. *If you don't try, you'll never know.* I grasped the handle and opened the door.

Dimmer than the hallway, the room had a hushed air, broken by the whisper of a breathing machine, the beeps coming from the monitors and Quatie Raincrow's labored breathing. My eyes filled with tears to see her, sunken-cheeked, tube taped to her arm, wires running away from the clip on her finger, and oxygen tubes taped to her face. For the first time, I realized Quatie Raincrow was old.

I stuffed my emotions down. She couldn't know my sorrow to see her in this condition. It would hurt her. I swallowed hard and shuffled to the chair next to her bed. The door closed and the room darkened.

When I placed my hand gently over hers, Quatie's eyes fluttered and she opened them. A smile wrinkled her face and she pressed a button to raise her bed.

"Praises be. Can I believe my aged eyes?" Her weak voice was difficult to hear over the bed motor. She covered my hand with hers. "Melody, my *Atsila.*"

My breath hitched in my throat. Quatie Raincrow's special name for me had always been *Atsila.*

"I have been praying to see you, child. Every day I ask how you are doing."

She had been asking about me and no one had told me? "I've been asking about you, too." I wouldn't tell her they wouldn't let me call anymore.

"Happy Birthday. I'm so glad you shared this special occasion with me."

Sick as she was, she'd remembered. It took a moment to find my voice. "I couldn't think of anyone I'd rather see on my birthday." I squeezed her hand. "Remember, we had plans."

Quatie nodded and brushed her hair off her face. "Things have changed a lot in a short time, *Atsila,* but we must move forward."

I didn't want to move forward. I wanted Quatie to get well and for us to go back home.

"How are you doing?"

A coughing spasm racked her body. I grabbed the tissue box from her bedside table and ripped out a few sheets and handed them to her. She held them in front of her mouth and spat into the paper. When her head relaxed against the pillow again, I grabbed the glass of water and held it toward her.

She took a sip, then handed the cup back with the red-stained tissue to throw away. My heart lurched. Coughing up blood couldn't be good.

After tossing it, I sat next to the bed and gripped the rail. The blips and beeps of the monitors underscored how sick Quatie Raincrow must be. It had been a mistake to come. I didn't want to know she was dying.

She patted my hand. "Don't fret. Things will happen as God decides."

She always knew what I was thinking.

Pushing up with her hands, she resettled in the bed. "I want to hear how you're doing."

I tore my eyes from hers. She had a knack of looking straight into my eyes and seeing the truth and I didn't want her to know how bad things were at the Jacksons'. I stared at the white tile riddled with green specks. "Things are fine. I'm getting used to my new school."

Boyd made it hard to make new friends. He was such a little creep, the other kids stayed away from me, too. Like I was a carrier of his brand of nastiness. Or maybe they thought he'd unleash the ugliness if they tried to be nice to me.

"*Atsila*, look at me and tell me the real story."

I hung my head. She always knew. "I don't fit in with the Jacksons. I just want to come home and take care of you."

Her gnarled hand cupped my face. "Nothing would make me happier, but for now our higher power has different plans for us."

The room shimmered as I blinked to keep the tears from falling. "But I don't want a different plan."

"Listen with your heart. Learn from your experiences, and always be open to new ones. Such are the words of wisdom from our ancestors." She took in a raspy breath.

How could I listen with my heart when it was breaking?

"Never forget you are blessed, *Atsila*. Perhaps you have been put with the Jacksons to fulfill a purpose. Maybe you are to help them to be better people."

"They're not going to listen to me. They barely talk to me unless they have to."

I bit back the rush of words. All the things I wanted to tell Quatie about the Jacksons but couldn't. Not while every beat of her heart was monitored. Not while she needed help with every breath. If we were home and sitting on the porch, I could tell her everything, and then she'd say something to make everything seem right again. But we weren't home and might not ever be again.

"Never forget who you are, child. Keep the love you carry safe inside you and don't allow others to destroy it. You are strong and beautiful. Never forget."

I didn't feel strong or beautiful. Without Quatie Raincrow, I felt almost as empty as I had after Mama died. If this experience had taught me anything, it was as a foster kid, I had no say in what happened to me. How could I be strong when I had no voice?

When Miss Prescott left me with the Jacksons, she'd told me it would be a temporary placement until they could find somewhere else more permanent. They told me the same thing when they left me with Quatie Raincrow. But I quickly hadn't wanted to leave Quatie and they hadn't bothered moving me until she got sick.

And as far as beautiful went … Quatie saw me through the filter of love. She didn't see the gangly, just-turned-teen who hadn't developed much yet. She didn't see the girl who couldn't turn a boy's head with two hands and a crowbar. Not that I wanted boys' attention anyway, but still, I was far from beautiful.

In looks, I took after Daddy more than Mama with dark hair, eyes, and skin. Although Daddy always said the shape of my eyes came from Mama along with the wave in her hair, the dimple in her cheek, and the sparkle in her smile. I'd never match Mama's beauty.

"*Atsila*, what has happened to my whippoorwill?" Quatie stroked my hand. "You haven't been this quiet since you first came to live with me."

A wry smile tugged at my lips. Quatie called me her whippoorwill because she said I chirped around the house as much as the whippoorwill sang in the night. The first time she'd said it, I'd thought she meant I was talking too much. But she explained just as she enjoyed hearing the birds call to one another, she enjoyed my chatter.

"What is wrong, child?" Quatie's voice was its most soothing.

An inner struggle broke out. I didn't want to add a burden to Quatie Raincrow. She didn't need to worry about me. She needed to get well. But the want to tell her how awful I felt staying with the Jacksons swelled. I wanted to tell her my troubles, as I always did.

I bit my lower lip as the inner war raged—my will to do the right thing and keep quiet battled the child within. Today was the beginning of my journey toward adulthood, so I should be able to make an adult decision.

But one glance into Quatie's eyes and my will lost the battle. "I don't want to live with the Jacksons."

She gave me a sorrowful look. "Are you sure it's the Jacksons you don't like and not the need to adjust to living with them?"

"No, it's them. Mrs. Jackson might be okay, but she won't do or say anything Mr. Jackson wouldn't like. And he doesn't call me by name. He calls me *girl*."

Once I started, the words kept coming—I couldn't stop if I wanted to. "He is super strict and doesn't allow any back talk, but anything I say he thinks is talking back." No matter what, nothing I ever said was right.

Worse, he hated my heritage. I'd overheard him telling his wife that had he known I had Cherokee, white, and black blood all mixed together in me, he'd never have agreed to take me. He said nothing good ever came from that combination.

"And their son, Boyd, is the worst of all. He's twisted and cruel."

I closed my eyes for a moment and the flash of the guillotine blade burst into my head. He had graduated from cutting worms in half to executing insects. And I had caught him tying a stick doused in gasoline to the neighbor's cat while carrying a lighter in his pocket.

Quatie frowned. "Have you talked with Rebecca about how you feel?"

I nodded. "She says there isn't an appropriate placement yet."

Pressing her hands to her lips, she sighed. "*Atsila*, you know I would take you out of there if I could. I want you to be happy." She held her hands out toward me, palms up. "Give me both hands."

I placed my hands in hers. Maybe this would help warm them.

Her eyes closed, she breathed deeply and called on her spirit guides. Quatie was asking them to show her my future. She gave readings to those on the reservation who came to her for advice, but she had never read for me before.

Her grip tightened on my hands and her breathing took on a harsh quality.

She opened her eyes and a tear trailed down her weathered cheek.

My stomach twisted into knots. What she had seen couldn't be good.

She cleared her throat. "Oh, my sweet child. You have many challenges ahead of you. Be strong."

Another coughing spasm convulsed her. After it stopped, she opened her mouth to continue, the corners of her lips partly glued together, her face pale with a sheen of perspiration across her forehead.

"No. Don't speak yet." I gave her the cup of water and she sipped it through the straw. After a few sips, she looked stronger and some of the color had returned to her face.

When I put the plastic glass back on the tray table, I was startled to see a priest standing in the corner of the room, head bowed and hands clasped in front of him. Where had he come from? I hadn't seen him enter the room. I didn't want to interrupt his prayer, so I turned back to Quatie Raincrow.

"You don't have to tell me any more. Please rest."

She shook her head. "You know I cannot keep it to myself. It is my job to share what the spirits tell me." She swallowed, then took a ragged breath. "You will face great adversity. I want you to remember these words from an old Cherokee proverb. '*The pain you feel today is the strength you feel tomorrow. For every challenge encountered there is an opportunity for growth.*'" Tears flowed down her cheeks as she grasped my hand in both hers. "Do not forget your gifts. Music and singing will see you through. And you will get through even though it may not feel like it sometimes."

I had never seen Quatie Raincrow get so worked up about someone's future before. Fear made my heart pound faster. The tears I had yet to cry bubbled over.

The priest approached the bed and stood beside me.

Why was he there? Quatie wasn't Catholic. Maybe he visited all the patients and prayed for them.

She squeezed my hand. "Don't forget what I have taught you."

"I won't. But you need to get better so you can teach me more."

"I must warn you—" Her eyes widened as the priest placed his hand on her head. The beeps and blips on the monitors went crazy.

She crushed my hand and gasped as if she couldn't catch her breath.

The priest simply watched Quatie in her distress.

"Pray for her." The words I screamed briefly drowned out the mechanical sounds.

She took a huge shuddering sigh and her hand went limp and slipped from mine. The monitor stopped spiking and flat-lined and the noise changed to a solid *beeeeeeep*.

An alarm went off in the hallway. "Code blue. Room 232. Code blue. Room 232."

Running footsteps sounded outside the room.

I couldn't take my eyes off Quatie Raincrow. The tears flowed down my face unchecked. I grabbed her hand. *Please breathe again. Don't die on me.*

Please, don't die on me.

I closed my eyes and prayed as hard as I could, asking God and the Grandfathers to please spare Quatie Raincrow. I needed her. She was my second mother. I couldn't lose her, too. Not today.

Several people rushed into the room. My eyes flew open as hands gripped my shoulders firmly and moved me out of the way. They shoved a cart next to the bed, ripped the bedding down, and opened her gown. I scanned the room. The priest was nowhere to be found. How could he leave?

One glance at Quatie and I covered my mouth. Her spirit had left her body while I prayed.

"Clear."

The doctor held two paddles in his hands and placed them on her chest.

Stepping backward, I hit the wall. The jolt through the paddles caused Quatie's body to jump. I wanted them to stop. She was gone. Didn't they know?

After watching the monitors, the doctor readied to attempt to start her heart again. I couldn't watch anymore. Stumbling into the hall, I couldn't stop my tears.

I rubbed my eyes and hurried as quickly as I could away from the room. I couldn't listen to them torture Quatie's body anymore. A flash of black caught my attention as the priest disappeared around a corner. I chased after him because I wanted him to tell me why she had to die. I rounded the corner, ready to call out, and faced an empty hallway.

After bolting into the bathroom, I collapsed against the wall and sobbed. She died because I had come to see her and let her know I wasn't happy. Looking into my future had caused her too much stress. She wouldn't have read my future if I hadn't told her about the Jacksons. My legs wouldn't hold me any longer and I slid to the floor.

She was the last person on this Earth who loved me, and she was gone. And her spirit had left before I said goodbye.

CHAPTER TWENTY

Spring 2015 – Melody, age 16

Melody sighed.

Mrs. Langdon glanced her way. "What's wrong with you? Cat got your tongue?" She cackled like an old biddy hen fussing at her brood.

When would she get tired of the same old jokes? Melody clenched her hands and chose not to react. She'd had a lot of practice over the past few years; *never let them know they got to you.*

"Oh, you're givin' me the silent treatment. I get it." Mrs. Langdon snorted at her joke.

Melody stared straight ahead, counting the blocks to the doctor's office. Too bad they weren't close enough for her to walk.

It had become part of her ritual to jump out of the car as soon as Mrs. Langdon pulled it into a parking slot. Most days she made it through the door and into the inner sanctum before Mrs. Langdon managed to wrestle the suitcase masquerading as her purse out of the car. Today she didn't wait for the car to come to a full stop. Once out, she slammed the car door.

Lily grinned when she saw Melody. But her smile faded when Melody slammed the office door and rattled the windows.

"What's wrong?"

Melody didn't break stride as she pushed past into the office.

When the door bounced against the wall, Dr. Kane raised one eyebrow and smirked. "You're eager to get started today."

Without bothering to close the door, she reached the chair in front of his desk and toppled it over.

Dr. Kane jumped to his feet. "Whoa. What has you in such a temper?"

Melody crossed her arms so he couldn't see her shaking hands.

The thudding footsteps and asthmatic wheeze of Mrs. Langdon preceded her into the office.

Dr. Kane looked from Melody to Mrs. Langdon. "I see." His lips pressed into a thin line.

Mrs. Langdon dropped her purse in the upright chair. "Don't think you're getting away with this." She jammed her fists on her hips.

Dr. Kane held his hand up. "What is it this time, Mrs. Langdon?"

"Dory." She made the correction while continuing to glare at Melody.

Jutting out her jaw, Melody narrowed her eyes and stared back.

"I'll tell you what." Mrs. Langdon threw her arm out. "This one here decided to jump out of the car while it was still moving." She took a step forward. "What if something woulda happened to you? I'da been blamed."

Dr. Kane's mouth popped open. "Melody, is this true?"

She turned her back on his disappointed gaze.

"You shouldn't get out of a moving car. You could have been hurt."

"It's about time you sided with me, Doc."

The piercing tones of Mrs. Langdon's voice shot through her. Melody stomped to the couch and plopped on the cushion.

Dr. Kane cleared his throat. "This is not, and never has been, a contest or anything to take sides over. We are all here to help and support Melody. That is all."

Melody's insides churned. Something inside her had cracked and she no longer had the ironfisted control over her emotions she was used to having. She queued a Dixie Chicks song on the music player, plugged in the speakers, and turned up the volume.

Dr. Kane righted the tipped-over chair with a soft thud. "I'm sure you have things to do, and it's time for Melody and I to have our session."

Mrs. Langdon gave her usual grunt when she hefted her purse to her shoulder. "I can take a hint. Make sure you get her to understand about the car."

As the door closed, Melody moved to the bay window and stared out.

By leaning her forehead against the glass, she had a better view of the pond. The glass felt cool and soothing. Sunlight glinting on the rippled water and grass bending in the breeze gave her momentary peace.

The leather chair sighed as Dr. Kane settled in. "You seem to be having a rough day."

Her shoulder twitched and she turned her body slightly more toward the window. *Rough* wasn't the word. Shadows cast by fluttering leaves undulated across the grass, echoing the ripples on the pond.

"I'm sure that woman said something to set you off."

She pushed play on "Not Ready To Make Nice" and glared at Dr. Kane while she sang along. When the song ended, she faced the window.

"I get it. You're mad as hell. That woman would try the patience of Job."

He didn't get it and never would. He couldn't. A winged shadow skimmed the grass and Melody looked skyward. It took her a moment to spot the hawk circling the treetops.

To be free to soar …

"Melody, we need to get started."

She closed her eyes and didn't move. The afternoon sun shone through the window and warmed her skin. He could start. She didn't want to do this anymore.

Not that she had a choice. She never did.

The note app clicked when he started it. "I'm still blown away by your voice. Have you had singing lessons?" He waited a moment for her response. "Last session we talked about why you left your first foster placement."

She hadn't left, she had been forced to leave. And it had been her home, not a placement.

Papers rustled as Dr. Kane shuffled through them. "Even though it was an emergency placement, there were several qualified applicants, so I'm not sure why you were placed with a woman too old for long-term placement care. There aren't any notes to explain why you were left with that woman for nearly four years."

That woman?

Quatie Raincrow had been *nothing* like Mrs. Langdon. Tears bubbled up and her breath caught in her throat.

With one sweep of her arm, Melody toppled the books from the top of the bookcase and growled. How dare he? She pulled individual books off the top shelf and flung them across the room. *Dead Cert, Risk,* and *10LB Penalty* by Dick Francis landed near Dr. Kane's desk. She scooped up an armful of Agatha Christie and threw them like Frisbees. *And Then There Were None* skimmed the top of the couch before scudding along the floor. *Murder on the Orient Express* and *At Bertram's Hotel* quickly followed suit.

Too slow. Melody grabbed the bookshelf and pulled. It didn't budge. It had been bolted to the wall.

Rage ripped through her like wildfire as she pummeled the bookcase.

Arms encircled her from behind. She thrashed and struggled against his hold. Dr. Kane clamped her arms to her sides and kept her from lashing out. Years of pent-up emotion overpowered and sobs escaped—her dam had burst. Her knees weakened and she sagged against his chest and slid downward.

He stopped her descent with a bear hug and rocked back and forth. "That's right. Let it out."

Settling back on the couch, Melody dabbed her eyes with a sodden tissue. Stinging eyes, headache, and stuffed-up sinuses—she hadn't cried like that since Quatie died.

"Here." Dr. Kane held out a cup of water.

The first sip eased the throat pain and helped calm her. She rested her head against the couch and closed her eyes.

After several minutes of silence, Dr. Kane cleared his throat. "I'm sorry, Melody. I didn't mean to upset you."

She drew her knees up, hugged them, and rocked.

"Sometimes we react more strongly to a trigger than we expect and what we're reacting to isn't about the specific trigger, but more about everything else."

The rocking motion soothed. She didn't want to stop.

"In your case, anger is to be expected. We've been working hard to dig deep to get to the root of why you stopped speaking. In doing so, you've been facing a lot of memories—things from your past you'd like to forget. We're ripping the scabs off your wounds and it hurts."

Her rocking slowed and she gazed at him through a curtain of hair.

Dr. Kane leaned forward. "You have done an amazing job so far, and I'm proud of you."

Melody released her knees and raked the hair out of her face.

"If you're feeling up to it, we have some time left and I'd like to go back to your placement with the Jacksons."

Melody shrugged. Her outburst had left her numb.

"You were angry about being placed with them and didn't like your time there. Why?"

She stared at her hands as the moment stretched into minutes. At least he didn't push her to answer. Before fifteen minutes had passed, she made up her mind.

As she reached for the music player, he stretched his arm toward her. "If you can, sing with whatever song you select. The more you sing, the easier it will be to talk."

Melody navigated back to "In Control of Me" and forwarded to the chorus. Nothing told her pain with the Jacksons like it.

Never fitting in
Held back by chains
Alone in hell
Where the devil reigns
I want to move on
I want to be free
I want to be
In control of me

She hit the pause button before it continued to the verse. Releasing her emotions about the Jacksons through song felt good. Singing always made her feel better.

"The case notes mention an altercation with Grady Jackson which precipitated your removal from there. What was the argument about?" He squinted as he read the page.

Melody didn't bother to use the music player. Since "Rattlesnake Song" was *a cappella* anyway, she didn't need the music.

On your belly, slither on by
Rattlesnake don't bite, don't make me cry
The hills are full, in the green green grass
Please leave me be, let me pass

Dr. Kane stopped reading, looked at her then back at the case notes. He shook his head. "I am horrified by what I just read. How does someone justify those actions? How do you feel about what happened?"

Melody pressed play to continue to the next verse of "In Control of Me." Nothing needed to be said.

I don't need
Another sinner on earth
To tell me
What I am worth
With my head down
There is God above
Rain down on hate
God show me love

CHAPTER TWENTY-ONE

April 7, 2012 – Melody, age 13

I strolled alongside the creek, the ground soft underfoot. The air still had a nip, although it was supposed to be warmer in the afternoon. The week had been an odd one with temperatures ranging from 80F a few days before to near-freezing last night.

Every Saturday, I left the house as soon as I could and stayed away as long as possible. Grady Jackson and Uncle Harlan would probably be good buddies if they knew each other. Except Grady never went to church and Uncle Harlan cloaked his nastiness in the word of God. Both filled with hate, taking everything to self-righteous extremes.

Uncle Harlan always wore a shirt and tie, while Grady wore jeans and a T-shirt most days. Despite their superficial differences, they'd recognize their kindred spirit—the desire to make everyone around them miserable and filled with fear.

I pulled the music player out of my pocket and slowly unwound the headphones. Miss Prescott had had to intervene when Grady wanted to take it away from me. He thought music gave people bad ideas and wouldn't allow me to sing around the house. I scooped up a rock and threw it as hard and far as I could down the creek.

Every week I asked about a new foster family and every week the answer was the same. Be patient—they were looking, but the right placement hadn't come up yet. Miss Prescott should know better. I'd given up on having the right placement when Quatie Raincrow died.

I wanted someplace better than the Jacksons', nothing more.

Hooking the headphones over my ears, I pushed the buds in, then picked one of my favorite songs and hit play. Something about music spoke to my soul. I touched the treble and bass clef music charm hanging from the silver chain at my throat. The notes themselves captured the emotion I felt. Even songs with no words tapped depths that could move me to tears. Mama, Daddy, and Quatie had understood my need for music. Without music, I might as well be dead.

Ahead a patch of tall grass waved against the breeze. I instantly stilled. A small animal must be hiding in the grass and I didn't want to spook it. I yanked the headphones out and draped them around my neck. I needed all my senses to help identify what hid in the grass.

Placing my heel softly on the ground, I rolled forward on my toes. I moved slowly toward the rustling grasses. With as quietly as I moved, the critter still might feel the vibrations of my footsteps. I needed to stay alert against attack.

The grasses parted in a serpentine pattern. Judging the width of the gap, it was probably a snake, which meant extra caution should be used. At least I wasn't wearing shorts. Not that Grady Jackson would allow shorts. But I wore thick jeans, which meant if it attacked, as long as I wasn't stupid enough to stick my hand down low, I shouldn't get hurt.

Based on the sluggish movement, it might be hurt. I picked up a stick from the creek bank and used it to spread the grass. The rattle sounded. I froze. I didn't want to cause it more alarm. The canebrake pulled back into a half-striking position, its tongue licking the air.

"Oh no." The underbelly of the snake was blistered and raw-looking. No wonder it moved slowly. It must hurt to drag your body across the ground when your front was all blistered. It needed help or it would die.

I crooned to it to help it relax. Without a bag or can, I couldn't transport the snake. And I'd need something to hold the head while I got a better look at the blisters. Daddy had nursed a snake with blister disease once. He'd been angry the snake had gotten in that condition.

Turned out one of the congregation had taken the snake home and kept it in a damp shed and had brought it back when he noticed the snake getting sick. But instead of letting someone know, he'd put it back with the rest of the snakes.

Pastor Wolfson kept the snakes segregated, but Daddy said he hadn't kept the snakes in their own box, but whatever box was handy at the time, so disease had more of a chance of spreading. Daddy's sick snake hadn't been nearly as bad as the blisters on the one in front of me.

The snake lowered to the ground and stopped shaking its rattle. I took a slow step backward. I couldn't help it without the right supplies. Since it was so hurt, it wouldn't get far while I was gone.

I retreated a few steps before turning around and running back to the house. Once the house was in sight, I slowed and crept forward watching to make sure no one would see me through the windows. I needed to borrow a few things from the shed. If I asked, the answer would be no, so why bother?

Daddy would want me to heal the snake. That was all the permission I needed. And I didn't want them to know what I was doing. If Boyd knew, he'd do something to the snake just to be mean.

I skirted behind the bushes to get to the shed in the back. Once inside, I grabbed a pair of heavy-duty gardening gloves to protect my hands. My cheeks puffed out as I exhaled. I had to find something to use like a snake stick. The Jacksons didn't have anything close to a snake stick, except the tree trimmer, and I'd clip the poor snake in half with it.

My gaze fell on a coil of paracord. If I could use the rope to lasso the snake, I could keep it from striking while I nursed its wounds. But trying to use the rope alone would be too difficult, even with a sick snake. I needed something to help me create a noose I could tighten.

Grady's shed was full of stuff from home improvement projects and preparing for any and every disaster he could possibly imagine. There had to be something in here I could use.

PVC pipe would work. Once I had captured the head, I could tie the tail and see what I could do about the sores.

The thought of trying to dress the blisters while the snake writhed all over the place gave me a weird feeling. Besides, Daddy immobilized the snake he helped with blister disease, so it must be the right thing to do.

Did I have everything I needed? I grabbed a couple of rags, in case.

Wait. I couldn't nurse the snake back to health if it could slither away while I was gone. Daddy always kept the snakes in cases of some sort. Grady had wood, but it'd take me too long to make a case. I picked through the shed looking for something … anything I could keep the snake in.

At the back, piled under a bunch of junk that looked as if it hadn't been touched in years, I saw a cardboard file box. I carefully dug down to the box and lifted the lid. Total score. The box was empty.

Why would someone keep an empty box buried beneath a pile of junk? I poked air holes around the top of the box with a screwdriver then put a couple in the lid so I could tie it on with some rope.

Outside the shed, I sneaked back around the house and went to the closest drug store to pick up antiseptic iodine, a plastic tub to use as a bath, antibiotic ointment, and swabs to spread the ointment. Good thing I had my wallet with me. I never left it in my room because Boyd had a bad habit of going through my things. He had stolen some money from me once. Not again.

I ran back to the creek, having tossed everything into the box. I slowed as I approached the place where I'd last seen the snake. The grasses didn't move except to sway in the breeze. Standing still, I scanned the area for any sign of movement. Nothing.

Poor thing. Where was it? If I couldn't find it, the snake would die. I placed the box on the ground and picked up a stick, prepared to sweep the grasses until I found it. I did one more search looking for the smallest movement. The sun shone and the temperature rose quickly from the morning chill.

Movement to my left caught my eye. Nothing in the grass. Wait. On the rock. I sighed. Smart snake to know it had to get out of the damp. It might be easier to catch while lying on the rock.

I transferred the cleaning supplies to the plastic tub, drew on the gloves, and grabbed the box and makeshift snake stick. Silently, I walked toward the rock. When I reached it, I set down the box and made the noose on the end of the stick a little larger. As I held out the stick, my hand shook.

Nothing to be afraid of. The snake needed help and I was the only one who knew it. I closed my eyes.

Big mistake.

Fangs and a wide-open snake jaw filled my head.

First strike to the face. Next to the throat. Blood oozing from the wounds.

My eyes flew open. I hadn't been close enough to a snake to see its scales since Uncle Harlan had locked me in the shed. And before that … Mama.

My heart raced and my mouth went dry. Maybe I couldn't do this.

Daddy's voice filled my head. "Snakes are sacred to the Cherokee, Melody. Do a good turn for a snake and you invite good fortune."

As always, Daddy calmed me—even when he wasn't here.

Tremors still pulsed through my arm, so I took a deep breath. Inch by inch I moved the noose over the snake to position it in front of its head. My stomach tightened with each passing moment. I lowered the noose with care until the rope touched the rock.

I slid it toward me. The noose slipped over the snake's head and I pulled the rope snug.

The snake wriggled as it hung from the stick. I swung it around to the box, dropped the snake in, and slammed on the lid. Tying the top, I listened to the angry rattle inside.

"This is for your own good. I'm gonna guess someone caught you and kept you locked somewhere damp." A snake in the wild was a lot less likely to get blister disease because it could move out of the damp area.

I took it to an abandoned shack in the woods across from the Jacksons' house. I set the snake box on a shelf and poured the antiseptic iodine into the plastic tub. The shack's interior was dark with the door closed. I didn't want anyone to see the open door and come to investigate. With my luck, Boyd would be the one who would see it.

Would the window give me enough light? The panes were so dirty, the light barely penetrated. I didn't want to wash the snake's wounds in the dark. The latch had so much dust and rust it took all my strength to get it to budge. The wood creaked and felt like it might break as I tugged open the window.

Rays of sunshine flooded in. Thank goodness.

I loosened the ties on the box, grabbed my snake stick, and readied it for capturing the snake quickly. Once the snake had been captured, I put it in the tub, careful to keep its head away from the antiseptic. Using one of the rags, I washed off the snake's belly.

Blistered throughout the entire underside, the skin pulled and was close to bursting where pus filled it. The blisters filled with blood made my stomach churn. The snake writhed as I dabbed, and I was afraid I might burst a blister as it fought against me.

"I'm sorry. I know it hurts, but it's to make you well. If I don't get all the dirt off and clean all the blisters, you're not gonna get better."

After washing off the snake, I put it on the shelf next to the tub and used another rag to blot it dry. I tried to open the antibiotic cream one-handed, but it was impossible with the thick gloves on. I shook my hand until the glove fell off, squeezed the ointment onto the swab, then dabbed it on the infected scales. This part made me squeamish. What if the blister popped and pus spurted onto my hand? Or worse, the bloody ones popping? I shuddered.

Finished, I put it back into the box. "I'll see whether I can find a better case for you … Something with a little light and a little more room to move. But it might take me a while."

I secured the top, closed the window, and left.

April 14, 2012 – Melody, age 13

While crossing the road, I checked to make sure Boyd wasn't spying on me. I had caught him following me earlier in the week during one of my after school visits to the snake. Fortunately, the snake had healed enough, so I could probably release it today.

I opened the door. The snake case laid on its side, door open. No snake.

My heart pounded. Hoping against hope it would still be inside the shed, I searched the ground and all the shelves. Nothing. And no warning rattle.

Someone had been here. Only one person was mean enough to steal a sick snake.

Boyd.

I ran back to the house and rushed into the kitchen, then skidded to a halt.

Mrs. Jackson's hand flew to her throat. "Melody, you scared me."

She was scared of her own shadow, so no big surprise.

"Have you seen Boyd?"

She pulled a tissue out of her apron pocket and wiped her nose. "I think he's across the way working on a science project for school." She tucked the tissue back in her pocket.

Talk about being completely out of touch with her own child. Boyd never did any homework unless forced to, and never on a weekend.

I ran back outside, not sure where to look next. And then it hit me. Boyd had a fort he'd built in the woods. Well, calling it a fort was more than it deserved. Ramshackle lean-to that would be blown apart in the first stiff breeze was more like it.

Instead of going directly there, I skirted the woods so I could surprise Boyd. Using the trees for cover, I snuck in close.

Boyd hunched over a board on the ground in front of his fort.

I inched forward and drifted to the side to get a better view.

Boyd had the snake strapped to a board and used a knife to make small cuts along its body. I shook with anger. How dare he torture it? If I made a noise, Boyd might slip with the knife … or he might deliberately kill the snake. How could I get him to stop?

"Boyd? Where'd you get to?"

Probably the only time in my life I was happy to hear the roar of Grady Jackson's voice. I'd have a chance to steal the snake back and take it somewhere safe. Hopefully, the wounds weren't too bad, and I could still release it back to the wild. I couldn't keep it in the shack anymore.

Boyd drove the knife into the board next to the snake's head. "Coming Dad."

He rose and dusted his knees off before heading toward the house.

I let him get past the first line of trees before moving in. When I reached the snake, I covered my mouth with my hand.

The poor thing. Droplets of blood glistened on its skin and stained the board beneath it.

Boyd had it tied to the board and I couldn't get the knot undone, so I pulled the knife out and carefully sawed through the rope at the tail end, making sure I didn't nick the snake in the process.

With the release of the rope, the rattle sounded. I grabbed it quickly to still the sound.

"Hey!"

I turned as Boyd charged back toward the fort. I stood and tried to block the snake from him.

"Whaddya think yer doin'?" He skidded to a stop, kicking up a cloud of dust.

"Me? You're the one who stole the snake." My face turned hot. "I'm not the one who's torturing one of God's creatures."

He sneered. "I wanted to see if cold-blooded meant it bled blue instead of red."

My jaw went slack, and words failed me. How could someone be so intentionally cruel?

"Get outta the way. It's *my* snake now."

I folded my arms. "No. You're going to leave this poor creature alone."

"Boyd." Grady hollered for him as his boots clomped through the grass. "What the hell are you doin', son?"

When he reached us, he smacked the back of Boyd's head. "I tol' you to get to the house." He glared at me. "What're you doing here, girl?"

For once I wasn't going to let this man intimidate me. "Saving a snake from Boyd. He's been torturing it."

He stepped forward and shoved me to the side to glare at the snake.

"Boyd, what did I tell you 'bout playing with your food?"

Food?

Grady scooped up the knife, twirled it between his fingers, and grinned. Then *whoosh*. He whirled the knife through the air and cut the snake's head off. "Take this to the house, Boyd."

My stomach heaved. "Noooooo." Tears sprang into my eyes and my hands curled into fists. I lunged at him.

He caught my fist in his hand, spun me around, and yanked my arm behind my back. "Girl, don't think you can take me on." He leaned in and talked directly into my ear, his sour breath hitting my nostrils. "I'm not taking any guff from some half-breed mu-lat-to."

He drew the word out.

"You try and I'll smack the mongrel outta ya. You're gonna learn who's in charge around here. And it ain't you."

He shoved me forward, and I stumbled but managed to stay on my feet. When I turned to face him, he backhanded me to the ground.

His upper lip curled. "Let this be a lesson to ya. Don't back talk me, girl. You get up and come back to the house. We're gonna have lunch." He kicked some dirt in my face and strode away.

Holding my face where he had smacked me, I pushed up to a sitting position with my other arm. The snake's head stared at me. Tears streamed down my face. After all I had done to save it, it had died anyway.

I couldn't leave the head there. Some other animal might come along and try to eat it. The thought nauseated me. Boyd had brought the gloves from the shack for handling the snake before it had been tied on the board. I pulled them on and picked up the head.

As I walked toward the creek, I grabbed a stout stick. I used it to dig a hole in the soft ground. I dug as far as I could, dropped the head in the hole, said a silent prayer for the snake, and covered it with dirt.

My arms and face streaked with mud, I approached the house. Grady stood on the front porch, hands on hips, glaring at me.

"What took you so long, girl? Lunch is ready." He shook his head. "You look like the dirty mutt you are. Clean that filth off and get to the table."

I cleaned the mud off, but couldn't clean the dusky red mark left by Grady's hand. I'd have a bruise in a day or two. My stomach knotted tighter. Something was wrong. Grady never called me into lunch. He had been waiting for me. And nothing good would come of it.

As I sat at the table, Mrs. Jackson brought out a plate covered in breaded and fried meat strips, almost like chicken fingers, and placed it on the table.

Grady forked a few pieces onto his plate. "It's not often we get to have such a delicacy."

He drew the word out like he didn't say it often. Which was probably the truth.

He took a bite and pointed his knife at me. "You should fill your plate."

Boyd grabbed some strips and squirted ketchup on his plate.

Grady nodded. "That's some of the best rattlesnake I've ever had. Eat up, girl."

I pushed away from the table. *He had cooked the snake?*

"Whassa matter? Do you think you're too good to eat what we put on the table?"

I shook my head. "I'm not hungry. Please, excuse me."

He stood and his chair fell over. "No. You're gonna sit right here until you eat some of this fine food we provided."

"Grady."

Mrs. Jackson to the rescue?

Though soft, her tone held admonishment. "I don't think—"

"I didn't ask you to think." He slammed his fist on the table. "This girl is not allowed to turn her nose up at what we place before her." He strode over, grabbed some pieces of snake and put it on my plate. "Now eat."

I stared at the brown strips and my stomach lurched. The memory of the blistered underbelly rose in my mind.

Grady grabbed my jaw, forced it open, and shoved in a chunk of meat.

"Chew."

All I could think about was the pus and blood draining from the blisters and my stomach lurched again. I spat the meat out and covered my mouth. Rolling off my chair, I ran for the bathroom.

I reached the toilet and heaved. Wave after wave hit until I thought I'd never be done purging my system. When the dry heaves finally subsided, I hauled my body up to the sink. Knees trembling, I scrubbed my teeth and splashed water on my face.

A soft knock sounded on the door. "Melody? Are you all right?" Mrs. Jackson cracked open the door. "Miss Prescott will be here soon, so you'll need to pack your things. Grady says you can't stay here no more."

Relief flooded through me. I wanted to curl up on the floor and cry. Finally, I would be released from this hell.

CHAPTER TWENTY-TWO

Spring 2015 – Melody, age 16

Melody opened the door and shuffled to the couch with her head down. After her outburst yesterday, eye contact would be too embarrassing. When she sat on the couch, she glanced at the bookcase. All the books had been put back as if they had never been disturbed.

She stared at her hands folded in her lap. Maybe he wouldn't bring up yesterday.

"Are you okay, Melody?"

Her fingers twitched, so she tightened her grip. No matter how much she wanted to pick a song, she couldn't. Not without letting him know how embarrassed she was. She'd never thrown a book in her life, but she had been so angry.

Dr. Kane closed his laptop and stood. "I ask because you didn't lock the door as you came in." He strode to the door and turned the lock.

Today marked the first time, other than the first day, she didn't want to be there. How could they get past her complete meltdown?

He sat and she saw him cross his legs out of the corner of her eye.

He clapped his hands together. "Let's get started, shall we? Where's your music player?"

The player was still in her pocket. She couldn't bring it out. He'd expect her to play a song in response to his questions. She didn't know where to start. They had opened too many wounds and she couldn't stop the hurt.

"Ah, I get it. You're having a little emotional backlash from yesterday."

He drummed the stylus against the tablet cover. "You got angry, threw things around, but nothing catastrophic happened. If you're worried I might be angry because you threw my precious paperbacks around, I'm not. In fact, I consider your anger a sign we're making progress, so I'm pleased."

He wasn't upset? Relief coursed through her. She leaned back against the couch and snuck a look at him.

"Well, since I don't like talking to myself, I'll have to carry your end of the conversation." He raised his voice to mimic her. "Oh, Dr. Kane, thank you. You're so wonderful to me."

"Roger." The whispered word barely escaped her lips. Her heart beat rapidly. She hadn't meant to let the word out.

He froze. "What?"

Oh, God. He'd heard her. What was she going to do?

He leaned forward and gazed into her eyes. "You don't need to be afraid."

She trembled but couldn't look away.

Soft and tender, he kept his voice low. "Take a few slow breaths. You're going to get through this."

She couldn't stop shaking. *What had she done?*

"This is just like the books. You got angry, you threw books around, and nothing bad happened." He swept his arm toward the window. "The sun is still shining. No thunder and lightning—not a cloud in the sky. The roof didn't fall in."

Her shakes subsided.

"And we didn't get an unannounced visit from your foster mother. Seriously, the biggest tragedy I can think of." He leaned back.

She tried to hold back a smile, but the corners of her mouth twitched up anyway.

"I knew that'd get you." He smirked. "Now, since you know nothing disastrous is going to happen, maybe you can give it another try. Say the same thing, but a little louder."

The tremors flooded back. If she started talking, would she be able to stop? What happened if he got disgusted with her?

His blue eyes pierced hers. "Melody, you can do this. I have faith in you."

She took a deep breath. "You said I could call you Roger." Her voice gained strength with each word.

He gave her a cockeyed grin. "I did at that. But don't you dare tell Mrs. Langdon or I'll never hear the end of it." He ruffled his hair and drew a breath imitating Mrs. Langdon's wheeze. "'*Roger*, I found this great pamphlet on how to get kids talking … mebbe you should read it sometime.'" He crossed his eyes. "'*Roger*, are you ever gonna get her talkin'? I mean that's the point, ain't it?'"

Melody stifled a snicker. He sounded just like her.

"Or my favorite … '*Roger*, the librarian helped me find some books about how we're gonna make this girl talk.'" He snorted. "I've been waiting for her to tell me gathering the bark of a eucalyptus tree at midnight, boiling it into a decoction along with eye of newt and wart of toad, is the best and most surefire way of making someone talk."

The more ridiculous the statement, the more she relaxed.

"So now that we have the tough part out of the way, let's dig in." He ran a thumb along his jaw. "I want to go back to yesterday and talk about what made you so angry trashing my office was necessary."

Heat rose in Melody's cheeks. She wanted to forget her outburst, not dig into why she'd gotten angry to begin with.

"You've reacted strongly twice, now, to mentions of Quatie Raincrow, so I'm going to guess she has some significance in your life."

Significant? Outside her parents, Quatie was the only one who loved her.

"You certainly didn't like me saying she was too old to foster you."

More than too old. He had put her in the same category as Mrs. Langdon. Quatie Raincrow was family. The words churned inside her, but she couldn't get them out. She rocked, opening her mouth, but closing it again before speaking. Emotion choked her and closed her throat.

Roger placed a hand on her arm. "It's all right. I don't want you to push. The more uptight you are with trying to talk, the harder it becomes. Remember, when we started our journey together, I told you my job was to get you to relax to the point where you were comfortable talking."

She wanted to, but speaking had made everything worse in the past. When she'd spoken about the man who had given her a weird feeling, Mama had died and Daddy had disappeared. When she'd told Quatie about the Jacksons, she died. When she'd spoken up about the snake to Grady Jackson, she had been sent to live with the Hatchets. And when she'd told Miss Prescott about Hatchet...

She couldn't risk it. The only good thing to come of speaking out was leaving Uncle Harlan's house and living with Quatie Raincrow.

Mrs. Langdon annoyed her, but so far she hadn't been hurt.

"Let's try visualization to help you relax. I want you to close your eyes and rest your head against the couch back."

Melody bit her lower lip, but then closed her eyes and rested her head.

"Oops. I forgot. I need your music player. We need one of your nature tracks for this."

Without opening her eyes, Melody reached in her pocket and pulled the music player out. After he connected the player to the speakers, the sounds of a brook filled the room.

"Now, take a deep breath in and hold it for a count of five ... four ... three ... two ... one ... and exhale."

He had her take ten slow, deep breaths. Her heart no longer raced.

"Let your imagination wander along the brook. See moss on the rocks, sunlight on the water as it gurgles past, and shadows cast by the leaves on the trees."

The babbling brook sounds transported her to the brook running past Quatie Raincrow's property. She and Quatie used to go for walks along the water's edge and pick leaves or flowers to decorate the house with. Sometimes they gathered small branches or vines for creating a wreath. She had been happy there.

She imagined walking beside Quatie once again. Quatie dressed in a long skirt, with her worn outdoor boots, and the ever-present headscarf with her spectacles perched on her nose.

Tears wet Melody's lashes. She saw Quatie so clearly, she didn't want to move and break the spell. Something warm pressed against her hand. Almost like Quatie had taken it.

Then Quatie faced her and her eyes twinkled. "*Atsila*, you have more courage and strength than you think. Remember, only an open heart will catch a dream."

Melody's breath caught in her throat. It had been so long since she had heard Quatie's voice. And it was so fitting for her to give Cherokee advice about catching a dream.

"It is time to break your silence and let your voice soar in song."

The younger Melody in her vision answered. "But Quatie, what if I can't? What if I'm not good enough?"

She smoothed the girl's hair. "Child, you have been given a gift in your voice. The Grandfathers say you have kept silent for too long. Let it loose and they will bless you."

"But what if I'm afraid?"

Quatie cupped young Melody's face, but current-day Melody felt the soft leathery touch of Quatie's calloused hands on her cheeks.

"Having fear is not a problem unless you let it stop you. Your mother named you Melody because you are the song of her heart. It is time you fulfill God's destiny for you."

Quatie smiled and the scenery wavered, and she faded.

"No. Don't go." Melody clapped a hand over her mouth and fought back the tears. Two escaped and rolled down her face.

Roger straightened in his chair. "What just happened?"

She pressed stop, cutting off the gurgling noise. How could she possibly tell him Quatie Raincrow had visited them? He'd think she had been hallucinating. He might want to give her drugs to stop her from doing it again. But she wanted Quatie to come back.

"All right. You're not ready to share with me yet. We'll go back to what has been working … with a twist." He raised an eyebrow. "Are you ready?"

She barely dipped her chin in assent.

"We'll use music like we've been doing where you play and sing the song, but then you'll say a few words about the reason behind your selection." He handed her the player. "I want you to tell me why Quatie Raincrow is so important to you."

Melody bit her lip. She knew the right song, no question, but would "If Not For You" reveal more than she wanted? She was comfortable with Dr. Kane—Roger—but what if he expected her to start communicating with Mrs. Langdon? The thought of having a conversation with her current foster mother took her breath away.

She'd never be left in peace ever again. Mrs. Langdon would hound her with question after question trying to make her talk more. Was she ready to face what she had lost when Quatie Raincrow had passed away? She glanced down at the screen on the music player. While thinking about whether she wanted to share, she had navigated to the song.

Her fingers had made up her mind. She pressed play.

Didn't start out good
But turned out great
When I met you
God changed my fate
Sent me an angel
With the kindest eyes
To correct the past
Of heartbreak and cries

If not for you
Who would I be today
If not for you
Would not have found my way
If not for you
I wouldn't be who I am
If not for you

Who would've gave a damn

The chorus made her choke up a bit. Where would she have been if it weren't for Quatie taking her in and showing her love? She took a deep breath to steady herself to sing the next verse.

Can't thank you enough
You made me whole
I was nothing but a scared
And broken soul
You put me on a path
To find my road
Taught me to fly
You were my path to gold

As she launched into the chorus again, Melody let the music flow through her and dedicated the song in her heart to Quatie. Too bad Quatie had passed away before this song was released. She would have enjoyed hearing Melody sing it around the house and they would have talked about the meaning behind the words.

My future is strong
On a rock I stand
Because you cared
And lent a hand
To someone lost
Thought so much of
Because of you
I believe in love

The vibrations on the final notes had completely stopped before Melody snuck a look at Roger.

Forefingers pressed against his lips, eyes closed, he had his head slightly bowed in an attitude of prayer. When he opened his eyes, he ran his hands through his curls. "You did an amazing job with the song. It obviously means a lot to you, so tell me why you connect it to Quatie Raincrow."

Her stomach tightened and her forehead prickled with sweat. How would she find the words to describe what Quatie meant to her? How would she say them? Picking songs and singing them was easy compared with putting her feelings into words.

She opened and closed her mouth a few times but couldn't get any words out.

He held up a hand, palm facing her. "Don't get agitated. Try singing the words instead of speaking them."

Relieved, she reached for the player to navigate to another song.

"No, I don't want you to sing something from your player. I want you to use your own words but sing them to me instead of speaking. Make your own song."

Melody nodded, gulping down her fear. Threading her fingers into her hair and bowing her head, she took a deep breath. She imagined the sound of Gregorian chants and brought Quatie Raincrow to mind. "She was the one who took me in when I was afraid and alone." She hummed while thinking about what to say next. "I thought love had been taken from me forever. She loved me until I believed I had a family again."

Roger gave her a crooked smile. "You're doing great. Keep it up."

"She taught me family was a matter of the heart and was not determined by blood."

Quatie's face rose before her and smiled.

CHAPTER TWENTY-THREE

March 3, 2008 – Melody, age 9

The darkness stretched around us for miles. Even though it wasn't late, the pitch black made it feel like the middle of the night.

Miss Prescott drove down the road, the blue-white light from the dashboard highlighting her frown lines.

When I'd woken up in the school office after napping on the cot, Miss Prescott had been waiting for me. We faced each other across a card table. She'd given me a cup of water and asked me to go through what had happened the day before. At first, I hadn't known what to say, but she'd waited and pretty soon I had told her the whole story. Her lips had tightened into a flat line when I got to the part where Uncle Harlan wanted me to prove my faith to God at church.

When I'd finished, she said girls were not supposed to be locked up with poisonous snakes so I would be taken to another house to live until everything could be sorted out. I didn't care, as long as they knew where to find me when Daddy came back. Not having to live with Uncle Harlan anymore made me happy.

We had gathered my clothes from the house and stuffed them in garbage bags. We didn't have any suitcases, so Miss Prescott said the bags would do the job. We pulled off the highway and passed the *Welcome to Cherokee* sign.

Miss Prescott's voice cut into my thoughts. "The only placement we could find for you on such short notice is on the reservation."

Living on the reservation wouldn't be a bad thing. Daddy used to have business out here, and he'd bring me sometimes. I always had a good time.

"The woman we're placing you with is named Quatie Raincrow."

My stomach tightened. I wanted to be away from Uncle Harlan, but the thought of staying with a total stranger made me nervous. What if she didn't like me? I hugged Raksha Waya tighter.

"Her place is outside of town, so it'll take a few minutes to get there."

I settled back in the seat. Not being in town was fine by me.

After about ten minutes, Miss Prescott pulled onto a side road. Then five minutes later, we pulled off the paved road onto a gravel drive. The darkness, with the exception of the headlights, was complete.

We rounded a curve and the beams lit up a house. The front of the house had a porch with wooden wheels hung on the railing as decoration. Miss Prescott pulled to a stop. The light turned on and the front door opened, followed by the creak of the screen door.

A short woman with hunched shoulders waved from the porch. She wore a shawl across her shoulders and a bandana covered her head. She leaned forward as she peered through her glasses, then called out as Miss Prescott got out of the car.

"Hello, Rebecca. I thought you'd be 'long 'bout now."

Miss Prescott strode up the steps and gave the woman a hug. "It's good to see you again, Quatie. Thank you so much."

I slid out of the car, hugging Rakkie to my chest with a shiver. I wore a sweatshirt jacket, which had been fine while the sun was out, but now I wished I had my heavy jacket on.

The woman beckoned me with the wave of her arm. "Come on, Melody. Let's get you inside. Leave your stuff. We'll get it once you've warmed up a bit."

I clung to Rakkie and made my way up the steps.

The woman opened the door wide for Miss Prescott to pass through, then held it for me, smiling so big her eyes crinkled.

When I crossed the threshold, the warmth thawed my nose. A fire crackled in the hearth and the reflection of the flames danced on the glass screen.

"Why don't you sit by the fire, Melody? I put a pot on for tea when you pulled up the drive." She winked. "I thought you might need a bit of a warm-up."

Miss Prescott followed her out. "Let me help you, Quatie."

I sat on the edge of the sofa, closest to the fireplace. I smiled at the wooden fawn lying on the hearth. It reminded me of the one I had saved from the coyote. The carved fawn was so lifelike, it felt like it was looking at me.

An inch at a time, I scooted back on the couch until my back touched the brown plaid pillow behind me. I couldn't relax against it, no matter how much I wanted because I was still nervous. I was in a total stranger's house, with no hope of going home.

But at Uncle Harlan's, I couldn't relax unless I was alone. So I guess it didn't make a difference.

Tears sprang into my eyes, and I swallowed hard to keep a sob from escaping. I missed Mama and Daddy so much. I squeezed Raksha Waya, then kissed him on the nose. "You'll never leave me, will you Rakkie?" Every time I thought about Daddy, my tummy got a pain and I couldn't breathe right. When would he come back for me?

I gazed around the room to keep from thinking about Daddy and Mama. The floor-to-ceiling stone fireplace had a poker and a bellows next to the screen along with a fireplace broom. A moose, a bear, a deer, and a log cabin were on the half-circle hearth rug. Across the room, a basket full of yarn sat next to an armchair with a half-finished project laid across the top. Brown, dark green, and maroon yarn mingled together. I couldn't tell what it was supposed to be, though. Definitely not a scarf or blanket.

"Here we go." She shuffled into the room carrying a tray with a teapot, three mugs, a pitcher, and a sugar bowl. She set the tray on the coffee table then straightened to her full height.

Miss Prescott still towered above her.

She waved her arm toward the couch. "Take a load off, Rebecca. I'll pour."

Miss Prescott sat next to me and patted my leg.

"Do you take milk and sugar in your tea, Melody?"

I nodded.

Miss Prescott tapped my arm. "Speak up, Melody."

The woman shook her head. "Don't pressure her, Rebecca. She's had a rough day from the sounds of it, and sometimes after a rough day, we need some quiet."

She brought me the mug of tea. I tucked Raksha Waya next to me, against the armrest, and took the warm cup from her. Once she gave Miss Prescott her cup, she went over and sat in the armchair.

The first sip of the hot tea made my insides shudder. Its warmth spread through me, and my spine eased against the cushion.

The woman took a sip of her tea, then set the cup on the end table. "I expect Rebecca told you my name, but I should have introduced myself anyway. I'm Quatie Raincrow, an' you can call me Quatie or Ms. Raincrow. Or mos' folks call me by both names for some reason."

Miss Prescott snorted. "Most folks are in awe of you, and they don't want to offend you."

"Tchah." She shook her head in disbelief. "Now, why would folks offend me by callin' me by my name?"

Miss Prescott set her cup on a coaster on the coffee table and smirked. "Maybe they're afraid you're going to wither their crops or something a little more personal."

More personal? And how would she wither someone's crops? I took another sip of tea.

"Rebecca. You're gonna confuse this child into thinkin' I'm somethin' I'm not." She shook her finger at Miss Prescott. "And while we're on the topic … when are you gonna do what I've been tellin' ya to?"

Miss Prescott sputtered into her tea and her cheeks reddened. "I've been busy. My workload—"

"Uh, uh, uh." She wagged her finger. "No excuses. Your workload ain't gonna keep you warm at night and fill you with delight."

Miss Prescott's eyes opened wide. "Quatie." She glanced at me. "Now is not the time for this discussion."

Ms. Raincrow gave her a stern look. "We wouldn't have to discuss it at all if you'd mind what I tol' you. An' since you don' come visit often, I have to take my opportunity as I see it."

"But my work—"

"I know … your workload. When are you going to understand you will only be truly fulfilled when you take some time for yourself?"

Miss Prescott's mouth opened and closed a couple of times. I quietly snickered because she looked like a fish chasing bait.

"Can't I be fulfilled by my work?" She pressed her lips together for a moment. "Someone has to be there for kids like Melody. They need help … someone has to."

"Humph." Quatie Raincrow raised her eyebrows. "Don't you know you'd be better at your job—more compassionate—if you'd refresh once in a while?"

Miss Prescott fell silent and drank some tea.

"Come see me next week, Rebecca. We'll have a little chat and get you back on track."

Crack.

I jumped when the popping wood hit the fireplace screen. Thank goodness I had just finished my tea. Otherwise, I would have spilled it. Not the first impression I wanted to make.

Quatie Raincrow stood. "Should we get your things, Melody? Let's get you settled so you can make yourself to home."

The temperature had dropped while we had been inside, and the wind kicked up. I hurried to the car, grabbed a trash bag and hauled it inside as quickly as I could. After we had brought everything in, Quatie led the way to my new bedroom.

The bed had a carved wooden headboard and matching carved chest at the foot. A colorful thick comforter and matching pillows covered the bed. The wooden nightstand had a wooden lamp with a blue Tiffany square shade.

Miss Prescott opened the closet—empty and waiting for my things. She opened a bag and reached inside.

Quatie Raincrow touched Miss Prescott's shoulder. "Let's leave putting things away until tomorrow. Melody and I will work on it together. It'll give us a chance to get to know each other a little better."

A look passed between the two I didn't understand. This was so overwhelming. I liked this room much better than the room I'd had at Uncle Harlan's, but it wasn't home. Having my things here would be weird.

Miss Prescott rested her hand on my shoulder. "Melody, I'll have to get you registered for your new school before you can attend. Hopefully, I'll be able to get that done tomorrow, so you'll be able to start later this week. I'll keep you posted."

I walked her to the door. She couldn't stay, and she was as much a stranger as Quatie Raincrow, but I felt like she was abandoning me. She left with a spurt of gravel kicking out from the tires as she reversed.

Quatie Raincrow joined me on the front porch and we watched the taillights disappear around the bend. After a moment, she placed her hand on my back. "We'd best get in the house before you freeze."

When she opened the door, the warmth greeting me caused a shiver to run down my spine. I hurried in, surprised I hadn't felt the cold while watching Miss Prescott drive away. But once inside I didn't know what to do.

"Are you hungry, Melody?"

I shook my head. Miss Prescott and I had stopped for something to eat on the way over.

A twinkle sprang into her eyes. "How 'bout another cup of tea with a chocolate chip cookie?"

I nodded.

"Go back in by the fire. You don't wanna leave your friend alone for too long."

I couldn't believe I had forgotten Rakkie on the couch. I scooped him up and hugged him and sat in the corner of the couch closest to the fire. The flames danced in the hearth. Maybe if I sat and watched the fire long enough I'd forget all the bad stuff that had happened over the past two weeks. Maybe I'd wake up and find out this had all been a dream.

Quatie Raincrow shuffled in with the tea tray. Once she set it on the coffee table, she put a plate with two cookies in front of me and fixed a mug of tea. Then she settled into her chair and picked up the yarn project from the basket.

"I hope you don' mind my doin' a little knittin'. My slippers are 'bout to fall apart an' mornings are too cold. So I thought I'd try my hand at knittin' a pair."

The needles clicked as she wrapped yarn around them and slid them back and forth. Her hands flew through the motions, yet she didn't watch them. She kept her gaze fixed on me.

"That's a mighty fine wolf you have there."

I took a bite of cookie and chewed slowly.

"I remember when Rebecca came here ... she was about your age. She sat right where you are now and drank her tea and ate her cookie without talking, either. She sometimes forgets how hard it is to talk when your life has been turned upside down."

Miss Prescott had been in foster care with Quatie Raincrow? Then she was like me. Washing the cookie down with a sip of tea, I finally found my voice. "His name is Raksha Waya."

She nodded. "Such a good, strong name for a wolf." She tilted her head. "I'll bet he keeps you safe and stands guard while you sleep."

Relief washed through me. She understood about Rakkie and didn't make fun of me for having a stuffed wolf like Jeb and Samuel did. I leaned against the pillow and finally relaxed. My eyes closed. A wave of tired overwhelmed me.

"Melody?"

My eyes flew open.

"Would you like to go to bed? I'm sure you're tired after your long day. You don't have to stay up to keep me company."

I nodded.

She put her knitting aside and before I knew it, she had tucked me into my new bed. She smoothed my hair from my face. "We'll have a chance to get to know each other better tomorrow. I'm so glad you came to stay with me, Melody. Dream sweet, child."

At the door, she stopped and turned toward me. "Do you want me to leave the door open a crack?"

I must have answered because she left it cracked open, but I don't remember nodding before I fell asleep.

A scream tore at my throat and woke me up. The snake. It came at my face, jaw wide and fangs long and sharp. Its yellow eyes glowed as it attacked. My heart raced as I sat bolt upright. I squeezed Rakkie and gasped for breath. And as I realized it was a dream, the tears started. A nightmare about Mama's death. Would God hear my prayers at Quatie Raincrow's house?

I couldn't stop the sobs that shook my whole body.

The door swung open. "What's wrong, Melody?"

Quatie Raincrow offered me a tissue and sat on the edge of the bed.

I clutched the blankets and drew them under my chin as I sat up. "I had a nightmare. And I miss Mama and Daddy so much it hurts."

She gathered me into a hug and stroked my hair. "I know, sweetheart. And if you need to cry, you go ahead and do it. As my mama always used to say, 'The soul would have no rainbow if the eyes had no tears.'"

I didn't know why, but the thought comforted me.

The wind howled and the roof creaked as if it might tear off. My head jerked up and I stared at the ceiling. Such a lonely sound.

"If you listen hard enough, you can sometimes hear voices of those who have passed in the breeze, whispering their love."

I closed my eyes and listened with all my might. Anything to hear Mama speak to me again. The wind did sound like it carried voices with it, but I couldn't make out what they said.

Quatie Raincrow hummed a tune I didn't recognize, but it helped get my tears under control. After I had calmed down, she brought me a drink of water and stayed until I fell asleep again.

CHAPTER TWENTY-FOUR

March 16, 2008 – Melody, age 9

Frantic squawking and flapping noises came through the screen door. I jumped up from the kitchen table where I had been doing my homework and dashed outside. Two feathers floated down to the rain-soaked ground.

Quatie joined me on the porch and placed her hands on her hips. "Somethin's been in the chicken coop."

I ran to the coop and peered through the wire. One of Quatie's hens lay on the ground, wings stretched at an odd angle, blood dappling the breast feathers. My breath caught in my throat. Poor chicken.

Quatie held her hand in the air, index finger outstretched, silently counting. "The bugger got a chick and took off with it." She stepped back and surveyed the coop. Her foot touched a wire near the door. "That's how it got in, the little devil. I'll call Thomas and have him bring something to patch this up."

"But the wire is only bent a little. How'd the chicken disappear?"

Quatie frowned. "It took one of the chicks, so it weren't fully grown. It's been eaten by now."

Oh no. Not a baby. "But that's so sad."

She put her hand on my shoulder. "That what took it is tryin' to survive. Just like the rest of us."

But it ate a baby. A fuzzy little chick with its feathers coming in.

"Why don't you keep an eye on the coop and build a bonfire while I go make some calls."

A glance at the ground, which was still wet from the storm the night before, told me I'd have to search for dry tinder to get the bonfire started. The light smoky scent in the air meant one of Quatie's neighbors had started a fire. If they could do it, so could I.

I'd use the wood under the tarp because at least it would be dry. A few of the trees closest to the clearing had enough dry leaves and needles to use. I gathered them and laid them on the paving stones Quatie had for bonfires.

If we didn't dispose of the chicken, more predators would be drawn by the scent. I didn't want any of the other chicks to be eaten. As I arranged the wood, a small head poked out from underneath the porch. Its black beady eyes stared at me.

A weasel. How dare it be so cute? I wanted to hate the critter for killing the chick, but Quatie was right. Survival meant finding food. I'd have to kill it so it wouldn't harm any more of Quatie's fowl. Or at least tell Quatie, so she could kill it, but its whiskers trembled and my resolve failed. Weasels were fast and smart, and it'd probably get away before I could do anything anyway.

But it couldn't stay here. It'd probably fit in the squirrel trap Quatie had in the shed.

"Stay put, weasel. I'll be right back." I walked to the shed, expecting it to run away when I moved, but it stayed where it was, half hidden behind the post.

When I returned with the trap, I lit the bonfire and sat cross-legged on the side closest to the porch. I set the trap in front of me, with the door open toward the weasel.

"All right, Mr. Weasel, it's time for you to get in the trap so we can take you into the mountains where you can't kill our chickens anymore."

It stretched its head farther out and the whiskers wiggled. It wanted to come to me. I felt it.

Quatie came out of the house and at the creak of the porch, the weasel disappeared.

"Oh, no." If we didn't trap it, Quatie would have to kill it.

"What's wrong, child? And why do you have the squirrel trap out?"

Quatie would think I was crazy. "It's a weasel trying to kill your chicks."

The corners of her mouth twitched. "Weasels are too smart to get caught in a trap."

My face got hot. "I was going to coax it into the trap. I don't want to kill it."

Quatie pulled on her thick gloves and pulled the dead chicken out of the coop. "I know you don't want to kill any critter, but if you let a predator live, they kill again."

"Can't I at least try? If I can trap it, can we take it far away and release it?" I clasped my hands under my chin and put on my best begging face. "Please?"

Quatie laughed as she put the chicken on the fire and poked the wood to get the blaze higher. "The weasel is probably half a mile down the road by now, but if you want to try, no harm will come from it."

"Thank you, Quatie."

A small movement in the dark under the porch told me the weasel was still around.

Quatie Raincrow sat on the rock she used as her bonfire chair. "Go ahead, child. I'm waitin' to see how you coax a critter, who is known for being a twisty little devil, into a trap."

I closed my eyes and felt a song well up inside. Opening my mouth, I sang the song as it came to me.

First the nose poked out, followed by the weasel's whole head, its whiskers going nonstop. I kept singing the song my heart gave me. The words didn't matter—the feeling did.

The weasel left the protection of the porch and edged toward us. It paused and looked up. A red-tailed hawk circled overhead. Then, as if making a decision, the weasel scampered straight into the trap and the door clicked into place, keeping it safely inside.

"If I hadn't seen that with my own eyes, I wouldn't have believed it." Quatie's brows rose to be hidden by her headscarf. "I've never seen someone who could sing a wild beast calm."

I pushed off the ground and stood. "I sang snakes calm before."

"You have a true gift, *Atsila*."

Atsila? Daddy had taught me some words in Cherokee, but I didn't recognize this one. "What did you call me?"

She smiled. "*Atsila*. You're my mustard."

My head drooped. I didn't want to be called a sandwich spread. "But why did you call me mustard?" I barely mumbled the words. Had I done something wrong?

"Don't be upset, child. Mustard is a good thing."

Mustard was yellow goop.

"Mustard is a field of bright yellow flowers, the color of sunshine, amid the sea of green that ripples like the ocean in the merest breeze."

I tilted my head. Mama used to talk about how beautiful the mustard fields were when we'd pass them.

"Mustard is a spice and will take root and grow anywhere you plant it. The short time you have been here, I have watched you grow roots and blossom and you are the spice in this old lady's life."

When she put it like that, mustard wasn't so bad.

"But the biggest reason is for what I witnessed here today. You demonstrated tremendous faith. And in the book of Matthew, it says, 'He replied, "Because you have so little faith. Truly I tell you, if you have faith as small as a mustard seed, you can say to this mountain, 'Move from here to there,' and it will move. Nothing will be impossible for you."'"

She reached her hands toward me and I gripped them. "When I watched you coax the weasel into the trap, it reminded me of the mustard seed and moving mountains. So, you are my mustard, my *Atsila*."

CHAPTER TWENTY-FIVE

Spring 2015 – Melody, age 16

Melody pushed open the door to the waiting room and waved at Lily. After yesterday's session, her spirit had lifted, and she felt freer than she had in years. And best yet, Mrs. Langdon hadn't pulled into a parking space but told her she'd be back to pick her up. She'd tell Roger … it'd brighten his day.

Lily nodded toward the door. "Go ahead. He's waiting for you."

She pushed the door open but halted after a few steps. Why was Miss Prescott sitting in front of Roger's desk?

"Come on in, Melody." Roger's smile showed off his straight, white teeth framed by the three-day scruff he always wore. "I asked Miss Prescott to join us today because she has a few things to tell you, and I thought it best we worked through things together."

A huge lump formed in Melody's stomach. *Work through things* didn't sound good. She scuttled to the couch and perched on the end, arms crossed over her midsection.

Miss Prescott moved the chair next to the couch at an angle facing Melody before sitting. She clasped her hands and leaned forward. "Dr. Kane has been telling me how well you're doing. No specifics, of course, but how much progress you've made. I'm proud of you."

If her stomach didn't hurt so much, Miss Prescott's praise would have made Melody feel good.

Miss Prescott ran a hand through her short, red hair, ruffling it.

Melody bit the inside of her cheek. The hair ruffling was always a sign

Miss Prescott wasn't sure how to break news to her.

"Dr. Kane called me about your current placement and we both agreed a change was in order."

Another move meant another house, another family that didn't want her, another school once she could return, another round of not fitting in anywhere. Why bother?

"I told Dr. Kane the difficulty with finding a new placement and he helped me figure out what I hope is a good and permanent home for you."

Yeah, right. Since when had any of the placements ever been long-term? Not that she wanted to stay with Mrs. Langdon. It would be a relief not to have someone pestering her and making jokes about her every day. The next place wouldn't be any better. They never had been.

Whatever. Fill the plastic bags and move on. She sighed.

Miss Prescott reached out and took her hand. "It's not as bad as you think, Melody. At least I hope not." She gave her fingers a light squeeze. "I have something else important to tell you first. I won't be your caseworker any longer."

Melody stiffened and pulled her hand back. *Abandoned.* The word clanged against her brain like a stone ricocheting against cavern walls, echoing in the wave of emptiness. Miss Prescott had been the one constant in her life for the past seven years. Now she would lose her, too? She blinked twice.

"Hear me out. There's more to it."

Melody's fingers tapped rapid-fire against her leg.

Roger pointed to the speakers and raised an eyebrow. "Do you want to share a song?"

The urge to pick a song was overpowering, but she wasn't ready to sing in front of anyone but Roger yet. She folded her hands to keep them from pulling out the music player and shook her head.

Miss Prescott slid a file out of her tan soft-sided leather briefcase. "We have a couple things to talk about today, but we'll start with your placement. The reason I won't be your caseworker is I have filed a petition to have you stay with me. We received the approval today."

Melody's head snapped up and she stared straight into Miss Prescott's hazel eyes. *Please God, don't let this be a joke.*

"I remember the first day I saw you, sound asleep on a cot, in a rough, black dress, two sizes too big, exhausted from having been awake all night. You were so sweet, and I wanted to scoop you up and protect you from any further harm." Tears filled Miss Prescott's eyes. "I've done a poor job of keeping you protected over the years. My heart breaks for all the things you've been through and had to endure."

Roger ripped a couple of tissues from the box and handed them to Miss Prescott.

She dabbed her tears and blew her nose. "Do you remember how Quatie kept after me, when I came for a visit, to make time in my life so I could have a family?"

Melody nodded.

"When Dr. Kane called me and told me he felt it was time to change your placement to something better, I felt an overwhelming need to make you my family."

A tear rolled down Melody's cheek. She wanted a permanent home more than anything. And Miss Prescott wasn't a stranger—they shared a history. Melody grabbed some tissue from the proffered box.

"You're not allowed to stay with me if you're part of my caseload. Besides, I'd rather make you part of my family instead. More than anything." She reached a hand toward Melody. "Do you want to come live with me? I will leave it up to you."

Melody jumped from the couch and Miss Prescott stood, open-armed, ready to embrace her. Tears streaming down both their faces, they hugged each other in a tight embrace.

When Melody's tears finally slowed, Miss Prescott stroked her hair.

"You've made me very happy. We'll get your stuff from Mrs. Langdon today and you'll come home with me."

She brushed the tears off Melody's cheeks. "I'm hoping the only tears you have from here on out are happy ones. You've had too many driven by sorrow. But I have something else I think will make you smile." She held her arm toward the couch. "Why don't you sit?"

Miss Prescott settled in her chair and inhaled deeply. "Dr. Kane brought up something he feels will be beneficial for you and help you feel more comfortable communicating."

Melody shot him a look and he grinned at her like the Cheshire cat.

"We'd like you to start working with a vocal coach. John Ludloff, the premier vocal coach in the state is willing to give you an audition."

Anxiety flooded through Melody and she couldn't stop her knee from bouncing. She couldn't audition for anyone. She pulled out the music player.

No. She couldn't play any song. She quickly placed it next to the speakers and leaned against the couch back.

Roger sat up straight. "Do you not want to sing?"

Melody shook her head.

"Why?"

His gaze unnerved her. She didn't know how to tell him. Burying her face in her hands, she pushed down the urge to reach for the music player. She rocked for a moment, her breath short and shallow. She couldn't help it. She snatched up the music player and navigated to the song.

Fishing out her headphones, she plugged them in, hooking the bud in her ear.

"Hey. We agreed. You share your music with me."

She held up her index finger and shook it at him. After pressing play, Melody listened, fast-forwarded, stopped and rechecked. When she had the song queued up, she yanked the earbud out and plugged the speakers in. The haunting notes of Sarah McLachlan's "Fear" filled the room.

Miss Prescott tilted her head and narrowed her eyes as she listened.

Once the phrase she wanted had played, Melody pressed the pause button and glanced at Roger.

His mouth drooped. "Do you not understand how talented you are? Melody, you are one of the best singers I've had the pleasure of listening to. You have so much to give with your music."

Melody couldn't look at the disappointed expression on his face. She stared out the window. The sun shining through the leaves looked inviting. She'd rather be out on the green reading a book than inside right now.

Miss Prescott clasped her hand. "When I used to be afraid to do something, or afraid I wasn't good enough, Quatie Raincrow used to tell me, 'You will never learn to fly—'"

Melody squeezed Miss Prescott's hand. "'… if you let someone else carry your wings.'" Her whisper was swallowed up by the silence in the room.

Miss Prescott's eyes filled with tears and her lips quivered. "It's so good to have you talk to me again. Thank you so much."

Melody wiped her eyes.

"You know Quatie would want you to audition. She loved to listen to you sing. Will you try?"

She nodded, her emotions putting her in a chokehold.

Roger scribbled a few notes on his tablet. "We have one more thing to discuss before we start today's session. School."

Melody's eyebrows rose. What? She had been taken out of school after the incident.

"Don't look so surprised. I've been busy on your behalf." A smug expression crossed his face. "After talking to Miss Prescott about removing you from Mrs. Langdon's, I had a nice chat with the judge and convinced him a return to a classroom environment would help you to speak more comfortably with others."

Her emotions were on a rollercoaster.

Miss Prescott crossed to the couch, sat next to her and threaded her fingers through Melody's. "You have both Dr. Kane and me on your side. We'll make sure things don't get out of control like they did before. Since I'm not your caseworker, I can get involved in a way I couldn't before." She patted the back of Melody's hand. "If you feel too much stress and are having trouble coping, we'll work through it together."

Melody closed her eyes for a moment. "Miss… Miss…" The saliva in her mouth dried and her tongue stuck to the roof of her mouth.

"Why don't you call me Rebecca? We're family now."

Melody's chest heaved as she inhaled. Lips parted, she attempted to form the word, but nothing came out. She could do this. Maybe if she whispered it. "Rebecca."

Rebecca hugged her shoulders. "Thank you. It means the world to me. I promise you, we'll take things one step at a time. I want the happy girl who lived with Quatie back again. No more sorrow." She glanced at her watch. "I'd better let you and Dr. Kane get to work." She stood.

Melody grasped Rebecca's wrist. She struggled with speaking. It shouldn't be this hard.

"Sing what you want to say, Melody."

Relief flooded her. She brought the Gregorian chants to mind and picked a note. "Stay."

Rebecca glanced at Roger, who nodded. She retook her seat next to Melody.

"We've had an emotional time already, so let's talk about some pleasant things." Roger crossed his legs, set the tablet on top, and tapped the note-taking app. "Yesterday we talked about Quatie Raincrow. She was obviously a special person in your life."

Rebecca smiled at Melody and patted her hand again. "Quatie was a unique and special individual and I know we both miss her greatly."

Roger tapped the stylus against his lips. "How about you sharing your most special memory of Quatie Raincrow with us, Melody. What stands out?"

She threw him a panicked look. He wanted her to *tell* him her best memory? She wasn't ready.

Roger held up his hand. "Take it easy. Same as before. Go ahead and pick a song, then say a few words … sing them, if you have to."

Phew. She didn't have to think, she knew the memory she wanted to share. She queued up "Christmas Is" and pressed play.

Why is this time of year
Such a big deal
Few know the true meaning

How everyone should feel
About the One who was born
A long time ago
Away in a manger
The savior of souls

Melody pressed pause. This would be easier if she took it stanza by stanza. Nothing bad would happen if she spoke. Too bad her heart didn't believe that, no matter how many times her head said it. She stared at her hands and tried to muster the courage to say the words.

Rebecca took her hand. Somehow it made her feel better. Maybe the world wouldn't smack her down again. She took a deep breath. She could do it.

Just say the words, Melody.

Pitching her voice above a whisper, Melody couldn't look at Roger or Rebecca. It would make things too hard. "Quatie loved Christmastime. It was her favorite time of year, but she didn't like all the trappings. She carried the Christmas spirit in her heart."

She pressed play on the chorus before anyone could say anything to her.

Christmas is a time
For a blessing of the soul
The reason for the season
Everyone should know
Who needs lights
On the house or the tree
When Christmas is about
Who died for you and me

"She never put lights up because she said God put the stars in the sky and they were all the wise men needed to find the Christ child, so they were good enough for her." Talking was a little easier this time.

Jesus was born

On a bed full of hay
And that is why we
Should celebrate this day
Not for the gifts
That Santa may bring
But for the One born
The Almighty King

She hadn't felt the meaning behind this song since she had left Quatie's house. When she and Quatie celebrated Christmas together, she almost felt the angels. "Every Christmas Eve, we'd go to church and Quatie would recite the Christmas story while we watched it acted out."

God has given us
The stars in the sky
The moon glistening on snow
Brings a tear to the eye
I don't treasure things
Like so many do
But when I think of Jesus
Christmas comes true

Melody's voice strengthened over the dying notes of the song. "Quatie used to tell me by keeping our thoughts on Jesus at Christmas, God would always give a Christmas miracle. Like the time we had a Christmas rose. But it was Quatie who gave me the only Christmas miracle I ever wanted." A tear rolled down her cheek.

"Do you feel up to sharing your miracle?"

She glanced at Rebecca, who put an arm across Melody's shoulders and squeezed.

"You can do it, Melody. I'm so proud of you. You brought so many memories of Quatie back with your words."

CHAPTER TWENTY-SIX

December 23, 2010 – Melody, age 11

After rounding the corner with the shopping cart, I checked over my shoulder to see what had happened to Quatie Raincrow. It never failed. Wherever we went, people always stopped Quatie and wanted to talk to her.

I sighed and leaned against the shelving unit to wait. When I had complained about never being able to go to the grocery store, or anywhere else, without having someone stop her, Quatie told me people in need didn't choose the timing. When someone needed spiritual counseling, she had to provide. God had given her the gift of a seer, so it was her responsibility to her community to share her gift.

"*Atsila.*" Quatie summoned me with a wave of her arm. "We're gonna have ta finish the shopping later."

I pushed off the shelf and grabbed the still empty cart. We hadn't put the first item in it yet.

"Elder Lowrey is ill and asked to see me. I'm sorry, but I don't have time to take you home first, so you'll have to go with."

Dwayne Kanuna took the cart from me and led the way out of the store. "The doc said to hurry. If you'll come with me, I'll bring you back after you're done and you won't have to move your car."

I trailed after Dwayne and Quatie as they entered Elder Lowrey's house. I had been here once before with Daddy. It seemed strange to be here without him.

Quatie faced me. "You'll have to wait here for me. I don't know how long I'll be."

She disappeared into the hall, following Dwayne. I shoved my hands into my jacket pockets. I didn't even have a book to read while I waited.

After looking at all the pictures on the wall, I flopped on the couch. As I waited, the temperature plummeted. It had to be colder inside than out. Crazy. I drew my arms tighter against my body and huddled inside my jacket.

I sat bolt upright at the sound of footsteps coming from the kitchen. I hadn't known anyone else was here. An old man wearing a wolf headdress rounded the corner and went down the hall.

My heart pumped as I stared. I had seen him before. Years ago. I searched my memory.

Oh yeah. I had almost forgotten. On Grandfather Mountain with Daddy the day I saved the fawn. He must be Elder Lowrey's friend. Weird that he wore the same clothes as he did then.

Before long, he came back out followed by Elder Lowrey. If Elder Lowrey was sick, shouldn't he still be in bed? Neither man looked in my direction, but Elder Lowrey's skin looked different. He glowed, almost like he was lit from the inside.

As they reached the front door, Quatie Raincrow came out. But when I glanced back toward the men, they were gone.

"What did you see, child?"

I stood. "Elder Lowrey. Where did he go?" My insides felt weird because the men had simply disappeared.

Quatie sighed. "I'll explain, *Atsila*, but after we're home. Now is not the time for explanation."

Dwayne shuffled into the room and pulled his keys out of his pocket. "I'll drive you back to the store." He sniffed. "I can't believe he's gone."

He died? But—

Quatie embraced me in a one-armed hug. "Let's get home."

I didn't understand, but Quatie wouldn't talk in front of Dwayne, so I choked back my questions.

When Dwayne dropped us off at the store, we went straight to

Quatie's car and drove home. We'd have to come back to get the groceries for our Christmas meal, but I wanted to know what had happened more than anything.

Quatie pulled into the drive and stopped the car. "You go in and put the kettle on. We're going to need some tea. I'll be in shortly."

The porch door banged as the water came to a boil. Quatie came in and put a teaspoon of leaves in the pot and poured the steaming water in.

As many questions as I wanted to ask, I knew better. Quatie wouldn't say a word until she was ready, and I had to wait.

I carried the tea tray into the family room where I set it down, then lit the fire. Even though I had questions, I didn't get nervous until Quatie sat next to me on the couch instead of sitting in her chair. Things must be a lot more serious than I had thought.

She raised her cup and took a sip of the hot tea. "Elder Lowrey went to be with the Grandfathers today while I was with him." She took another tiny sip. "This may be difficult to understand, but you saw his spirit leaving."

Other than the glow, he'd looked the same as he did before. My mind raced. It didn't make sense. I could see ghosts?

She peered over her glasses. "What else did you see?"

"A man wearing ceremonial wolf clan skins and headdress. I've seen him before."

"When?" Quatie rapped the question out.

"Hiking on Grandfather Mountain with Daddy. He stood behind Elder Lowrey."

Quatie's glasses slid down her nose and she pushed them back into place. "Death has tracked Elder Lowrey for quite some time." She settled against the couch back. "I had wondered …" Her words broke off when she pressed her fingers against her lips.

The warmth from the cup seeped into my hands. "Does seeing Elder Lowrey's ghost make me weird?"

She patted my leg. "No, *Atsila*. You have been blessed with a gift from God and the Grandfathers. Just like your gift of song." Closing her eyes for a moment, she breathed deeply. "God gives us gifts for a purpose. With your voice, you are meant to bless many. Having sight is to help you."

But how did seeing dead people help me? Confusion was the only thing the *gift* had brought me so far.

"Do you remember what you told me about seeing your mama walking beside the creek before she died?"

I nodded. "I saw a man wearing robes walking beside her … but she swore no one was there."

Quatie took a sip of tea. "Death comes to us in many ways, but he will always come to take the spirit onward."

I shivered. "So the man in the wolf skins and the man walking beside Mama was … Death?" No wonder Mama denied walking with a man. My throat tightened. If I hadn't said anything about the man would she still be alive?

"Drink some tea."

My hand shook too much. "But—"

"When Death comes there is no stopping him. You are not to blame."

I wished I could believe that.

"Today, you saw spirits to help prepare for the future. I can't say more'n that."

The tea, drinkable now, calmed some of my inner turmoil. At least Quatie didn't think Mama's death was my fault or that something was wrong with me. But I still had more questions jumbled like a big ball of yarn in my mind. But one question flashed in bright neon letters, separate from all the others.

She smiled. "You won't know about your father until you ask."

Quatie always knew. The day had uncovered so many memories.

"My daddy is dead, isn't he? He'll never come back." Tears filled my eyes. Deep down I knew … but I had never said it before.

"I'm sorry, Melody."

A tear escaped and ran down my cheek. The fire cracked and a piece of wood pinged off the glass screen. It had been almost three years since Daddy had walked out the door, leaving me behind, so why did it feel like my heart had been ripped in two again? "How could he leave me?"

Quatie put her arm across my shoulders. "I don't think your daddy meant to leave you … not for long."

I couldn't hold back the tears any longer. "Why did he go?"

"When two people are connected at the soul like your father loved your mother and one passes away, the departed soul can call to the one left behind."

My breath came in short bursts. "But why would Mama take Daddy away from me? Why didn't she call me, too?"

"Shhh." Quatie hugged me to her and rocked. "Your mama knew you had a bigger purpose here on Earth. She didn't want to take your daddy from you. She only wanted him to accompany her to the land of the dead's door."

I sat up and wiped the tears from my eyes. "How do you know? Is she here?" I jumped up from the couch and searched the room. "Mama? Mama, where are you? Please don't hide from me."

Everything looked exactly the same. Nothing out of place … not even a shimmer to show where a departed soul might be hiding. "Why can't I see her?"

"She's not here, *Atsila*."

The hope filling my heart died.

"Come back and sit down."

After staring at the fire for a long moment, I shuffled back to the couch and plopped down. "I wanted to see her, so much."

"She comes to me in dreams to check on you."

I had to swallow the rest of my tea before I could talk again. "Why doesn't she visit me in my dreams?"

Quatie's eyes watered. "She doesn't want you to live in the past. She wants for you to look forward and fulfill your destiny."

Swirling the dregs in my cup, I stared at the bottom, mesmerized. "I still don't understand why she called Daddy."

"Your mama was afraid of following Kanati's trail alone. When they reached the mouth to the underworld, your daddy meant to turn back, but the Grandfathers took him with her through the veil."

I understood. A little. *Poor Mama.* She'd died in the way she had feared her entire life, so she was probably afraid what else might happen.

"I miss them so much it hurts."

Quatie gathered me in a hug. "I know, *Atsila.* Let me share some wisdom from Chief Dan George. 'May the stars carry your sadness away, may the flowers fill your heart with beauty, may hope forever wipe away your tears, and, above all, may silence make you strong.'"

CHAPTER TWENTY-SEVEN

December 24, 2010 – Melody, age 11

The storm clouds gathered as I hurried home from the woods. A white plume escaped my lips with every breath. If it got any colder, I swore my breath would freeze into ice chunks. Nosesicles had formed and I couldn't feel my feet as my boots crunched across the ground.

A trickle of sweat rolled down my back. It never failed—my nose was so cold it felt like it might snap off if I touched it, but with my heavy coat on, gathering the branches made me hot. As I left the shelter of the trees and brush, the wind cut sharply across the yard.

I gave the mud chucker at the bottom of the porch a workout so my boots wouldn't leave tracks. When I went inside, my nose thawed and started running. I set the branches on the hearth, peeled off my coat, and grinned.

I loved decorating Quatie's mantle with boughs for Christmas. And this year I found holly berries to help make things more festive. After yesterday's emotional storm, I hadn't thought I'd get the Christmas spirit, but I wanted to celebrate more than ever. I stood in the middle of the room and gazed at my creation. My best effort yet. Quatie Raincrow would love the red touch of the holly berries.

Now for the final decoration. I pulled the crystal bowl out of the cupboard and set it in the center of the mantle, then filled it with pine cones. Last year I had wanted to paint the pine cones silver and gold. But Quatie said their natural beauty was good enough for her.

She had left early that morning, saying she didn't know how long she'd be. Humming carols, I fussed with a few of the branches. The wind moaned as it crossed over the chimney. Only one log left in the andiron. We'd definitely need more.

I grabbed my coat and put my gloves back on. We wouldn't want to bring in wood on Christmas Day.

Quatie came home as I brought the last load of logs up on the porch.

"Thank you, Melody." She climbed the steps. "We'll need those logs 'cause we're gonna have a very white Christmas."

She always knew. Better than the weather forecasters. "But the weather report says it's supposed to be clear tomorrow with a chance of snow on Sunday."

Quatie snorted. "They'd be able to predict the weather better if they'd stick their head out the winda once in a while." She leaned against the porch rail and peered at the sky. "Look at those clouds. They're full of snow and they're not gonna hold off just because it's Christmas."

The wind whipped through and I shivered.

"Let's get inside. It's been a long, cold day." She put her arm across my shoulders and opened the screen door.

I put the final logs in the andiron while Quatie changed her coat for her Christmas apron. The apron was the one festive article of clothing she wore. It always made me smile to see her put it on. It was the first gift I had given to Quatie Raincrow.

I had wanted to buy her something special but hadn't had money. She'd found me pouting in my room and told me she'd much rather have something I make for her because then she was sure it came from my heart. I still hadn't known what to make. The weekend came and Quatie Raincrow had taken me into town to the recreation center where they had a craft room.

When I saw the stack of aprons waiting to be decorated, I'd known exactly what I wanted to give her for Christmas. She loved to cook. It had taken me all day to get it exactly how I wanted it. After I carefully folded it, I slipped it in a bag with some tissue paper to wrap it in later. I remembered how nervous I'd been waiting for her to open it. What if she didn't like it?

But when she'd opened it, she'd told me it was perfect and she'd wear it every year on Christmas Eve and Christmas Day, and had.

Quatie hummed in the kitchen to the scrape and clunk of pots and pans on the stove. "Why don't you get a fire started?"

I grinned. The logs were on top of the special pine cone fire starters we'd made to help give us that Christmassy smell. I grabbed the fireplace matches, pulled the screen away from the opening, and shook out a couple of rolled newspaper spills from the holder. After the first spill caught fire, I held it to the tinder under the logs.

The cones flared an orangish-red at the tips. I rested the edge of the spill on the grate, lit the next, and started the fire on the other end. I rocked back on my heels and waited until the log caught. The heat made my face toasty as I put the screen back into place.

"You did a right nice job on the mantle this year, *Atsila*. Those berries are the perfect touch."

The warmth of pride spread through me. Quatie never went overboard in her praise, but she always made me feel good about myself.

"Do you know what you're wearing for your solo tonight?"

I nodded. "My red sweater, black skirt, and tights."

She straightened the Christmas throw across the couch back. "And what will you sing this evening?"

Heat crept into my cheeks. "'O Holy Night.'" Mama used to sing it to me on Christmas Eve before tucking me into bed. She said it was her favorite hymn to remind her about the true meaning of Christmas. I'd never sung it in church before, so was a little nervous about it.

"A beautiful choice. The Grandfathers will be pleased." Quatie closed her eyes for a moment. "You're gonna do a fine job. Don't worry so much, Melody."

The knots in my stomach relaxed a little. Quatie always knew.

We spent the evening before the service singing carols, as we usually did on Christmas Eve. After the service, we hurried home just ahead of the storm. I stomped my feet on the porch before opening the door trying to get the circulation running in them. My shoes were no match for the cold. I needed my boots.

"Go get into your PJs and stoke up the fire while I make our hot cocoa."

I stoked the fire first to take the chill off the family room. Then slipped into my pajamas and huddled into my robe. I snickered as I grabbed the Santa cap I had from our school program. I pulled Quatie's gift from the shelf in my closet. Clutching it gently to my chest, I didn't have to wonder whether she'd like it this year … she would.

I hid her present behind the couch and, stifling giggles, put the Santa cap on the fawn on the hearth. Then I sat on the edge of the sofa and waited.

Quatie shuffled in carrying the cocoa tray. She wore her full-length, maroon plaid robe and a pair of knitted slippers. She set the tray on the coffee table and straightened. When she glanced at the fireplace, one eyebrow rose. "Now that's the first time I ever saw a fawn in a Santa cap."

I couldn't hold the giggles back any longer.

"It won't hurt anything, I guess." She frowned. "Did you ask the fawn whether he wanted to wear your cap?"

"He said it would make him festive. And he's always wanted to be a reindeer."

Quatie shook her head. "Child, I surely don't know where you get your imagination from. In all my years I never once thought that putting a hat on a deer would make it a reindeer."

She handed me my cup of cocoa then settled in her chair with hers.

I reached over the side of the sofa and closed my fingers over her gift. "Are you ready for your present?" I didn't wait for her response as I jumped up from the sofa and held the package out.

Back on the sofa, I took a sip of the cocoa and enjoyed the warmth as it slid down my throat. Quatie Raincrow never ripped the paper off. She carefully peeled the tape back until she could open the gift without tearing any of the paper. Then she'd keep the paper and reuse it somehow.

My knee bounced as she finally removed the tape and opened the wrapping to reveal the gift inside.

"Oh my, Melody. You made this?" She pulled the pine cone wreath out of the paper.

"Do you like it?"

"It's the most beautiful wreath I've ever had." She held it at arm's length. "We won't put it on the door until after the storm blows through. I don't want it to tumble off in the wind and break. Thank you."

I knew she'd like it.

"Your present is in the cupboard. Go ahead and open it."

When I opened the cupboard, there were two gifts. I turned my head toward Quatie. "Both of them?"

She nodded. "Open the big one first."

I ripped the paper off a new hand-knit sweater and Quatie cringed. She had always told me the Grandfathers didn't like anything to be wasted. "Don't worry … I'll roll these into spills to use for the fire. The paper won't go to waste."

She laughed. "You do my soul good."

"Thank you for the sweater." I held it against me. She'd bought the yarn I'd been eyeing every time we went to the shop. A variegated green, blue, rust, orange yarn knitted into the most gorgeous sweater I'd ever seen. She must have knit it while I was at school because I'd never seen a scrap of the yarn left out.

I laid the sweater aside and turned the other package over in my hands.

"Go ahead. Open it."

After I tore the paper off, I was shocked to see a music player and headphones inside. I glanced at Quatie Raincrow, my mouth wide open. "Are you serious?" She'd never given me a store-bought present before.

She smiled. "Music is your gift. You should have something to keep it with you always."

Wow.

She cleared her throat. "I already started your collection for you. I've been writing down songs that you sing around the house and asked them to help me load it at the music store."

With trembling fingers, I turned the unit on and scrolled through the artists. My grip tightened at one of the names. I couldn't catch my breath. "My name is on here."

My voice sounded weird, like it was trying to squeeze through my closed-off throat.

"I tracked down Thomas Hill. He still had the track you made of 'Amazing Grace', so I asked him to put it on your player."

Tears rolled down my cheeks. *Mama and Daddy were on my player.* I plugged the headphones in and navigated to the song. And there we were. Daddy playing guitar. Mama on the piano. And the five-year-old me, who had no idea how her life would turn out, singing her heart out. The tears kept coming. I couldn't stop them.

As soon as the song finished, I clicked back to play it again.

"I didn't mean to upset you, child. I thought you'd like it."

She didn't understand, but my throat was so choked up, I couldn't talk. I turned the volume up as the song came to a close.

There. At the end of the song, faintly, Daddy's voice. "*Good job, baby.*"

It had been so long since I had heard Daddy's voice; I almost couldn't remember it anymore. Now I didn't have to remember. I could hear it when I needed to. I wished Mama had said something, but I'd have to settle for hearing her play the piano and remember how much she loved me.

I took a couple of sips of cocoa to help me stop the tears. Then I ran to Quatie Raincrow and hugged her as tight as I could. "Thank you."

She stroked my hair. "Merry Christmas, Melody."

CHAPTER TWENTY-EIGHT

Spring 2015 – Melody, age 16

When she finished talking, Melody dared to peek at Roger. His eyes were wide and his jaw slack.

"Wait … the 'Amazing Grace' you played for me before was you singing? What about the *a cappella* song about snakes?"

She nodded. "It's my song." She bit back a laugh as the cute furrows between his brows appeared … a sure sign he didn't understand what she meant. "I made it up one day when I was out hunting with my daddy."

Roger straightened and gave her a sideways look. "How old were you when you wrote the song?"

Melody's smile faltered. The raging sense of loss and overwhelming heartbreak rose out of the desert of her past, like a snake ready to strike and swallow her whole. She buried her face in her hands to wait out the tidal wave of emotion threatening to drown her.

Rebecca smoothed the hair back from Melody's face. "Are you okay, honey?"

She jerked away from Rebecca's touch and dashed to the window. She begged the serenity and calm of the trees to act as a balm on her soul, to give her a sense of peace over the past. *Please God, heal my bleeding heart. Oh Grandfathers, hear my pleas and let me feel the stillness amid the storm.*

Melody poured her heart out in prayer. But the darkness roiled and slithered surrounding her, pulling her into its depths.

"Melody?"

Roger's voice barely penetrated the blackness enveloping her—the sound muffled and indistinct.

"Don't shut us out. Use music if you need to, but tell us what is happening."

Her fingers closed on the music player in her pocket. "No Power In Me" described where she was, but the walls closed in. If she didn't get out of there, they'd crush her ... or the darkness would swallow her whole. She couldn't catch her breath and sweat drenched her body.

She turned from the window and the door lit up like a beacon—safety and escape rolled into one. She bolted past Rebecca and Roger, unlocked the door and raced through the waiting room to the outside. Once outside she could breathe, but couldn't stop running. The darkness would catch her and consume her.

She dashed around the building and sprinted past the pond. Stopping for a moment, she looked at the sky. Her mountains were calling. It had been too long. The road to the left went downtown. She turned to the right and ran along the side of the road.

Free from the city, Melody still had a long way to go, but her steps faltered to a walk with a stitch in her side. At least she had worn sneakers and jeans today. She had outrun the darkness but needed the solace of the mountain laurel alongside the streams. Too much had happened. And when Roger had asked her how old she was when she'd made up the rattlesnake song, the day had flooded back—the thrill of hunting with Daddy, being chased by the vipers, seeing Mama walking with the strange man—with Death, the snake biting Mama, Daddy making her sing the snake song while Mama died, and Daddy leaving her ... never to return.

Rebecca being there made it worse. She had been there through too many of the losses Melody had had throughout her life. The loss of Quatie Raincrow was second only to Mama and Daddy.

A car behind her slowed instead of passing. Melody shot a look over her shoulder. Adrenaline flooded through her. Rebecca. How had she found her?

Melody veered into the brush beside the road and forced her feet to run.

Rebecca pulled the car onto the shoulder and stopped. The car door slammed. "Melody, wait."

Melody didn't bother to look back but sprinted forward. Over her ragged breath, Rebecca's footsteps crunched in the gravel. The ache in her side clawed at her lungs like the swipe of a bear's paw. Clutching her side, she dashed into the trees.

Her feet hit a tree root while her eyes tried to adjust to the sudden change in light. She sprawled into the moss and dirt. Before she could get her feet back under her, Rebecca caught up.

"Please stop running, Melody." Rebecca leaned forward, propping herself up by her knees and panting. "I'll take you where you want to go. Just get in the car. We'll do this together."

Melody stared into her eyes. Could she trust Rebecca?

Rebecca held out her hand. When Melody grabbed it, Rebecca pulled her to her feet. "Where do you want to go?"

"Home." Melody bit her lip, hoping Rebecca understood.

Rebecca gave her a wry smile. "You don't mean my house." She glanced at the road. "And based on your direction, I'm going to say you were headed back to the mountains."

Relief made Melody's knees weak. She wouldn't have to explain. She wasn't sure she could.

Rebecca put her arm across Melody's shoulders. "Let's get in the car. I can't take you to your old house. Someone else lives there now. But we'll find a good place for you to refresh."

Forty-five minutes later, Rebecca pulled off the highway on the road to Grandfather Mountain. How could she have known?

"I thought maybe if we hiked on one of the mountain paths you used to climb, it would feel like home."

Melody struggled to find her voice.

Rebecca held up her hand. "Quatie told me you used to talk about Grandfather Mountain and I made a note in your file. I'm glad I did."

When they got out of the car, Melody glanced at Rebecca's shoes. She wore a skirt suit, and usually dress shoes weren't good for hiking.

Rebecca smirked and held her foot up to show off a leather shoe with a square heel. "In this job, if I've learned nothing else over the years, I've learned the value of wearing shoes that can go the distance." She raised an eyebrow. "After all, you never know when you're going to have to chase a teenager down a mountain road."

Melody turned her head and bit back a smile. At least Rebecca didn't seem angry.

They walked together along the path in the afternoon sunlight. Just breathing the mountain air helped the tension from the day fall away. As they crossed the creek, Melody saw umbrella petals ahead. She rushed forward, tears standing in her eyes. She touched the blooms and remembered when she used to "play music" on the mountain laurels and sing the song in her heart at the time.

Rebecca placed her hand on Melody's shoulder. "The laurels are beautiful. Well worth the hike."

A gentle breeze kissed the leaves and ruffled through the flowers. Melody's soul felt at peace and speaking was easier.

She asked what she'd never had the guts to ask Rebecca before. "Do you ever think about Quatie?"

Rebecca massaged the base of Melody's neck. "All the time. She was like my mother for half my childhood and beyond … even when I left her care. I'd give anything to hear her voice one more time. To talk to her and tell her how life is going." She wiped a tear from her cheek. "We've never talked about the day you called me because Quatie was sick."

The words hung in the air. Melody's throat closed. She couldn't talk about the second most horrific day of her life.

"Dr. Kane told me songs hold meaning to you for events in your life. You don't have to share it with me if you don't want to. I won't pressure you. But do you have a song for that day?"

Melody faced Rebecca and stared into her eyes. After a long moment, she nodded. After pulling the music player out of her pocket, she stared at it. Without speakers, she couldn't share it with Rebecca. She wasn't sure she wanted to.

That wasn't true. Rebecca was the one person she could share with who would truly understand. Roger listened and understood far more than she had expected, but he hadn't known Quatie Raincrow and had already proven he didn't understand how important she was.

Rebecca knew. Daddy had told her true understanding came when you could walk in someone else's shoes. As a child, she hadn't understood what he'd meant. But standing here in front of the laurel, she remembered his words.

She and Rebecca had shared the experience together, so she was the best person to understand how much the song meant.

"Melody, it's all right. If you're not ready to share… I shouldn't have asked. But like you, I miss Quatie and hoped you had something to help us both feel her presence more closely." She squeezed Melody's shoulders. "Like you did with the Christmas song. I'd heard it before, but never knew why I loved it so much. You showed me that today, so thank you."

Melody fished out her headphones and uncoiled them. Fully extended, there were about three and a half to four feet between the earbuds. Maybe if they both used a bud? She stuffed the left bud in her ear and handed the right to Rebecca.

"Are you sure?"

Melody took a deep breath. "Yes. I want to share with you." She navigated to the song while Rebecca put in her earbud.

As if time sat still
While the Earth still turns
With fire in the sky
Tragedy burns
Minutes ago
There was peace in the air

Blood on the ground
Too much to bear

Melody paused the music. The stream gurgled as the water flowed past and the scent from the mountain laurels danced on the breeze. Quatie loved nature and Melody felt her presence with them. She would have loved hiking Grandfather Mountain, just as Daddy had.

"Quatie had never been sick before. Not in the nearly four years I lived with her." She stroked a blossom and inhaled the sweet perfume. "Not even a case of the sniffles ... not until then. She wanted creosote tea and I felt as if I were moving through molasses. I couldn't get there and back fast enough. Everything moved in slow motion."

Rebecca squeezed her hand.

Melody pressed play.

Heart beating fast
Body goes numb
Feeling so helpless
I cannot run
Oh God please help
Stop what I see
I pray but there's
No power in me

"That's exactly how I felt. What power did I have to help? I was just a kid."

Rebecca used two fingers to rub out the wrinkles in her forehead. "But honey, I felt so much the same trying to get to you and Quatie as quickly as I could. Never has the drive taken so long."

Knowing Rebecca had felt the same way helped somehow. She sang along with the next verse and chorus.

So close I can taste it
But can't change a thing
My mind is in motion

But I have a broken wing
Pinning me down
To damaged ground
Above the flames
Where the devil's bound

Heart beating fast
Body goes numb
Feeling so helpless
I cannot run
Oh God please help
Stop what I see
I pray but there's
No power in me

"I prayed so hard … to both God and the Grandfathers … but if they heard it, they didn't answer."

Sirens cry
Piercing ears
Paralyzed
And raining tears
Red lights spinning
Round my dizzy head
Can't do a thing
But bury the dead

CHAPTER TWENTY-NINE

December 22, 2011 – Melody, age 12

I dropped my bike at the edge of the road and splashed through the puddles across the yard. My chest heaved from the fastest bike ride I'd ever taken. I checked to make sure I still had the package safely tucked inside my jacket. Though I was soaked to the skin from the rain, I didn't worry about the package because it was in a plastic bag.

Movement beyond the house caught my eye. Who would be walking through our woods on such a dreary day? I didn't have time to worry about it. I needed to get back to Quatie Raincrow—fast.

I barely stopped to use the mud chucker before pounding up the porch steps. I pulled the packet of leaves out of my jacket and tossed it on the counter, grabbed the kettle and filled it. I lit the burner and put the kettle on to boil.

After racing into the family room, I skidded to a stop. Quatie Raincrow sat under a blanket in her chair, head lolling forward, eyes closed, skin pale, unmoving. I couldn't catch my breath.

A rumbling cough racked her body.

Thank God and the Grandfathers. I slid on my knees next to her chair and patted her arm. "I have the creosote leaves and the water is heating." She made no response. "Quatie?"

Her labored breathing marred the quiet.

I shook her shoulder gently. "Quatie … please wake up."

A scream sounded from the kitchen. I had forgotten about the water. Tearing myself away from Quatie, I dashed back to the kitchen. The steam poured out the spout and the whistle hurt my ears. I flipped off the burner, put some leaves in the pot and poured in the hot water.

I glanced out the window as I reached for a big mug from the top shelf. A strange man stood at the edge of the woods, watching the house. I set the mug on the counter and rushed to the door to make sure it was locked. We'd never had any problems out here, but he creeped me out. Standing there, staring. What did he want?

I placed the tea strainer over the mug and poured the tea. A quick glance out the window showed the man standing in the same place, hand in his pocket, waiting. *For what?*

Taking care not to spill, I took the hot tea into Quatie. I set the mug on the side table and tried to rouse her, but couldn't.

I grabbed the phone and ran back into the kitchen to dig out Quatie's phonebook. *Why did she even have the thing?* She never used the phone unless she couldn't help it. She said she had to have a phone or I couldn't stay.

I flipped through the mostly clean pages to find Miss Prescott's number. Relief coursed through me when I saw Quatie had both her office and her cell phone. I didn't bother with the office phone number. With the holidays approaching, Miss Prescott was unlikely to be at work.

I held my breath as the phone rang, waiting for her to pick up. As soon as I heard the answering click, the words tumbled out of my mouth. "Miss Prescott, this is Melody. Quatie Raincrow is sick and she won't wake up. I made her creosote tea, but …" A sob escaped. "I can't …"

"Melody, slow down, hon. I can't understand you. Take a deep breath."

I took a huge, shuddering breath. "Quatie Raincrow is sick and is asleep in her chair, but I can't wake her up to drink the tea she asked me to get."

"Is she …?"

"She coughed and it sounded horrible, and her breath gurgles."

"Melody, I'm going to call the hospital to get Quatie some help. I want you to stay with her. I'll be there as quickly as I can. Make sure you hang up the phone so we can call if we need to."

I clicked the phone off and hurried back to Quatie's side. Perspiration glistened on her forehead. I tore into the bathroom, wet a washcloth, wrung it out, and returned to place the compress on her forehead. When I touched her skin, heat radiated from her.

The compress fell off as she doubled over with another coughing spasm. When the attack eased, she opened her eyes. "Melody?"

I grabbed her hand. "I'm right here, Quatie. I made you some creosote tea."

She closed her eyes and relaxed against the chair back again. "Thank you, child."

I gripped the cup. "Why don't you drink some? It might help with the coughing."

She struggled to lift her head, so I held the cup to her lips. Her hand trembled as she held it against the bottom to tip the cup forward. After a tiny sip, her head plopped back against the headrest.

Where was Miss Prescott? How long would it take her?

Quatie closed her eyes. "Warmth feels good. So cold."

But she was sweating. The fire crackled in the hearth, heating the room. She was covered with a big knit blanket.

"Take another sip, Quatie. It will help."

After I helped her drink more tea, she slumped in the chair. My fingers fluttered against the cup. She didn't look good. It frightened me.

A faint siren wailed in the distance. Quatie had fallen asleep again, her breath rasping in her chest. I placed the barely tasted cup on the side table and took her hand. I wanted her to know I was there, even while sleeping.

The sirens came closer. We usually didn't get sirens this far from town. I focused on warming Quatie's hand between mine. Maybe if her hands were warm she wouldn't feel so cold.

The sirens cut off mid-wail as they pulled into the drive. Swallowing the lump in my throat, I ran to the door and swung it open. The EMTs jumped out of the ambulance and ran to the back to pull out a stretcher. The red lights flashed, glinting off the puddles, and washed over the house staining the walls as they pulsed.

Numb as the EMTs rushed up the steps with the stretcher, I held the door open for them and pointed to the family room. As I followed them into the room, my ears buzzed and I couldn't feel my feet. They set the stretcher next to Quatie's chair and lowered it.

The EMT with his dark hair pulled back in a ponytail knelt next to Quatie and asked her questions. As she answered, she had another coughing spasm and he signaled to the EMT with the short hair. The short-haired guy pulled a cylinder out of a case. He connected some hoses, then put a mask on Quatie's face. Then ponytail guy scooped her up, blanket and all, as if she didn't weigh a thing, and laid her on the mattress.

They raised the stretcher and started toward the door. As they passed, Quatie Raincrow held her hand out to me. They halted.

I took her hand. "I'm here, Quatie."

"Don't leave me, my *Atsila*."

"I won't."

They continued pushing her through the door, then collapsed the wheels to carry her down the porch steps.

I followed them, taking a moment to look at the spot where the stranger had been standing. Thank goodness he was gone. Maybe the ambulance had scared him away.

I raised my leg to step on the bumper and grabbed the rail to join Quatie in the back of the ambulance.

The ponytail EMT put his hand on my shoulder. "I'm sorry, miss. You're too young to ride in the ambulance."

I shrugged off his hand. "But I promised her." Hauling myself up, I stepped inside.

He put an arm around my waist and lowered me to the ground. "It's against regulations." He gazed at me with sorrowful eyes. "I really am sorry. We'll take good care of her for you."

I bit my lower lip as an inner struggle raged. I wanted them to get Quatie to a doctor as soon as possible, but I couldn't break my promise to her. If I jumped in the ambulance, they'd only delay.

She called my name.

"I'm right here." I swung up on the ledge again.

The EMT grabbed me with both arms this time. I grabbed the handrail and held on as he tugged. A car pulled off the road and skidded to a halt, spewing mud, water, and rocks as it did.

"Put her down."

Thank goodness. I released the handrail and as soon as my feet touched the ground, I ran to Miss Prescott. "I promised I'd stay with her, but they won't let me ride in the back."

Miss Prescott gave me a hug. "Get in the car, Melody. We'll follow." She released me and strode toward the ambulance. "What are you waiting for? Get her to the hospital."

The EMT's head snapped back like he'd been hit. He shut the doors, secured them, then hustled to the cab.

Miss Prescott hurried back to the car. I hopped in and buckled my seatbelt. The ambulance circled around and hit the road, sirens wailing once more. We followed and I prayed the whole way to God and the Grandfathers that Quatie would be well.

We arrived at the hospital not more than two minutes after the ambulance. Miss Prescott spoke to the intake nurse and told me to wait in the lobby. I sat on a couch and hunched forward. A TV on the wall played a commercial. The screen could show nothing more than the Emergency Broadcasting symbol for all I cared.

I chewed on my fingernails and my knee bounced as Miss Prescott paced in front of the entrance talking on her cell phone. She told me she had to make a few calls outside. Every time the double doors swung open, my head jerked around. I wanted the doctors who were working on Quatie to come and tell us something … anything.

Miss Prescott finally clicked off her phone and put it back in her purse. The double doors swung open again. A woman doctor signaled to Miss Prescott. I jumped up and joined them.

"We've stabilized her condition. We need to bring her fever down and reduce the fluid in her lungs. She has pneumonia and will need to stay with us for a few days."

Miss Prescott put her hand on my shoulder and gave me a squeeze.

"Can I see her?"

The doctor's lips pressed tight. "If you keep your visit to no more than five minutes. She needs her rest."

I nodded.

We went through the double doors and when we reached Quatie's room, I went straight in while Miss Prescott stayed in the hall with the doctor. Sitting next to the bed, I took hold of Quatie's hand.

"I knew you'd come."

I tried to smile. "I promised you. You had me worried. The doctor says you're sick and will have to stay for a few days."

Quatie looked through the doorway. "Listen to me, Melody. You will have to go with Rebecca. Be a good girl and do what she says. I'll work on getting better so we can both go home."

The tears in my eyes made everything in the room shimmer. "I will."

Miss Prescott joined us. "You've given us a scare, Quatie. Melody and I will have to leave you now. Get better." She stroked my hair. "Come on, Melody. Time's up."

I squeezed Quatie Raincrow's hand. "I love you, Quatie. Get better."

CHAPTER THIRTY

Spring 2015 – Melody, age 16

Rebecca pulled the car into a slot at the front of the school and turned off the engine.

Melody played with the snap on her book bag, pulling it open and snapping it shut repeatedly. The thought of getting out of the car made her queasy stomach want to lose her breakfast. Not that she had eaten much.

Rebecca opened her door. "It's going to be okay, Melody. If you have any problems, we'll get them taken care of right away." She got out of the car. "I know this is tough, but you can do it."

New school, new teachers expecting her to talk and participate, new kids taunting her—her breath caught in her throat. If only everyone would leave her alone.

Rebecca came around and opened the passenger door. "You'll see. Things are going to be different this time. I've already had a chat with the administrators and your teachers. No one is going to push you to talk before you're ready. And if they do, they have to answer to Dr. Kane and me."

Melody swung her feet out and stood. Why did she feel like she was walking the last mile? Rebecca had better be right.

"Let's go get your schedule and get you to homeroom."

Melody trailed after Rebecca. The bell signaling the start of school hadn't sounded yet, so kids were still arriving, hanging out in clusters, talking, texting friends. One guy sat on the planter wall, wearing a fedora and sunglasses, strumming a guitar. She smiled. He was completely absorbed in his music and oblivious to all the activity around him.

She followed Rebecca up the steps and into the administration office.

Rebecca greeted the receptionist by name and waved to a few office workers as she passed through the gate and marched directly into the principal's office. "Hey, Phil. This is Melody Fisher."

Principal Ward stood and held out his hand.

Goodness, he must stand 6' 7" and he had a firm grip.

"Miss Prescott and I have had a nice talk about you and what will best help you settle into our school. We're here to help you get acclimated and make you comfortable with continuing your education." He smoothed his suit coat. "One of the rules we have here is no use of music players or any digital device."

Melody's neck knotted. She couldn't leave her player at home.

"But Miss Prescott tells me music is part of your therapy, so we will make an exception to the rule." His brown eyes twinkled. "Do me the favor of keeping it low profile so I don't have to deal with a revolt."

Melody nodded.

He clapped his hands together. "Well, let's talk about your schedule." He glanced at Rebecca. "In reviewing her schoolwork, we've placed her in senior classes. She has already completed all the junior coursework and most of the senior work. Do you see a problem with that?"

Rebecca put her hand on Melody's shoulder. "I think it will be fine, Phil. What do you think, sweetie?"

She'd be able to finish school this year and never have to face another day in high school? She searched Rebecca's eyes.

Rebecca arched a brow. "Yes, I really mean it."

Melody bit back a smile.

Chuckling, Rebecca patted her shoulder. "We have a yes from Melody, too." She plopped her satchel on the chair back and extracted a file folder, flipped through, pulled out a few pages, and handed them to Principal Ward. "Here are the court documents approving Melody's return to school and the specific parameters. She will need to continue her daily therapy sessions."

Principal Ward took the documents and added them to the file on his desk. "Since we had already discussed the therapy sessions, I crafted her schedule to cover mornings and one class after the lunch period."

"Excellent. One last thing … I want to stress that no one is to pressure Melody to speak during class or any other time. Her therapist is adamant Melody be allowed to communicate and participate at the level she is comfortable with." She slung the satchel strap back over her shoulder. "She speaks during therapy and has said a few words at home, so we're hopeful speech will transition to the classroom soon, but pushing the issue could cause irreparable damage."

Principal Ward held out his hand. "All of her teachers are clear on the importance of allowing Melody to set her own comfort level."

Tension drained from Melody's shoulders. She wouldn't be forced to speak before she was ready.

Rebecca shook the principal's hand. "Thanks again, Phil. Keep me posted. I want to know every little thing as it relates to Melody."

"I'll keep in touch, Rebecca." He held his hand out. "Welcome to Laurel High, Melody. I look forward to helping you further your academic career."

As she entered the quad outside the administration building, the lump of fear Melody had been trying to suppress all morning grew. The students milled through the campus. Her stomach clutched and her breath came faster. Which of them would be the first to hurt her?

"Take a deep breath. You're going to be fine. I'll walk you to your first class." Rebecca checked the campus map and class schedule.

"I'll be here at a quarter 'til two to pick you up. Meet me in the parking lot." When they reached the classroom door, Rebecca hugged her. "You have the cell phone I gave you?"

Melody patted her purse.

"Good. If you need anything or if anything happens, text me." Rebecca strode away, trench coat flapping with every step.

Melody fought down the panic that she had been abandoned again.

Rebecca would be back for her. She had to be.

"Excuse me."

A boy reached around her for the door handle.

"You're new to this homeroom?" He pulled the door open. "After you."

She walked into the class and the teacher came to greet her.

Melody exited the building and faced the quad. Too many students. She needed somewhere quieter for lunch. She wasn't ready to be around the other kids outside the classroom. So far, the day had been all right, but she now had forty-five minutes to fill and needed some solitude. Two hours left until Rebecca came to pick her up.

The athletic field might be the best place to find a little space to read and eat her lunch. Melody focused on the campus map and her steps slowed. The field should be to the right. She turned and took a step forward.

A big guy wearing a letterman's jacket plowed into her.

James?

He grabbed her arm to steady her. "Sorry, but next time look before you step in front of someone."

Melody's cheeks flamed as he walked away. The same short blond hair, swaggering steps, and spiced cologne reminded her of James like a punch in the gut. She should have known better because James didn't go to Laurel and would have graduated already.

Taking a deep breath to get her rapid heartbeat under control, Melody checked to see whether anyone else had noticed the encounter. She shuddered. What if he had looked like Troy?

Her heart jumped again when a guy with curly brown hair strode past. It wasn't Vince, but for a split second, it could have been. Haunted by the past, she hurried away from the quad.

She rounded the corner of the locker rooms then pulled up short. The guy she had noticed at the front of the school this morning sat on the ground in the middle of the volleyball court, strumming his guitar. Hat pushed back on the crown of his head, sunglasses pulled down to the end of his nose, he went through a few chord progressions, then scribbled something on the notepad next to him.

When he played a few more notes, Melody inched closer. She wanted to hear him play. She settled on the ground, out of his range of vision, unpacked her lunch, and ate while listening as he worked through his song. Completely absorbed in his music, he didn't seem to realize anyone else was around.

She smiled when he hit a point not quite right. He played it then nearly knocked his hat off, running his fingers through his brown hair. He caught the hat and put it back in place. Then he gripped the neck of the guitar, positioned his fingers, and played the notes again, making a minor adjustment. Three times through, and he resolved the conflict and made another note on his pad.

The hour sped past and the bell rang signaling the time for her next class. Before she had packed her things, the boy looked up and saw her.

He slid his sunglasses back up his nose and stood in one smooth motion. "I didn't realize I had an audience." He brushed a few small pebbles off his slacks. "How long have you been sitting there?"

Melody froze. She had been so relaxed, but the direct question caused her throat to close off.

He snapped the guitar into the case. "Doesn't matter. You're the new girl, right?"

Melody fiddled with getting her things packed. Maybe if she ignored him, he'd leave her alone. At least he'd stopped talking to her. She gathered her books and took a moment to hope he had gone to class. A hand appeared in front of her face. She placed her hand in his.

"Of course you're the new girl." He pulled her to her feet. "I'm sorry. Where are my manners?" He gazed directly into her eyes. "I haven't introduced myself. Kelly Garland, at your service." He bowed. "Since you're new, I'll be your escort. What's your next class?"

She handed him her schedule.

He ran a finger down the page. "We have a class in the same building, so come with me, Miss Melody Fisher."

She had forgotten he would see her name on the schedule. But if she hadn't handed him the paper, she'd have had to say something. He hadn't reacted to her name, so maybe he hadn't heard of her.

"I always come out to the athletic field during lunch to get away from all the chatter in the quad. I'm as sociable as the next guy, but I am serious about my music and need time to work on it." He shifted the guitar to his other hand so it was no longer between them. "And honestly, it's a little ironic, but the sometimes homophobic jocks are all over the quad during lunch and completely absent from the athletic field, so the guy who nearly fails PE every year takes refuge on his field of shame."

He glanced at her and raised an eyebrow. "Oh, yes, honey. I'm as gay as the day is long. If I didn't tell you, someone else would have."

They reached the building door and he opened it for her. "I get along with most everyone, but I try to avoid the situations where mob mentality can come into play." He led her to a door. "Here you go, Melody. Your class awaits. I'll see you around."

She waved as Kelly went down the hall. Having a friend again might be nice. She missed Vince more today than any other. Maybe things would turn out differently this time.

CHAPTER THIRTY-ONE

February 8, 2013 – Melody, age 14

Hunching my shoulders forward, I pulled my books tightly against my chest. Wherever I went this afternoon to stay away from home had to be warm. I should have worn a heavier jacket, but it was upstairs, and Hatchet was on the move up there. I couldn't stomach seeing him and had grabbed the first jacket from the coat closet and ran out the door.

A shiver made me quicken my pace. Another afternoon in the library sounded like a good idea. I could always say I was working on homework. My grades had slipped, and Miss Prescott hadn't failed to mention it at our meeting this week. She had been sympathetic when she first took me out of the Jacksons'. She housed me in a temporary shelter for a few days before she placed me with the Hatchets—Wade and Evelyn, but everyone called him Hatchet.

Miss Prescott had asked me to give them a chance—Hatchet and Evelyn were good people. No matter where she placed me, to Miss Prescott, they were good people. Maybe because they were willing to take a kid when no one else would.

But things were so different. I didn't like living in the city—too much concrete and not enough nature. Because my test scores were good, they had jumped me ahead a grade when I'd moved schools, so I had started high school in the fall instead of spending another year in middle school. The youngest in my grade and I felt out of place. It had been nearly a year, and I still didn't fit in.

Though she didn't say it, Miss Prescott wanted me to stop being a problem. Both of us avoided mentioning the last time I had been happy in a placement was with Quatie Raincrow. Thinking about her still hurt. I should have called sooner, when Quatie refused to go to the doctor and she'd been so sick. And I should never have told her what had happened at the Jacksons' …

This time Miss Prescott told me to stop moping; she knew I could do better, and I needed to get my grades back up.

Schoolwork wasn't the problem. But I couldn't tell her.

"Hey, Melody. Wait up."

Vince sprinted toward me, his brown hair flopping with each step.

I smiled. He'd been the first person to talk to me at this school. We'd met when loneliness followed me everywhere. I'd had a few months at the middle school before summer, so hadn't had a chance to make many friends. He was the closest friend I had.

Vince jammed his hands in his jacket pockets and flipped his bangs out of his eyes when he reached me. "What're you doing this afternoon? Wanna hang?"

I shrugged. "I'm going to the library to get out of the cold."

Vince wrinkled his nose. "You don't want to sit in a moldy old library on a Friday afternoon. We should do something."

"Like what?" Shivering, I headed toward the sidewalk on the other side of the parking lot to get my blood moving.

Vince fell in step beside me. "Whatever you want. We could go see a movie, wander around the mall, or go bowling."

"Bowling? I've never bowled in my life." The only thing I knew about it was the balls were big and rolled down a lane.

"That's it. If you haven't bowled, you have to try it. It'll be fun."

"As long as we're indoors and I can thaw out, I'm good."

"Vince. Hold up."

A guy with short blond hair walked toward us. Well, as Daddy used to say, he walked like a rooster strutting through the henhouse. His hands rested in the pockets of his varsity jacket and his head swung from side to side, acknowledging greetings from classmates. He sure wasn't in a rush to catch up, but expected us to wait on him.

I cocked my head toward Vince and raised an eyebrow. He gave me a sheepish grin and shrugged. Another shiver ran through me. Vince whisked off his coat and put it over my shoulders.

The warmth from his trapped body heat felt so good. But I couldn't let him freeze. "Aren't you going to be cold?"

He shoved his hands in his pockets. "Nah. I'll be fine. I'm wearing a sweatshirt." His rigid stance belied his words. His friend finally made his way to us. "Hi, James."

James punched Vince on the shoulder. "Where are your manners, dude?" He held his hand out to me and his grin made his blue eyes sparkle. "James Davenport, nice to meet you. I'm a buddy of Vince's."

I placed my hand in his. "Melody Fisher." His cologne had a hint of spice to it.

James backhanded Vince on the chest. "Where have you been keeping this one?"

Vince stumbled back a step. "I haven't been hiding her." He reached for my books. "We're going bowling. Wanna come?"

"Bowling?" James laughed. "Are you kidding?"

Vince's shoulders drew forward and he glowered at his friend.

"I gotta go do weight training anyway." James winked at me. "I just wanted to meet your friend and say hello."

My smile faded as I saw Sadie walking toward us. I hadn't made my escape from school soon enough. She never wanted to be near me; whenever she looked for me it was bad.

James followed my gaze and sneered. "What do you want, Sader tot?"

Her dark eyes gleamed through the narrow slits between the long black lashes and the heavy black liner.

As Sadie glared at him, James smirked. "Still trying to think of a comeback?"

"No. Trying to figure out why you need to use a cheap grade-school insult. You don't have anything better than that? Really?" She rolled her eyes. "Are you sure you graduated from elementary school?"

The corners of his mouth turned down, and his face reddened. "Are you calling me stupid?"

She clapped her hands slowly. "Well done. You figured it out."

"It's on, bitch." James took a step forward, cocking his arm back.

Vince grabbed his bicep. "Don't be a douche. You don't want to hit a girl. Especially on school property."

James pulled his arm out of Vince's grip and snarled at Sadie. "You're lucky Vince was here to save yo' ugly ass."

Sadie wasn't ugly. She used too much heavy, dark makeup, and wore nothing but black, but at home, I saw the real Sadie. Her dark hair set off her pale, almost translucent skin, dusted lightly with freckles.

Sadie put up her arms and gave James a "come on" wave of her fingers. "Any time you want a piece of me and you're feeling lucky, go ahead and bring it. I'll serve your ass back to you on a platter."

James snorted. "You wish I wanted a piece of you. I don't need anybody's sloppy seconds." He made a face. "I'll never be *that* desperate."

"Who do I need to thank for small favors?" She turned her back to him. "Mom said you need to come straight home. You've been told. My job's done."

As she made to walk past Vince, he stopped her. "Melody said she needed to go to the library."

She shot me a look over her shoulder. "Do I care?"

"Miss Prescott wants me to bring my grades up. I have homework."

She sighed. "All right, I'll tell the Madre you're studying. Don't say I never did anything for you."

She gave a last look at James, raised her middle finger to her lips, kissed it, moved her arm in an arc and placed her finger on her butt. "You know what you can do."

He jerked his head back. "Not if you were the last girl on the planet."

"That's not what you said last year when your only goal in life was to get in my pants." Her lip curled. "Still upset I turned you down?"

James spluttered. "I … I never …"

Sadie held up her hand, palm facing James, and walked away.

James shook his head as he watched her walk off. "How did you get mixed up with Sad Sadie? Don't tell me you live with that bitch."

I bit my lip. It never failed, I'd meet someone and when they found out I was a foster kid, they looked at me like a second-class citizen. I was so over those sad looks, but I had at least four more years before I could break free from the system. "The Hatchets are my foster family." I waited for the inevitable questions.

"Foster family? Like you have no parents?" James's eyebrows rose.

At least he didn't give me the same look you give someone when they tell you their puppy just died.

Vince smacked him on the shoulder. "Dude, don't be a jerkwad."

"Don't worry about it, Vince. I'm used to it by now." That was a lie. I'd never get used to the questions, the prying, and worse, the pity. "No. My mama died when I was nine, and my daddy disappeared."

"But—"

Vince cut off the next question. "I thought you had to go workout. And it's freezing balls cold out here."

The warmth of Vince's coat made me feel guilty. I wriggled my shoulders.

"Yeah, I should get going." James grinned. "It was a pleasure to meet you, Melody. Don't be a stranger." His right eyebrow raised and a mischievous gleam crept into his eyes. "You're someone I want to get to know better."

"Nice to meet you, James." I gave him a shy smile.

He ran off and Vince and I continued to the parking lot.

"I should give your coat back, Vince. You shouldn't have to freeze because I grabbed the wrong thing this morning."

He shoved his hand back in his pocket. "No, keep it on. We'll be out of the cold soon."

When we reached his pickup, he opened the door and helped me in. He turned the key and the radio blasted out the latest rap song. Vince lunged for the knob to turn it down.

"You like rap?"

He shrugged. "Some. It hit my mood this morning. Not so much now." He fiddled with the knob until he hit the latest pop station.

I pressed my lips together to keep from smiling. I didn't want him to think I was laughing at him. He got so self-conscious when we were alone together. In a group or in the quad during breaks or lunch, he did fine, but he got nervous when no one else was around.

The bowling alley was like a warm blanket after the cold outside. With the weather and the hour, I didn't expect too many people to be at the alley, but several lanes were already taken. Some bowlers looked like their life depended on the score—they focused on nothing but the lane and pins ahead. Others were there for the fun of it. Vince and I took a lane on the far end, so I didn't have to be embarrassed since I had no idea what I was doing.

Vince went to the food stand and brought back nachos and sodas, and helped me pick out a ball. We spent the next few hours rolling a ball down the lane and chatting and laughing more than I'd laughed in over a year. For once I was able to push out reality so that nothing outside the bowling alley existed. Too bad it couldn't last for the rest of my life.

But all good things come to an end. When we finished our last line and had changed our shoes, I sat on the bench, staring at my feet.

Vince sat next to me and gently turned my head toward him. "What's wrong?" His big brown eyes were full of concern. "You look so sad."

I broke away from his gaze. "I'm sorry, Vince. It's just that we've had so much fun. And now …" I took a deep breath. "And now it's time to face reality again."

Vince's forehead crinkled. "Are things at home okay?"

Life with the Hatchets would never be okay. I waited as a ball rolled down a lane for the inevitable crash of the pins or *thunk* as it hit the gutter. The pins scattered and the electronic arm came down to sweep the fallen pins to the back.

"Not really." I closed my eyes. Hatchet's angry face flashed in my mind and my stomach clenched. "But I can't talk about it."

Vince stood and held out his hand to help me up. "You know if you ever need to talk …" He hugged me. "I'm always here for you."

I clung to him. I had never wanted to talk to anyone more than I wanted to talk to Vince right now. Biting my lower lip, I choked back the words. "I know … I just can't." I squeezed him and let go.

His hands dropped to his sides. "Then get ready for the big freeze until we get in the truck." He grabbed his coat and put it around my shoulders again. "You'd better put your arms in the sleeves this time."

As I put on the coat, I asked what I had wanted to ask all afternoon. "What's up with your friend James? Is he always such a jerk?"

Vince's cheeks flushed. "He's all right, but yeah, he can be a total douche when he wants to be."

He was cute when he got embarrassed. "What does he have against Sadie anyway? I know she can be a pain, but it's because she hates everyone. She's not bad if you don't take her attitude personally."

Vince opened the door for me. The winter air rushed into the bowling alley, biting any exposed skin it could find. We ran to the truck. Vince clicked the remote before we reached it, so he could open the door for me without wasting time fumbling for the keys.

After he climbed in the cab, he slammed the door and rubbed his hands together. "It's colder than a witch's …" He stopped and his forehead wrinkled as his eyebrows rose.

Before he started apologizing, I put him out of his misery. "… tit in a brass bra." I grinned. "It's not the first time I've heard the expression. But you haven't told me what's up with James and Sadie."

He shrugged. "They've always taunted each other. Sadie kinda said it. Last year James wanted to go out with her." He reversed out of the parking spot. "But when things got physical, Sadie told him no, so things got ugly." Vince pulled into the home-from-work traffic. "James has always turned into a total jerk when she's around."

When he pulled up in front of the house, Vince insisted on walking me to the door. He took me into his arms. "If you need anything, give me a call."

I threw my arms around him and wanted the embrace to go on forever because then I would never have to set foot in the Hatchets' house again.

CHAPTER THIRTY-TWO

Spring 2015 – Melody, age 16

Rebecca pulled into the parking lot right on time. Melody hopped in the car and put her backpack between her feet.

"Did things go okay today?" Rebecca wheeled out of the parking lot.

Melody shrugged. "Yeah."

"Things will get better, sweetie. Today was probably tough for a lot of reasons. You're going to do great, though."

How could Rebecca be so sure? It would take one person to make the connection between her and Troy Alexander before the whole school would know. Just thinking about Troy made her sick to her stomach. The memory of the disgust on James's face when he'd confronted her afterward burned in her brain.

All the kids in school would react the same way … even her new friend, Kelly. They didn't know the truth and she couldn't tell them. As ridiculous as it was, she had been told by her defense attorney not to talk about the case. Not that she would anyway. So, like everyone else, they'd listen to the lies.

"Are you all right, Melody?" Rebecca met her gaze in the rearview mirror. "It seems like something is bothering you. Talk to Dr. Kane about it, okay?"

Melody looked out the passenger window. She couldn't talk to anyone about Troy. Not even Roger.

When she walked into Roger's office, she couldn't settle. She picked up a few books, flipped through the pages, put them back, stared out the window and wished she could be outside.

Roger cleared his throat. "You're a little agitated. You're not planning to run off again, are you?"

She gave him a deadpan stare.

"Ouch. Be careful. You might hurt someone with that glare of yours one of these days." He motioned to the couch. "Why don't you take a seat? Talking about why you ran off is as good a place to start as any."

She crossed her arms and plopped down on the couch.

Roger wrinkled his forehead. "Exactly what did I say to bring on this snit?" He leaned back in his chair. "You ran out like you were being chased by a wild boar with a sore tusk last time you were here. I think it bears a little discussion."

Melody couldn't keep the sullen tone out of her voice. "I already talked with Rebecca."

His eyebrows shot up. "You did?" He smiled. "Very good. I'm glad you felt comfortable enough to tell her why you ran. So what else is bothering you?"

She rolled her eyes. He should give it a rest.

"All right. If you're not going to tell me, I'll pick something for us to talk about. How about school?"

She relaxed her arms and dropped her hands into her lap. "Nothing to say."

Roger crossed one leg over the other. "It was your first day back in the classroom after having been homeschooled. I'm sure there is something to say. How did your teachers treat you? The other students?"

She shrugged. "Fine."

"You are a fount of information today. We have two hours, so take your pick. We can either talk about why you ran out of here during our last session or you can talk about school." He waited for a moment. "Up to you. I'll keep badgering you until you pick one."

"School." She and Rebecca had shared with each other about the loss of Quatie Raincrow. Roger didn't need to get in the middle of their moment.

"You know, things would go better if you tried words longer than one syllable." He smirked. "At least I get a response when I piss you off. Now try putting some of that energy into words."

She hopped off the couch and went back to the window. "What happened to making me feel comfortable until I was ready to talk?"

He gave a hoot. "Finally. Words. Strung together to make a sentence." He sighed. "Making you comfortable enough to speak *was* the goal, but we've crossed the line. Trust has been established, you've shared your past through music, but now we need to talk about the past rather than sing about it."

She turned and scowled. "What if I don't want to?"

Shrugging, he frowned. "Ultimately, I go back to the judge and tell him you have spoken, but deliberately refuse to talk. The judge will set the case for trial. Because of your age, you'll most likely be tried as an adult, you'll be found guilty, and you'll go to prison for stabbing a boy."

Her shoulders slumped.

"You need to be able to tell the judge what happened. I have a job to do. I know you don't want to go to jail. You've been working your butt off, so why are you giving me grief today?"

She shuffled to the couch. "I don't know. I guess going back to school stirred up a bunch of feelings I thought I had buried."

Roger smiled. "That's my girl. Talk to me about those feelings. Let's see if we can slay the demons."

A puff of air escaped her lips as she silently laughed at the image of Roger as a demon slayer.

"Go ahead and mock me." He mimed pulling an arrow out of his heart. "I can take it. Now talk."

Melody's mouth went dry. She swallowed a few times but still couldn't get the words to come out. Roger pointed at the speakers. How did he know she was having a problem and not just stonewalling him?

She fished the music player out of her pocket and connected it. Pressing play on "In Love with an Angel", she held her breath through the opening bars.

He stood by me

When he shouldn't have
Lifted me up
When life was bad
Around every corner
His smile I'd see
No matter what
He was there for me

When she pressed pause, Roger leaned forward.

"So, who is the *he* in the song?"

She couldn't continue looking into his blue eyes. She picked at the cuticle on her thumb. "An old friend. Vince."

"Was Vince a special friend?"

"Yes … no." She stopped, her jumbled emotions tying her tongue. Roger waited while she untangled her feelings. "Vince was my best friend." She turned her head to the side and shot him a look. "Do you know what it's like to always be different? To be the one who has bounced from family to family?"

Roger stroked his stubble. "No, because I grew up in a stable, if slightly dysfunctional, household. But I imagine it is difficult to go from house to house, changing schools, leaving friends, never feeling like you fit in."

"When I lived with Quatie Raincrow, things were better. On the reservation, I wasn't the odd one out because of my heritage. And I had friends because I was in one place long enough to make them." She listened to the ticking of Roger's watch. Even while living in Cherokee, she spent more time with Quatie than friends her age.

"When I had to go live with the Jacksons, their son went out of his way to make sure I didn't make any friends. So when I was with the Hatchets and met Vince, I thought it was possible to have friends again."

Roger made a note on his tablet. "You lost touch after you moved on from the Hatchets'?"

Melody rubbed her temples. "Not exactly. Vince was the best friend I've ever had."

CHAPTER THIRTY-THREE

February 8, 2013 – Melody, age 14

I unlocked the front door. Vince waited on the front porch to see me inside. If only he knew I was safer outside. Once in, I closed and locked the door and leaned against it for a few moment's respite before having to deal with the family. With any luck, Hatchet wasn't home yet, and I could have a bit of peace.

Sadie poked her head around the corner, widened and crossed her eyes, then cocked her head toward the family room. My heart sank. It meant one thing—Hatchet was home. I shrugged off my jacket and put it and the book bag in the closet.

Hatchet stood by the family room windows, twitching the curtains shut as soon as I walked in. His folded suit coat laid across the couch back. His crisp, white shirt didn't have a single wrinkle, as if it had just come off the hanger instead of having been worn for the entire day. He hadn't loosened his tie.

After glaring at me for a moment, he widened his stance and shoved his hands in his pockets. "I thought you were told to come straight home from school."

I shot a look at Sadie, but she averted her eyes. I shouldn't have expected any help from her; she'd made it clear I was on my own. I met Hatchet's angry stare as deadpan as I could. "I had homework to catch up on."

His jaw pulsed. "Is that why you were making out with a boy on our doorstep?"

My mouth popped open. I hadn't been making out with Vince. I sensed rather than saw Sadie stiffen. What was going on? Sadie never reacted to anything, except with surliness and disdain. I kept my words level. "I wasn't making out with him. He gave me a ride home."

"Like hell. You don't think I watched while you groped each other?" He flung his hand toward the window. "Who is he?" The last words came out in a growl.

My heart thumped. I wasn't going to let him rattle me. I hadn't done a thing wrong. Except for the borderline lie. I did have homework to catch up on … I just hadn't done it.

"Who?" Hatchet's face turned red.

My mouth went dry. I unstuck my tongue from the roof of my mouth. "He's a guy from school. And we weren't groping. He hugged me. That's all."

"Wade, leave the girl alone." The doorjamb held Evelyn upright as she drew her bathrobe closer around her thin frame.

It took me a moment to remember Wade was Hatchet's first name. Evelyn was the only person I'd ever heard call him Wade. Everyone else, including Miss Prescott and Sadie, called him Hatchet.

"I was just trying to find out why Melody didn't honor your request to come home after school." Concern replaced the anger on Hatchet's face. "Are you sure you should be out of bed, sweetheart? I thought you weren't feeling well."

She tucked a lock of dishwater-brown hair behind her ear. "I'll go back up in a moment. Melody, I'd like to talk with you." She turned to head back upstairs. "Sadie, can you get dinner?"

"Sure, Mama."

The question and answer were both given as if Sadie hadn't already started dinner. She made dinner every night because Evelyn didn't feel well enough. After having lived with them for almost a year, I still didn't know what was wrong with her. No one ever said, and I hated to ask.

Hatchet treated her like pure gold—extremely valuable, but easily broken. Precious beyond all else. Nothing was ever too much trouble when it came to what Evelyn wanted. Nothing in the world mattered more to him than she did.

When Miss Prescott first placed me with the Hatchets, I'd seen why she said they were good people. Hatchet's devotion to Evelyn, his active service in his church, and dedication to his job all showed what an upstanding member of the community he was. So Sadie was a little on the dark side, I hadn't thought anything of it. I'd thought maybe the Jacksons were an anomaly and I had once again found a loving home.

I followed Evelyn up the stairs. On the landing, she swayed and I thought she might fall, but she righted and continued on.

Her room was lit by a single, heavily shaded lamp, so it took my eyes a moment to adjust to the gloom. Evelyn sat on the edge, adjusted the bed to a sitting position, leaned against the pillow, and swung her legs up.

"Have a seat, Melody." She pointed to the chair next to the bed.

I sat on the edge, not sure what Evelyn wanted. I'd only spoken with her separately two or three times since I'd been living with them.

"How are you doing?" She took a sip of water from the glass on her nightstand.

She hadn't brought me up to her room to find out how I was doing. I didn't know how to answer the question. What did she know?

Evelyn shook her head. "I'm sorry. I told myself I wouldn't start off with social niceties, yet they're so ingrained I did anyway." Her lips flattened. "I'm just going to come out and tell you."

I braced myself.

"I had a conversation with Rebecca Prescott a few days ago."

Oh. My stomach unclenched a little.

"She's concerned because your grades have been slipping." She paused.

I held back for a few moments while Evelyn waited for me to speak. "She talked to me about it. I'll bring them up." I couldn't meet her gaze, so I stared at the bedspread instead.

"I'm worried advancing you a grade is causing the problem. Are you getting along with the other kids at school?"

The quilted bedspread had been made in blues, greens, and purples in the double wedding ring pattern. Calm, serene, traditional, like Evelyn herself. I was afraid to say anything because once I started talking, I might not stop. If telling Quatie Raincrow why I was unhappy with the Jacksons had caused her heart attack, I couldn't risk the same with Evelyn. I couldn't take another death on my conscience.

"Melody, honey, I'm not upset. I just want to know what's wrong so I can help fix it." She pulled the blankets a little higher. "Sometimes all you need is to talk about what's wrong with someone else and it puts things in perspective."

First Vince, now Evelyn. I wanted to say something … anything … but what?

"Have you made friends?"

I nodded. "School's okay. Really." I didn't have a lot of friends, but it didn't matter. I had a few and they were enough.

She looked at me with a slight frown. Her eyes implored me to share more with her. "I don't think you're happy and haven't been for a while. At first, I thought you needed time to get over your horrific experience with your last foster placement."

She grabbed a tissue and blew her nose then wadded the tissue into a tight ball. "But you've been with us for ten months, and I think you're more unhappy than ever. I don't want you to be miserable."

My insides writhed as I battled the urge to tell her the truth.

"After I spoke with Miss Prescott, I called the school and found out your teachers feel you are shy; a good student not working up to your potential."

The only sounds in the room were the occasional ping of the radiator against the background hiss of the humidifier.

"Then I contacted your school before you came to live with us and heard what a good student you were, and how you might be quiet but were confident in your studies."

I had studied a lot then to keep my distance from the detestable Boyd. I did all the extra credit I could get my hands on as an excuse to stay in my room by myself.

"Then I called your school on the reservation."

My eyes briefly met hers before I looked away.

"I found it interesting that your teachers described you as outgoing and talkative. These days you barely say a word unless we ask you a question." She touched my hand. "Are you being teased or bullied at school? We'll support you in taking care of the problem."

I couldn't let her think school was the problem. "No. I'm not being bullied." She wasn't going to be happy until I told her something. "I miss Mama, Daddy, and Quatie Raincrow. I loved them all so much, and they left me. And as I get older, I miss having a mama."

Evelyn clutched the wadded tissue against her heart. "Oh, sweetheart. I can't imagine how much pain you've been through. I hope you can think of me as a surrogate mama to you. If you ever need to talk about anything, my door is always open." Tears brimmed in her eyes.

"Thank you. If I need to talk, I'll come see you." I swallowed hard, wanting nothing more than to escape the dim emotion-charged room. "I should go see whether Sadie needs any help with dinner."

She wouldn't. Every time I asked her what she needed me to do, she responded with a single word.

Leave.

If she only knew how much I wanted to.

CHAPTER THIRTY-FOUR

Spring 2015 – Melody, age 16

"Melody, wait up."

Kelly sprinted toward her, his unbuttoned blazer flapping with each step. He held his hat on his head and had his guitar strapped on his back.

He grinned when he reached her side. "Thanks for waiting. Thought you might want an escort to class." He took a step and kept talking. "'Why, thank you, Kelly. You're the sweetest thing to walk me to class.'"

Melody tried to suppress a grin and failed.

Kelly slid his hands in his pockets. "You'll have me blushing, Melody. I'm just being a good friend." He kicked a rock in their path out of the way. "'You're not just a good friend. You're the best. And so talented.'"

The snort escaped before she could stop it. He reminded her of Roger when he pretended to speak for her.

He kept up the chatter. "Now you're going too far. I mean, I'm a good guy, but best? You're right about me being talented, though."

A guy called across the quad to him. "Hey, Kelly."

Two guys with short haircuts stood with hands on hips. Her stomach sank.

Kelly pointed at himself and mouthed, "Me?"

"Yeah, I'm talking to you." The tall guy with the short brown hair took a step toward them. "You wanna watch your back with that chick."

Melody's cheeks burned and she stared at the ground. Somebody had figured it out.

Kelly pointed at me. "Her?" He made a face like the guy was crazy. "She's sweet as punkin pie, Rich. You should get to know her."

Rich came closer while his buddy waited behind. "Dude, I'm serious. You don't know who she is."

She had no doubt Rich would enlighten Kelly and in about two minutes she'd have no friends … again.

"I know who she is. This is Melody Fisher."

Rich curled his fingers into a fist next to his leg. "Kelly, be serious for a sec. I'm trying to give you a heads up. She's the one who stabbed Troy Alexander a few months back."

Stomach acid hit the back of her throat at the mention of Troy.

"Troy and I train in the same off-season football camp. He told me all about what happened. So dude, get a clue and leave the crazy chick alone."

The burning hatred coming from Rich's eyes was exactly why Melody hadn't wanted to return to school. Why couldn't Rebecca have let her stay homeschooled? She clenched her jaw and tried to keep her knees from shaking.

Kelly wrinkled his forehead. "Rich, you don't have the whole story. Melody told me things didn't go down the way Troy said."

What? She hadn't said a single word to Kelly. She hadn't told *anyone.*

Rich's eyebrows shot up and his mouth dropped open. "She talked to you?" He pushed Kelly on the shoulder. "She's a mute, jerkwad."

"Her?" Kelly gave a short laugh. "When we're together I barely get a word in edgewise. You must be thinking of a totally different Melody Fisher."

Why was he lying?

Rich threw his hands up. "Look, just trying to do you a favor. When you end up with a knife in the back, don't say I didn't warn you."

"Don't you mean a pair of scissors?"

He knew?

Kelly's face went blank. "Thanks, Rich, but I've got this covered. We're good."

Rich stalked back to his friend and Melody couldn't stop the shakes.

Kelly ducked to gaze into her eyes. "Hey, you gonna be okay?"

Melody sniffed and nodded.

His lower lip slid out. "You're not lying to me, are you?"

She smiled through the tears standing in her eyes.

"We've got to get to class, so come on. I said I'd escort you and I will." He took hold of the crook of her arm. "Don't worry about guys like Rich. He means well, but is a bit misguided by knowing that jackass, Troy."

The way he said Troy's name … he had a history with him, like she did.

"Actually, a bit surprising, but nice of Rich to try and warn me. He must be worried about his end-of-year party. He hired me and some guys I jam with to play." He nudged her. "Most of the time he pretends he doesn't know my name, so yeah, that was an encounter of the bizarre kind."

He opened the door to the building. "You'll be fine during classes. When it's break time, you come find me. People will leave you alone then."

When Rebecca picked Melody up for her therapy session, the unpleasantness of the morning had faded. But it rushed back when Rebecca asked how her day had been.

She pulled out of the parking lot. "I thought things were going pretty well for you in school. What happened?"

How did she know? Melody hadn't given anything away. Where did she start? With Kelly? With Rich?

"Talk to Dr. Kane and tell him about it. Please?"

She didn't want Rebecca to be irritated with her. She had intended to tell her. Rebecca might give up on her if she didn't talk. If that happened, Melody would give up. She cleared her throat. "I'll tell you … tonight."

Rebecca smiled. "Fine, sweetie. But talk with Dr. Kane anyway, okay?"

Melody nodded.

Rebecca pulled into the parking lot. "Have a good session. I'll be waiting out here for you when you're done."

Roger was pacing the office, muttering, when she entered. She checked the time. She wasn't late. He reached the wall, spun around, and looked startled to see her standing there.

"I'm sorry. I must have lost track of time." One corner of his mouth curled up. "You caught me working through a speech I have to give for an upcoming convention." He grabbed his tablet off the desk. "I may wear a hole in the carpet before I get it right." He sat in his chair and did a double take. "What happened to you?"

She shrugged.

His right eyebrow rose. "Not good enough. Come on, you can tell me. And I'll help you out. You didn't have a fight with Rebecca." He leaned back in his chair and raised his voice a notch. "'How on earth did you know, Roger? Are you psychic?'"

He grimaced. "Psychic? No. If you'd had a fight, you'd have been seething and ready to throw things around. So my guess is something happened at school to hurt you and made you sad."

She glanced from the floor to his eyes and to the floor again. "Some kids at school know who I am."

"Oh."

Yeah, oh. He should have realized this would happen. The story had made a big splash when it happened because Troy was a high school superstar. It didn't matter whether the media kept her name out of the papers and off the airwaves—Troy had a big mouth and ran it to anyone who would listen.

Roger drummed the stylus on the chair arm. "If you can stick it out, and they aren't heckling you, I still think it's best for you."

She took a deep breath. "A boy named Kelly stood up for me."

"Fantastic. See, Melody? Not everyone in life is horrible. I'm glad you found a friend." He made a note. "We should probably get started with our session."

Melody relaxed against the couch back. She had been afraid he'd want all the details, and she wasn't sure she could tell him. Not yet. Too fresh and cut too deep.

"I think we're to the point we should start talking about why you stopped talking. From everything I can gather from your history, you stopped talking after your placement with the Hatchets."

Her spine stiffened. She didn't want to talk about the Hatchets. Some things were meant to stay buried.

CHAPTER THIRTY-FIVE

February 8, 2013 – Melody, age 14

Snuggling under the comforter, I stretched until my toes hit the icy part of the bed. It'd warm up in a few minutes, but until then my toes would be little ice cubes. I stretched my arm out and snapped the desk lamp off with a click. Miss Prescott would be happy I'd caught up on most of my homework. Going to the library to finish the rest would be a good excuse to get out of the house tomorrow. Finding reasons to stay out of the house on weekends was a struggle sometimes. Especially during cold weather.

The branches from the red maple tree brushed against the window. Instead of creepy, the sound brought comfort. It reminded me of home and the time I had been frightened when the tree branches had scratched against the window pane. Mama had stroked my hair and told me the tree just wanted to say hello. And that it wanted me to know it stood guard outside my room. Then Daddy had come in with a drink of water, picked me up, and all my fears went away.

My chat with Evelyn floated back to mind. My heart hurt with homesickness crushing it to bits. I used to be happy. I pulled Raksha Waya out from underneath my pillow and hugged him tight. His fur, worn at the seams, had been almost rubbed off on his nose, but I loved him as much as ever. He was truly the only one I had left. My steadfast protector.

I kept him out of sight because Hatchet wanted me to get rid of him. *Never.*

Raksha was the keeper of the things I couldn't say. And I had told him so much since moving here. Raksha, the protector was also Raksha, the secret keeper.

I tried to hold the memory back, but tonight I wasn't strong enough. Evelyn's questions brought everything to the surface. They brought back the night my personal hell had started.

A stair tread creaked. My heart pounded and I thrust Raksha Waya back under the pillow edge. Sadie had already come up and gone to her room. I closed my eyes and prayed to God and the Grandfathers—without hope of an answer. But I prayed anyway because it was the only thing I could do. *Please, not tonight.*

Hatchet came up the stairs slowly, each footstep on the stairs deliberate as he shifted his weight from one foot to the next.

I took a deep breath and tried to calm my racing heart. If I convinced him I was asleep, he'd leave me alone. My racing pulse and shallow breaths would give me away.

His footsteps stopped outside my door.

Please let him change his mind and pass on by.

He jingled the change and keys in his pocket. When he fumbled with the doorknob, I rolled on my side and faced the wall. A single tear rolled to the end of my nose before dropping to the pillow below.

The door swung open with a squeak and he halted. After a few moments, he exhaled and closed the door as softly as he could. The snick of the tongue clicking into place was barely louder than a pin drop.

I forced my breaths to remain calm and steady, belying the rapid thumping in my chest as he shuffled toward the bed. *Not again. Please, not again.*

His knees banged against the mattress and for a moment—nothing. Then a finger carefully pulled the hair back from my face.

Breathe slowly. You're sleeping. My nerve endings screamed and made me want to twitch.

He brushed his knuckles over my face with a touch as soft as down on a duckling.

A whimper escaped my lips.

He stroked my cheek. "I was afraid you had already gone to sleep." His hushed words held the huskiness of desire. He unbuttoned his shirt and folded it over my desk chair.

God forbid his shirt ever get wrinkled. The moonlight shone through the window and glinted on the gold Saint Christopher medallion he always wore. My throat muscles hurt from holding back anger over what was about to happen. My nails dug into my palms.

I no longer had the same fear I had the first time he'd come for a late night visit. The memory of the knife he had held at my throat flashed and made my stomach churn. I had been so afraid he'd cut me, I couldn't help but cry. All he had done the first time was stroke and touch me. A perverted form of cuddling. I had felt so dirty and ashamed after he left.

His slacks joined the shirt on the chair. Bile burned the base of my throat. He acted like it was his right and I had no say.

I didn't.

His threats to cut out my tongue if I told anyone about his visits had effectively silenced me. These had escalated with the intimacy of his attacks. But he no longer made any threats. He didn't have to.

He leaned over the bed and stroked my hair. A shiver of hatred ran down my spine. He kissed my cheek and I bit my lower lip willing myself to be unresponsive to his touch. It was the only power I had. The smell of his musky cologne washed over me, and I choked back a gag.

He pulled the comforter and blankets down and the cold air rushed in while he turned me onto my back. Straddling my legs, he leaned forward and kissed my lips and his medallion thudded against my chest. I stifled the urge to yank it off his neck and throw it across the room while screaming every obscenity I knew. I hated how it thumped against my chest—a mockery of two hearts beating as one.

His kisses increased in intensity, and his tongue forced its way into my mouth. I despised myself for kissing him back, but it kept him from getting violent. His hand trailed from my face down to my breast and he cupped and rubbed it through my nightgown. Slipping his hand inside my gown, he caressed my breast in a circular motion.

My skin burned at his touch and my breath caught in my throat as the tip became aroused. My body betrayed me and the hatred I felt for him.

He slid his hand down my back to my butt and worked my nightgown up. His hardness pressed against my leg as he softly moaned. The sour stench of his sweat overpowered his cologne the more aroused he became.

I couldn't face what came next. Not again. More than hating him for doing this to me, I hated myself for not fighting back. For allowing it. I loathed every moment, every touch, every caress, but lay there like a willing participant.

God, if you truly exist, please make everything the church tells us about our loved ones looking down and watching over us a lie.

My knees locked together. Not that it would make a difference. It never did.

He smacked my side when he couldn't get his hand between my thighs. He could do what he wanted to my body because he was bigger and stronger and would kill me if I even thought about telling anyone about these visits. I had to block the awful reality.

Music had always been my joy, but it had become my refuge.

He moved my thighs apart and positioned himself between my legs.

I escaped into the music in my head.

Someone who … I looked up to
But darkened skies … are never blue
Took my trust … threw it on the ground
You told me not … to make a sound

The Saint Christopher against my chest kept the tempo of each thrust.

Stole my spirit … but not my soul
In faith and strength … I'm in control
Thought I'd never … get up again
Now I'm stronger … than I've ever been

His neck veins bulged as he rocked over me.

The smell of sweat ... and cheap cologne
My fear of you ... when we were alone
Saying you owned ... every part of me
I prayed to God ... set me free

His dark hair flopped over one eye as he grunted and panted. He bit his lower lip, to keep from crying out.

Stole my spirit ... but not my soul
In faith and strength ... I'm in control
Thought I'd never ... get up again
Now I'm stronger ... than I've ever been

He climaxed and collapsed on top of me.

Bruised my body ... you made me bleed
You traded shelter ... for a wicked need
Took advantage ... of innocent eyes
But no one gets far ... on sin and lies

I sensed rather than felt his weight lift off me. He had finished—until the next time. I dragged the blankets up to my chin.

Stole my spirit ... but not my soul
In faith and strength ... I'm in control
Thought I'd never ... get up again
Now I'm stronger ... than I've ever been

Hatchet dropped to his knees next to the chair and folded his hands and bowed his head. "Lord God in heaven, hear my prayer. Please heal Evelyn or take these urges from me. I am Your servant and want to do right by You. But when You give me these urges, I am only flesh and blood."

I wanted to throw up. Hatchet usually asked for the Lord's forgiveness and for Evelyn to be healed. But now he blamed God?

"If it was not Your will, You would have made me celibate. Oh, God, give me the desires of Your heart and lead me to the path of redemption."

I bit my lip so hard, the coppery tang of blood touched my tongue. *Please God, just make him leave.*

Hatchet rose from his knees and paced by the bed, muttering. I wished he'd put his clothes back on. I didn't want to see his shriveled, saggy sack, especially in the cold. I couldn't move for fear it would draw his attention.

The branches scratched the window, the red maple's way of letting me know they were still protecting me from the evil outside. I gritted my teeth. But the evil wasn't outside. The scratching brought up the memory of Mama telling me about God. If feeling loved was a sign God was with me, I had been abandoned.

After a few minutes, Hatchet finally reached for his slacks and put them on. Slipping on his shoes, he didn't bother with the shirt. Evelyn wouldn't see him sneaking in because they slept in separate bedrooms.

As soon as the door closed, I couldn't hold back the tears. I turned to face the wall, the sobs sending shudders through me. I pulled Raksha Waya from under the pillow and clutched him tight. I couldn't take much more. The secret visits had to stop.

CHAPTER THIRTY-SIX

Spring 2015 – Melody, age 16

As her tears subsided, Melody clutched a sodden tissue in her fist. She stared at the blue and burgundy rug. Unable to meet Roger's eyes, she didn't want to see his disgust for not stopping Hatchet's visits sooner.

"Thank you for sharing your experience with me, Melody." Roger kept his voice low and soothing. "You know you were not to blame in any way for what happened, right?"

She couldn't keep the sob from creeping into her voice. "But I shouldn't have let him do that to me. I should have stopped him sooner."

Roger grabbed another tissue and handed it to her. She dabbed her eyes.

"I disagree. You were taken out of a bad situation and put in one where, on the surface, it was a better environment for you." He leaned forward and braced his elbows on his knees. "Hatchet was bigger and stronger than you, and he threatened you with bodily harm if you told anyone."

"But I shouldn't have been such a coward."

His eyebrows shot up. "You think trying to fight him off or defying him would have been the brave thing to do?" He shook his head. "No, you would have been foolish and would have wound up harmed or even killed."

She dropped her gaze to the coffee table. "Maybe I'd have been better off dead. Then I would have joined Mama and Daddy and Quatie Raincrow. No more pain."

His shoulders rose as he inhaled. "Melody, you are the most unique patient I've ever had the pleasure of working with. You're smart, talented, and found a brilliant way to communicate when plain words were too scary and had not served you well. You have so much to offer the world, it would have been a shame—no, closer to a crime—if you weren't here to fulfill your destiny."

The emotion behind his words took her aback. What had happened to the aloof, wise-cracking, even-keeled doctor who let nothing ruffle him?

"I know, I'm supposed to be the impartial, dispassionate physician. But you have been gifted with such tremendous talent, I'm not sure you realize how blessed you are." He jumped up and paced the length of the room in front of the windows. "Hypothetically, should Hatchet have harmed or killed you, I likely would never have had the opportunity to meet you. And my life would not have changed."

He faced her, hands on hips. "I've admired your strength and resiliency from the day you first walked into this office. And the way you've dealt with the lousy life circumstances which have been meted out to you." He brushed back his brown curls. "In someone with less strength, not only would you have stabbed someone, but I'd be dealing with a junkie or alcoholic, or both. Or someone who goes out of their way to inflict the same harm on the world that the world has given them."

Was that how he saw her? She didn't feel strong. She felt weak and beaten down.

"*But not you*. You met your troubles head-on and coped with them in the best way you could. And you never lost touch with your past. Your love of nature and music sustained you through your darkest times."

She couldn't live without music. It spoke to her in a way she couldn't describe. Even to herself.

"Hatchet was the one in the wrong. He knew it and proved it by his secrecy and threats. He is sick, but he had a choice. You didn't."

Choice. The word hit her hard. She hadn't had any choice. She hadn't wanted or asked for any of it to happen. Hatchet was the one who had always come to her.

The tears fell again, only this time they weren't the tears of shame, but of release. A huge knot in her stomach had come untied and the emotion leaked out her eyes. She yanked some tissues out of the box.

Roger brought her a glass of water. "I don't want Miss Prescott to blame me for dehydrating you during our session today. You need to replenish."

"Thank you." The words barely squeaked out.

He sat in his chair and leaned forward. "Hang on to the words of the song you shared with me. It got you through the worst … and the words are true. You are stronger than you've ever been."

The water helped the tears to abate and a measure of control crept back in. She had survived—not only Hatchet, but everything fate had thrown at her.

"I'll get off my soapbox now, but anytime you want to talk about this, I'll be ready to listen. And I'll tell you as many times as you need to hear it, you were not to blame."

Rebecca brought steaming mugs in from the kitchen. She handed one mug to Melody and sat next to her on the couch. "Quatie used to say hot cocoa was the best cure for your ills, and after all these years, I'd have to say she was right."

Melody wrapped her fingers around the hot mug and shuddered as warmth radiated through her hands.

"If you're cold, grab a throw. And while you're at it, I'll take one."

Melody set her cocoa on the side table and opened the cabinet to pull out the throw blankets. The day had been balmy, but when night fell, the temperature had plummeted and her jammies and robe weren't doing the job.

Snuggling under the blanket, she grabbed her cocoa and took a sip. The liquid spread warmth through her from the inside out. She took a deep breath and relaxed. Sitting with Rebecca in the evenings was nice. Content at last.

Rebecca raised the footrest and settled in with her cocoa. "It feels so good to put my feet up. Today was a long day. A lot of hurry up and wait. Had to go to court today with one of my cases. A long day with no results." She took a sip and sighed. "I did have some good news about you, though."

Melody's eyebrows rose and she waited for Rebecca to continue.

"John Ludloff contacted me today. Not only is he willing to take you on as a client, he wants to take an active role in managing your career."

Melody's knuckles whitened as she gripped the cup and her voice left her.

"Don't get uptight. We'll take things one step at a time. He wants to put together a plan and you and I will go through it together." Rebecca smiled. "It's fantastic to have someone so renowned get so excited about your talent."

Melody inhaled deeply. "I'm afraid I might not be able to sing in front of people anymore. I used to love it."

After a sip of cocoa, Rebecca set her cup down. "I am certain you'll find the joy in your voice again. And remember, that's why we put you in choir. So when you're ready, you can sing in an ensemble setting."

Being with Rebecca made Melody feel safe … at long last. The urge to share a part of her day welled up. "I told Roger about Hatchet today."

Rebecca grasped Melody's hand and squeezed. "I'm so proud of you. I'm sure it wasn't easy for you to talk about. How do you feel now?"

"Okay." Melody took another sip. "Better. Roger said it wasn't my fault and that I didn't have a choice."

"Of course you didn't have a choice." She faced Melody. "Hatchet is a sick man. I'll never forgive myself for placing you there. You did nothing wrong. And I'm so glad you told me what was happening so we could stop it."

Melody ran a finger around the rim of her cup. "But I didn't tell you right away."

Rebecca covered her mouth. Then she took a deep breath. "I'm not going to lie … I wish you had come to me the first time Hatchet touched you. But you're not to blame for not speaking out. I carry the blame because you felt you couldn't tell me."

Rebecca blamed herself?

"But I didn't say anything because Hatchet told me he'd cut my tongue out, so I couldn't speak."

Rebecca's head drooped forward. "If you had a reason to trust I would be there for you and would take care of the problem for you, you'd have told me. You didn't believe I had the power to protect you from him." She raised her head and gazed directly into Melody's eyes. "I want you to know you can tell me anything and can come to me with any problem and we'll get through it together. I don't care what it is. I will be there for you."

Tired of crying, Melody bit the inside of her lip to keep it from trembling. "What if I feel guilty over someone other than Hatchet?"

"Whatever it is, I am here for you. I'll listen to whatever you want to share with me, without judgment."

Her last two words helped calm Melody's churning nervousness. "I don't know where to start." She stirred her cocoa.

"I'm not going anywhere, so take your time."

"I guess I could call it *A Tale of Two Boys* after Charles Dickens. His opening line fits, except the politics." She dredged the quote from her memory to share the pertinent part. "'It was the best of times, it was the worst of times, it was the age of wisdom, it was the age of foolishness, it was the epoch of belief, it was the epoch of incredulity, it was the season of Light, it was the season of Darkness, it was the spring of hope, it was the winter of despair…'"

Her voice trailed off. Despair cut too close and reminded her of too much.

CHAPTER THIRTY-SEVEN

April 5, 2013 – Melody, age 14

Vince crossed the small stream using a log. Halfway across, he pretended to lose his balance. His feet flew back and forth while he waved his arms and leaned first one way and then the next. He stopped and held his hand toward me. "Join me?"

I shook my head. "Not if you're going to make me fall."

He stretched his arm closer. "Come, on. You know I'm kidding around."

When I placed my hand in his, he pulled me up on the log with him in one smooth motion. I hadn't realized he was quite so strong.

"This stream is so tiny we could jump across anyway. It's just more fun to balance on a log."

True to his word, Vince led me straight across, hopped off the end, spun and grabbed me, then lifted me down. With his arm around my waist, he pulled me forward. We were almost to the top of the falls.

When we reached the top, I walked toward the edge. The rushing water and beautiful valley filled me with a sense of peace. It felt so good to be back in the mountains. I'd forgotten how much I missed it. I filled my lungs with the crisp air and felt happiness bubbling through me.

Spring break was coming to an end. We had the weekend left before going back to school. The week had been filled with days spent with Vince and doing things with James at night. Hatchet didn't like letting me out of the house, but Evelyn had told him I had brought my grades up and deserved to have a fun break. She wanted me to be happier. And I still couldn't find the words to tell her the real problem.

Since we'd had the chat about my grades a few months ago, Evelyn had made an effort to talk with me on a regular basis. I understood why Hatchet and Sadie treated her with such adoration—Evelyn had such a pure and good heart. Hatchet approved because Evelyn was feeling better and not confined to bed so much. I had felt the same tug to do anything in my power to make things easier for Evelyn. Nothing was ever too much.

Our heart-to-heart talks felt so good, but I always had to hold back, and doing so filled me with guilt.

Overlooking my beloved mountains, I remembered traipsing through the trails with Daddy, walking beside the creek with Mama, and the pleasures of nature with Quatie. I couldn't face life at the Hatchets' anymore. Seeing how much I had lost brought the memories flooding back. I turned my face toward the heavens and closed my eyes.

God, how much more do I have to endure? I'm not strong enough. Please Grandfathers, save me.

Something inside snapped. I wanted to fly from the top of the falls like the red-tailed hawk. Then I'd soar over the mountains and glide through the valley, finally free. Arms spread like wings, my hair blew back with the wind and it buffeted my body. I leaned forward.

"Melody!"

Vince's panicked voice cut through my reverie a moment before he grasped me around the waist and pulled me back from the edge. He didn't stop pulling me backward until we reached the benches past the trail opening and he set me down.

"What the heck were you doing?" His frightened eyes probed mine.

Tears filled my eyes. How could I explain I was imagining the freedom of the hawk?

He brushed a tear off my cheek. "Don't shut me out. Tell me what's wrong." He flopped on the bench next to me and buried his head in his hands. "Please tell me you weren't going to jump."

"No." The despair I had felt surged again. "Maybe." I sniffed. "I don't know."

He took my hand. "Do you know how much your friendship means to me? I don't want to lose you." His thumb stroked the back of my hand. "What won't you tell me? I know there's something, so don't try to tell me you're fine."

"I wish I could, Vince. If I told anyone, I'd tell you." Two tears slowly made tracks down my cheek. "I was thinking about how good it felt to be back in the mountains and all the things I've lost overwhelmed me." I squeezed his hand. "I don't think I would have jumped. Daddy and I used to go for hikes over on Grandfather Mountain, and I'd watch the red-tailed hawk soar overhead and wonder how free it felt gliding through the air." The woodsy scent from the trail filled me. "I just wanted to feel like the hawk and for a moment imagined how it would feel to soar over the falls."

Vince whipped his hair out of his eyes. "You had me so scared. I thought you were going to fall."

As I'd leaned, I hadn't cared whether I fell, but it had been for a brief, fleeting moment. What had happened to my carefree day?

He stroked my cheek. "Don't do anything like that again, okay?"

I nodded. "I'm sorry I scared you. Give me a moment?"

He put his arm across my shoulders and the tension drained from him.

The sound of rushing water brought the thoughts of home back to me. Evelyn sensed there was something wrong, but she never pressured me to tell. She had arranged for me to see the school counselor weekly. She was concerned because I still only spoke when asked a question, both at home and school. Except when I spent time with Vince. I relaxed my head against his shoulder.

James Davenport made my life a little more exciting, but I was tongue-tied most of the time around him, as well. Spending time with James helped me forget those dark moments with Hatchet for a few minutes at a time. Kissing was a lot more fun with James and didn't make me gag. Except for the afternoon when we went to the movies.

SPEAK NO EVIL

March 2, 2013 – Melody, age 14

I swerved around a baby stroller and had to pull up short as a grandpa pushing a cart blocked the aisle. While grandpa and his wife debated the merits of the different brands of fiber supplements, I backed up and slipped around the center aisle display. Mama with a toddler on a leash straight ahead. Mama didn't notice her son gleefully pulling the boxes off the shelf and dropping them on the floor.

I dodged down the cosmetics aisle to get away from the people blocking the way. Mistake. Too many people trying to decide on mascara brand and facial cream. Apparently, half the town had come down to the superstore to get out of the house on a slushy, snowy day. Everyone wore heavy coats, which made the narrow aisles more clogged than normal. All I wanted was to get to the other side of the store so I could leave through the garden center.

Finally. I pushed through to the back aisle and it was free and clear except in the pet area, where I had to navigate around the dog food which had fallen off the end cap and was strewn across the floor. A light sheen of perspiration covered my forehead by the time I opened the garden center doors. I checked the clock on the wall. I had to hurry, but I'd make it in time.

The freezing temperature felt good since my trek through the store caused me to overheat. I still had to hike across the street. Quickening my steps, I picked my way through the snow-crusted back parking lot.

Shoving my hands deeper into my coat pockets, I checked to make sure there was no traffic and crossed the street. A smile grew. I couldn't believe I would get to spend a few afternoon hours with James. Just the two of us. Well, and all the rest of the people in the movie theater, but we never got to hang out after school because he always had conditioning or training or practice.

I couldn't stop the thrill that ran through me when I saw James waiting for me in front of the box office, facing the other direction. He hadn't seen me yet. A beanie covered his short, blond locks. I still wanted to pinch myself because he was interested in me and wanted to spend time together.

He turned and his face broke into a grin when he saw me. I waved and hurried faster. He pushed past a group of kids waiting in the ticket line and trotted toward me.

"I already bought the tickets." He grabbed my arm. "Let's get inside. It's freezin' ass cold out here."

He opened the door and I sped inside. The warmth mingled with the smell of popcorn and covered us like an aromatic blanket. James placed his hand at the small of my back and ushered me toward the ticket collector. We passed through the stanchions and went down a hallway lined with pictures of different movie moments over the years. We turned the corner and James grinned and pulled me into an alcove.

He wrapped his arms around me. "I've wanted to do this all day." He leaned in and kissed me.

The scent of musk cologne hit my nose and my stomach lurched and twisted. He put his hand up to cup my face and I stiffened. He wore the same cologne as Hatchet.

"What's wrong?" He touched the end of my nose and smiled. "Just relax and enjoy."

When his lips touched mine again, I felt the thump of Hatchet's medallion against my chest.

I pulled my head back. "I'm sorry."

I broke from his embrace and ran toward the ladies' room. Tears blurred my eyes. Once inside, I collapsed against the wall and couldn't stop shaking. James didn't know, and I couldn't tell him, but when his face came toward me, it was Hatchet's I saw. Moments from his visits kept playing through my head. My stomach gave another twist and I rushed into a stall and heaved.

"Melody? Are you okay?"

Arms and legs still shaking, I gulped air.

"Are you alone in there?"

After a huge shuddering breath, I regained a little control. "I'm fine. Don't come in."

I staggered to the sinks and filled my hands and splashed water on my face.

"Melody, we're gonna miss the movie. C'mon, babe. I'm worried about you."

I patted my face dry with a rough paper towel. The horrible moment had passed.

When I opened the door, James leaned against the frame, his forehead resting on his arm.

"Thank goodness you're okay. I was gonna go get some girl to go in and check on you."

He reached out to hug me, and I took a step back. Even from this distance, the cologne turned my stomach. A hurt expression crossed his face.

"I'm sorry, James." What could I tell him? I couldn't tell him the truth. "Uh …" There was no way I could spend the afternoon with him. "… I'm so sorry. But I think I'm allergic to your cologne."

My stomach lurched again and I covered my mouth to hold it back.

He looked horrified. "Should I go wash it off?"

Unless he showered, it wouldn't be enough to dampen the smell. "I think I'd better go home. I'm really sorry."

An irritated gleam crept into his eyes. "If you have to go home, I'll drive you." He took a step back so I could leave the restroom. "We'll have to see the movie another time."

The thought of being cooped up in a car with his scent brought the shakes back. "No, James. I'll find my way home. Thanks, but I can't … I'm too sick."

I bolted without waiting for him to answer. Running back through the parking lot, I didn't stop until I was back in the superstore. I called Vince. He told me he'd be there in five minutes, to stay inside until he arrived.

When he pulled up in front, I rushed out and hopped in the passenger side of his truck, slammed the door, and stared at my feet.

Vince pulled forward, but parked at the edge of the lot and turned off the car. He put his arm across my shoulders and cupped my face with his other hand and turned me to him. "What did he do to you?"

I shook my head.

"Melody, you weren't coherent when you called me, you were so upset. What did he do?"

I swallowed hard. "You don't understand."

He hugged me. "So tell me."

As much as I needed the hug, I pulled back. "I can't."

Vince gave me his woeful puppy expression. The one I couldn't deny.

"It's not that I don't want to, but I don't know what to say. James didn't do anything. I had a reaction to his cologne and couldn't let him drive me home because it made me too sick." At least I'd told him the truth. Just not all of it.

Vince ran a hand through his thick brown hair. "I don't know what to do with you. Do you realize how lame your story sounds?"

I turned my head to look out the window. "James will probably never want to talk to me again the way I ran out of the theater." I buried my head in my hands.

"If that's all you're going to tell me, then I'd better get you home." He turned the key in the ignition.

"It's true."

Vince brushed the bangs out of my eyes. "Do you really think it's the cologne? If you're feeling sick, maybe it's the flu or something."

I shrugged. "Maybe. But I think it's the cologne. I was fine before I saw him." If he ever spoke to me again, James could never wear that scent again. "Thanks so much for coming to get me, Vince. I didn't know who else to call."

He gave me a shy smile. "Of course. I can't leave my girl in a lurch."

April 5, 2013 – Melody, age 14

I couldn't ask for a better best friend than Vince. I jumped from the bench, grabbed his hands, and pulled him up. "Let's not waste the day sitting here. We have a trail to hike and some falls to walk behind."

He grinned. "Let's go."

I pointed out some of the plants to Vince and told him what they were.

"How do you know so much?"

A bittersweet pang hit my heart. "Because my daddy taught me. Spending time together on the mountain was one of our favorite things to do together."

"I'm sorry. I didn't mean to make you remember again."

I brushed the toe of my boot across the path. "I'm okay. Don't worry."

We reached the bottom of the falls and followed the path leading behind them. The water was like a curtain enclosing us in the rock alcove.

Vince kicked his heel against the rock behind him. "So, what do you and James have planned for tonight?"

Uh-oh. I knew the tone in his voice too well. Vince didn't like me dating James. Even though they were friends, Vince said James wasn't exactly the nicest guy in the world.

I shrugged. "I think we're gonna try and see a movie. Maybe go somewhere and look at the stars."

Vince's shoulders slumped. "You know what he's after, don't you?"

I sighed. "Give it a rest."

His lips pressed into a thin line. "I don't want you to get hurt."

I took his hands in mine. "You mean more to me than anyone else I can think of, but you need to stop worrying about me. James and I have fun together. And I don't want to lose my best friend because he can't drop it."

He pulled his hands back and shoved them in his pockets. "Damn it,

Melody. You don't know James like I do." He kicked a rock. It careened against the mountain and ricocheted across the path. "He's not a good guy when it comes to girls. He doesn't know the meaning of treating them well. He wants one thing and once he gets it, he moves on." He inhaled, held it a moment, then exhaled. "And don't tell me he's different with you. I've heard that from too many girls."

Vince didn't understand. I didn't care. If James only wanted one thing, maybe it was time to give it to him. I had a few memories to bury as deep as I could. "I don't want us to fight. Not today. Can't we agree to disagree?"

He threw his head back and growled. "Do you know how maddening it is to stand by and watch my best friend make the biggest mistake of her life?"

When he lowered his head, he faced me with tears in his eyes. "I don't know that I can watch. He'll break your heart and I'm helpless."

Vince was the one breaking my heart. And nothing I could say would change his mind or his feelings. "What are you saying? You don't want to be friends anymore?"

He stared at the ground. "I don't know. Maybe."

Tears sprang into my eyes and I choked back anger. "Some friend you turned out to be. I'd never give up on you." I couldn't stop the corners of my mouth from turning down. "Never!"

His head jerked back like I had slapped him, and his mouth dropped open.

I held up my hand to stop him from speaking. "You'd really let our friendship go because you don't like my boyfriend? You're the one who introduced us."

"No. I don't want to." Vince pulled his hands out of his pockets and ran them through his hair. "Don't blame me for this. Do you know how much it hurts to see you with him every day?"

As a tear rolled down his cheek, I felt like I had been punched in the gut. How could this be happening? I had to stop him from saying anything more. I couldn't handle it. Not now. Why hadn't he said anything? I hadn't thought he wanted to be anything more than friends.

"I never meant to hurt you. I don't want to lose you." My voice caught on the words.

Vince turned away from me. "Don't. Let's just leave it."

I closed the distance between us and laid my hand on his shoulder. "Where do we go from here?"

Vince stood with head bowed for a long moment. Then he spun around and hugged me tight and whispered in my ear. "We stay friends."

I held on, relief flooding through me.

I don't know how long we stood there, embracing each other, afraid to let go until we heard voices approaching.

Neither of us spoke much as Vince drove me home to get ready for my date.

CHAPTER THIRTY-EIGHT

April 5, 2013 – Melody, age 14

While I waited outside the library for James, a rush of traffic blurred past. My thoughts kept going back over the day. How could I have missed how Vince felt about me? I hoped I hadn't lost the best friend I'd ever had.

Before I had too much time to think, James pulled up to the curb in front of me. He leaned across the passenger seat and opened the door. I hopped in, and he merged back into traffic.

"I thought about you all the way through practice today." James took one hand off the wheel and patted my knee.

I laced my fingers between his.

He gave me a crooked grin. "I have something special planned for the end of spring break."

"I thought we were going to the movies."

He squeezed my hand. "This is better. You'll see."

Vince's warning came back to me. The urge to break free returned, so I settled into my seat, ready for whatever came.

When we reached the outskirts of the city, James turned the car onto the road into the mountains.

He shot me a couple of glances. "You told me how much you like the mountains, so I thought we'd get a little closer to the stars tonight."

My heart melted a little and I couldn't keep the grin from sneaking across my face.

James hit the button to turn on the radio and bopped his head in time with the beat that filled the car. “Oh yeah.” He drummed his hands against the steering wheel and joined in on the chorus.

A big smile held back the laugh building inside me. He sang with gusto, but off-key and couldn’t carry the tune with both hands.

When he noticed my smile, he sang louder. “This is one of my favorite songs.” He turned up the music.

“I can tell.” I had to yell to be heard.

When we turned off the main road onto an unlit poorly paved road, it reminded me of the night I arrived at Quatie Raincrow’s. I pushed the thought from my mind. Too much had happened since then. Remembering the good times hurt too much.

James stopped in front of a dark cabin. He shut the car off, unbuckled his seat belt, and twisted around to kiss me. Kiss melded into kiss. His tongue always had the tang of the cinnamon gum he chewed. Had he brought me up in the mountains just to make out in the car?

After a few moments, James broke off the kiss. “Now that’s how I like to say hello.” He brushed his index finger against the tip of my nose. “But let’s not stay out here all night.”

The fresh woody essence from the surrounding trees mingled with his sandalwood-scented cologne when he opened the door. He hadn’t worn musk since the afternoon at the movies.

“Come on, don’t stay in the car.” He ran around the car to open my door. He took my hand to help me out. “This is my Uncle Bill’s cabin. He let me borrow the keys.”

Hand at the small of my back, he led me up the porch steps to the front door. As James fumbled with the keys in the locks, I noticed a big round object past the rocking chairs on the end of the porch. My eyes were adjusted to the dark, but there simply wasn’t enough light to see what it was. A creek gurgled as the water flowed by.

“The creek sounds close.”

James looked over his shoulder. “That’s because it’s about twenty feet away.”

The lock finally clicked, and James pushed the door open. He reached inside, grabbed something, and flipped the porch light on. He faced me with his hand behind his back.

His blue eyes twinkled. "I want you to know how much spending time with you, getting to know you better, has meant to me." He pulled his arm from behind his back and handed me a bouquet of roses.

"Oh, James …"

"Uh-uh." He placed a finger on my lips. "Let me finish. Especially this past week. Spending time with you has been so much fun, I wanted to make tonight special."

He stepped back and held out his arm for me to pass. As I crossed the sill, he flipped the lights on. We walked into a big room which was divided into a combination kitchen and family room. Uncle Bill's log cabin walls were burled and polished to a high gloss; the floor was large rock tiles. A big stone hearth took up half of one wall.

James closed the door and led me to the couch. On the coffee table in front of the couch sat a bottle of wine and two glasses.

A flutter of excitement made my heart beat a little faster. "When did you do all this?"

He gave me a sly grin. "I have my ways." He peeled the foil from the neck of the wine bottle and then plunged the corkscrew in. "A little celebration for our eight-week anniversary."

Aw. Guys didn't usually keep track of things like anniversaries. How sweet. A flush crept into my cheeks.

"Take off your coat, have a seat, and get comfortable." He poured the wine, then went to the hearth, took the matches from the mantle, and lit the fire.

I sat on the leather couch, not quite able to relax. I couldn't believe James had gone to all this trouble. The reckless feeling inside me surged. I'd never had wine before, but maybe it would help me forget … everything.

Not seeing a vase, I laid the flowers on the coffee table. The red of the wine matched the deep red of the roses.

James flopped on the couch next to me, put his arm across my shoulders, and leaned his head back. "Pretty sweet place, right?" He put his feet on the coffee table. "Relax, babe."

Scooting a little closer, I nestled against him.

He stroked my hair. "That's better." His heels slid off the coffee table as he turned and cupped my face. He gazed into my eyes. "Do you know how beautiful you are?"

His eyes took on a hooded look and his face slowly closed in on mine. His lips brushed my cheek, the barest feathery touch. He closed his eyes and pressed his lips against mine. I kissed him and flicked my tongue against his lips.

He opened his eyes, a slow grin crossing his face, and my world faded to the sky blue of his eyes. His hands fondled my neck. As kiss followed kiss, my tension flowed away. I relaxed into the couch.

James shifted and slid me down until my head rested on the arm of the couch. He lay against me on the edge, trailing a hand down my back. Our breath mingled and I could no longer tell where one kiss broke off and the next began. I gave myself up to the moment. Nothing mattered but his lips caressing mine.

He broke off for a moment and smiled. "You may not talk much, but you sure know what to do with your tongue." His face dipped back toward mine. He ran a finger along my forearm and started a fire of desire. He cupped my breast and sighed.

My hands ran over his taut back muscles. I slid a hand under his shirt and his breath caught. He gave me a tender kiss, then sat up and ran his hands through his short hair.

"Wow, you are so hot tonight." He shook his head. "We haven't even had any wine yet. And I have another surprise for you."

At first, I was going to object because I wasn't ready to stop. Kissing James meant everything else went away, and I needed it to so much. I smirked. James couldn't keep his hands to himself when we were alone together so it wouldn't be long before we were making out again.

He raised his eyebrows. "That's a mischievous smile if I ever saw one. What are you thinking about?"

I tilted my head. "You."

"Perfect answer." He stood. "Don't you want to know what the surprise is?"

"Does it involve more kissing?"

He held out his hand. "If you play your cards right, it will."

When I placed my hand in his, in one tug he pulled me to my feet and up against him. His arms encircled me, and hands slid down to my butt and he kissed me deeply again. My pulse quickened.

He leaned his forehead against mine. "Surprise first. More making out later."

He grabbed my hand and led me out onto the porch. The night air chilled instantly. James strode to the big thing at the edge of the porch and pulled the cover off.

"A hot tub?" My jaw slackened.

He dipped his fingers in the water. "Perfect. I flipped the heater on when we got here. I thought it was probably warm enough." He put his hand in his pocket. "I promised you a chance to look at the stars while on the mountain. We're gonna stargaze from the hot tub while we drink our wine."

"But I don't have a suit."

He arched one eyebrow. "You've never heard of skinny dipping?"

Naked?

"Come on, Mel. It's just us up here. No one else is around for miles. We're facing the creek and I'll turn off the light so we can see the stars better."

I walked over and trailed my fingers in the water. The steam billowed from the tub. It felt good in the cold night air.

"You only live once." He gave me a rakish smile. "Be daring."

I narrowed my eyes at him. "So how do we do this? Strip in the freezing cold?"

His eyes widened. "Seriously, you will?"

"Surprised? Maybe I'm feeling a bit adventurous tonight." And maybe I needed something to help me forget—a sweet memory to hold on to when reality got ugly. I pushed my palm against his shoulder. "But you didn't answer my question. And I'm starting to get cold standing out here. You don't want me cold, do you?"

"No way." He opened the front door. "We'll change inside. I have some big towels."

Once inside, he grabbed a large towel and handed it to me. "You can go into the bedroom, first door on the left, to change. I'll be ready for you when you're done."

I threw the towel over my shoulder and marched into the bedroom. Once the door was closed, I slumped against it. Was I crazy? I liked James and had fun kissing him, but naked? Was I ready for this?

I took a deep breath. The reckless voice that had been with me all day piped up. Why not? It wasn't like I didn't know where James was trying to take this night. The roses, the cabin, the wine … at least he cared about me—not just a body to do his business with. This wouldn't be a guilty secret. I wouldn't feel dirty.

I refused to feel used.

Then why did my hands shake as I unbuttoned my blouse? Anticipation? It wasn't too late. I'd tell him I couldn't do it.

At the thought of the disappointment on his face, I shook my head. No. I was all in on this adventure. This was *my* choice and not something someone else did to me.

I stripped the rest of my clothes off and laid them on the bed. After wrapping the towel around me, I rejoined James in the family room.

He wore his towel wrapped around his waist, his chest bare. I gulped. I wanted nothing more than to run my hands over his bare chest.

He gazed into my eyes. "I thought you might have changed your mind." He opened the door. "I'm glad you didn't."

Standing next to the hot tub, I was hit by a bit of shyness. Should I just drop the towel? Why did I have to be so awkward? James might decide having a freshman girlfriend was more trouble than it was worth, and someone older would know how to skinny-dip without being so unsure.

"I'm going to turn my back while you get in. Then I'll turn on the jets and join you."

Oh, thank goodness.

When he turned his back, I pulled the towel off, draped it on the rocking chair closest to the tub, hurried through the freezing night and climbed in. Lowering into the water, I sighed. It felt so good.

The jets started.

"Whoops. I almost forgot the wine. Be right back."

He disappeared through the front door and returned moments later holding two full glasses. He had poured them half full before, so he topped them off before returning. He handed me a glass, then whipped his towel off and let it drop to the ground. I couldn't help but take a peek before turning my head while he climbed into the tub.

He scooted next to me and raised his glass. "To tonight and eight happy weeks of being together."

We clinked glasses. The wine had a slightly tangy taste. As it slid down, I felt the warmth spread from inside out.

"You can take a bigger sip than that. It's time to relax." James raised his glass and took another sip.

I looked at the sky. The stars were bright. Last night the clouds would have covered them. Tonight, the sky went on forever. I took another, bigger, sip of wine.

"That's it. You'll relax better."

The warmth from the wine and the hot tub did its job. The rest of the tension I'd been carrying around left. I could sit in the hot tub staring at the sky all night long. The only problem was the sun would come out in the morning and mask the stars.

Daddy always said everything in the world was Earth's reflection of the stars. For about the millionth time I wondered how the Grandfathers had taken him. Nothing but death would have kept him from me. But to never know how …

I had to block the past. Raising the glass to my lips, I drained it in a few swallows.

"Whoa, you don't want to drink it too fast."

I set the glass on the tub ledge and leaned toward James. Wrapping an arm behind his head, I pulled him in for a deep kiss. He broke off the kiss long enough to put his near-empty glass down beside mine. Then he cupped my face and kissed me.

I placed a hand on his wrist and pulled it down until it covered my breast. The intensity in his kisses increased. I let my hands roam over his back. He ran his other hand down my spine to my buttock and stroked it.

If Earth was a reflection of the stars, they must be sparkling bright tonight.

I tasted the wine on James's tongue and it mingled with the chlorine in the tub. I moved my hands to his front and explored. My heart raced and my breathing became heavy with desire. As my hand trailed down his abdomen, I accidentally went too far, and my fingers raked against his shaft. I pulled back.

James pulled me tighter to him and kissed me deeply while taking hold of my hand and deliberately moving it back down. When my fingers touched him, he moaned.

The jets turned off and the water cleared.

James pulled his head back for a moment and swept his gaze over my body. "Do you want to go in?"

Unable to look away, I nodded.

He kissed me on the forehead and hopped out of the tub. After he wrapped the towel around his waist, he picked up mine and held it out in front of him. When he wrapped me in the towel, he grabbed my butt and pulled me against him and kissed me. I shivered, but I didn't know whether it was from the cold or from the kiss.

Once inside, he led me into a different bedroom than the one where I had undressed. James turned down the covers, then dropped his towel. As he embraced me, his lips met mine and he loosened the towel so we stood naked front to front.

He sat on the bed and pulled me down with him. He stroked the hair away from my face while gazing in my eyes. Inching to the other side of the bed, he scooted under the covers and held them up for me to join him.

My stomach knotted. Would this be like it was with Hatchet? I didn't want to ruin what James and I had. But I'd come too far to turn back.

James brushed my cheek with his fingertips. "Don't tense up. It'll be okay."

He leaned over and I thought we were going to kiss again, but he took my breast and kissed it instead of my mouth.

I gasped. I never knew it could feel like that. My fingers raked up and down his back as he sucked on my breasts. His hand slid down my side, then to my inner thigh. My body felt on fire everywhere he touched. My breath quickened. When his fingers slipped between my legs and rubbed, it was my turn to moan.

James grabbed a condom off the nightstand and ripped the package open with his teeth. He knelt on the bed beside me. I took the condom from him and rolled it on.

He kissed me and knelt between my legs. "This is gonna be a night to remember." He positioned himself and entered me. Giving me a deep kiss, he started thrusting.

He grunted, but I heard Hatchet's grunt.

No, this was James. I wanted this.

Hatchet's straining face filled my mind.

I tried to focus on James, but my mind betrayed me and I kept seeing Hatchet. My body went rigid. James kept pumping away.

A tear escaped and slid down my cheek to the pillow behind. James's grunts became moans and his thrusting became frantic as he kept saying *oh yeah* over and over. Then his whole body shuddered as he came.

He slid out and collapsed next to me, panting heavily.

I couldn't stop the tears from flowing.

"Melody, what's wrong?" James used an elbow to prop himself up. "Why are you crying?"

The sobs wracked my body and I couldn't talk.

James hopped up. "What the hell?" He paced beside the bed. "You wanted it." He pointed at me. "You put the condom on me."

I couldn't catch my breath.

James strode out of the room. When he came back, he had his pants on and had my clothes. He tossed them at me. "Get dressed."

The disgusted look on his face was more than I could bear. A fresh wave of sobs erupted.

He put his hands on his hips. "Most girls like it. Are you some sort of freak?"

"No." I shuddered trying to get enough breath. "You don't understand."

"You're right. I don't." He shook his head. "You're supposed to enjoy it, not burst into tears." He threw his hands in the air. "Just get dressed. I'll take you home."

I had wanted this night to bury memories of Hatchet. Instead, Hatchet had screwed me again.

CHAPTER THIRTY-NINE

Spring 2015 – Melody, age 16

As soon as the lunch bell rang, Melody hurried out to the athletic field to join Kelly. Hanging out with him helped her avoid the whispers about her past. And her silence never bothered him.

When she rounded the corner, Kelly sat on the bleachers down by the track, strumming his guitar. Shoulders hunched, sunglasses sliding down his nose, hat perched on the crown of his head, he was completely immersed in his music.

Spending the lunch hour listening to Kelly play his guitar helped her get through the school day. Sometimes he worked on original songs and other times he played the well-known to the obscure. He reminded her of Daddy and the way he'd practice in the evenings. Kelly played an acoustic guitar like Daddy did, too.

He didn't hear her approach, but looked up and grinned when she sat on the bench next to him.

"If it isn't my number one fan." He laid the guitar across his lap and tapped his chin. "Now, what does Melody Fisher want to hear today?"

She glanced at her hands.

"No need to be shy. Request whatever you like and I'll kill it for you." He cupped his hand around his ear. "What's that? You want 'Every Heart Has Its Time To Fall'? Whose heart have you been breaking, darlin'?"

Kelly gripped the neck of the guitar and played the first few notes.

Melody stiffened. Maybe she shouldn't have come.

Kelly softly sang along.

No understanding
The truth ain't out
A bitter break up
What's it all about
There are two sides
To every story
For broken hearts
There is no glory

When he hit the chorus, she couldn't help it—she softly sang with him.

Making it public
A he said she said
Tears go to sleep
Alone in bed
When hurt, the tongue
Makes a fool of us all
Every heart
Has its time to fall

Tears streamed down her face by the time they finished the chorus.

"Oh no." The last note died away as Kelly leaned forward and used the back of his finger to wipe the tears off her cheeks. "Don't cry, Melody. I'm sorry, honey. I never meant to upset you."

Melody took a deep breath and tried to get her emotions under control. She hadn't listened to the song for a while. The hurt was still too much.

"Whoever he was, he's not worth it." Kelly wrapped his arms around her. "You let it all out … and then I want to know where you learned to sing like that."

The realization she had sung in front of Kelly hit her like a thunderclap. How could she have been so careless? She pulled out of his embrace.

"Whoa, darlin' … I won't tell anyone."

She searched his eyes. Could she trust him?

He put his hand over his heart. "I promise. Cross my heart and hope to die." His forefinger traced a small x over his heart. "You have a beautiful voice, but if it makes you uncomfortable for anyone to know, it'll be our little secret." He settled his hat more squarely on his head. "Now I know why they put you in choir. Thought it was a strange class for someone who doesn't speak. It'd be an honor to perform with you. Just sayin'."

Melody relaxed. Kelly was her friend and for once friendship didn't have teeth to bite her with.

Kelly took her hand. "We're friends, so I got your back. No worries." He grabbed his guitar and sang the chorus of "Stand By Me" at the top of his lungs.

She giggled, though the tears still stood in her eyes.

"Seriously, Melody, I figure you have a reason for staying silent and until you're comfortable talking, you shouldn't." He puffed out his chest. "And I got you to laugh. So there. Are we good?"

She nodded. The bell rang. The time always passed so quickly when she and Kelly were together. Like it used to with Vince. Before …

She pushed the thought away. Thinking about Vince was a quick trip through hell to regret.

Roger looked up from his tablet and pursed his lips. "You seem pensive today. What happened?"

Was he a mind reader? She should be able to keep some things to herself. "Nothing."

His eyes narrowed to slits as he studied her. "Nooo. There's something you haven't talked about. I sensed a hesitation when I asked whether you had spoken to anyone at school today."

She broke eye contact. Had she hesitated? She hadn't spoken. She wasn't ready to share what Kelly's song had uncovered. She'd already cried once today. She wasn't ready to rip that scar off. "I didn't talk."

He tapped his upper lip. "You did something to communicate. Why are you so evasive? You know you're going to tell me eventually."

"You're not gonna let it go, are you?"

He smiled and shook his head. "You know me better than that."

Melody strode to the window and looked out. The grass was overgrown. Roger should get the groundskeeper to trim it up. Although, their squirrel could run through the grass in stealth mode, ripples in the sea of green the only sign he was on the move beyond his tail bouncing above the grass tips with each step.

She bit the inside of her bottom lip. If she told Roger about singing with Kelly, then he'd want to hear the song, and the thought made her ill. But he wouldn't let up until she shared. Why did she always have to relive hell?

"I sang."

"What?"

The incredulity in his voice made her want to snicker, except she knew what was coming next.

"What song?" Roger spluttered. "Why? Wait, never mind why. I am so proud of you, Melody. This is a huge breakthrough."

He might change his mind. One slip didn't mean she was ready to be a chatterbox. She fingered her music player. She might as well get this over with. She returned to the couch and connected the player and played "Every Heart Has Its Time To Fall". Then she buried her face in her hands. She couldn't sing until the song hit the second verse.

Anger builds
Into screamers yell
Standing on
The edge of hell
No communication
Will make it worse
I don't believe
That love's a curse

Making it public
A he said she said
Tears go to sleep
Alone in bed
When hurt, the tongue
Makes a fool of us all
Every heart
Has its time to fall

Honesty could've
Cut it off at the pass
But regret in life
Seems to always last
Never forgetting
What you should've done
You continue to pray
But you still feel numb

CHAPTER FORTY

April 6, 2013 – Melody, age 14

Sadie screeched to a halt at the red light and took the opportunity to glare at me. "How did I get saddled with the job of taking you places?" She sneered. "And when did you get popular enough to hang out at the mall?"

I shifted uncomfortably in the passenger seat. "I'm not popular."

Sadie's anger blazed across the inches separating us. "I guess I should feel blessed you spoke to me. Is that your appeal to James? You never interrupt him as he's telling you how great he is."

My head snapped to face her.

Her dark-lipsticked lips curved into a smirk. "Do you think I'm stupid? He was after you day one." Her eyes flicked toward the light. "Did you give him what he's after yet?"

The light turned green and she put her foot down on the accelerator, throwing me back in the seat. At least it saved me from answering her mocking question.

My stomach was tied in enough knots already without her adding to it. James had barely spoken last night when he drove me home. And no matter how much I wanted to, I couldn't explain. Telling my boyfriend he wasn't the only one I was having sex with wasn't a conversation I could start. And I couldn't tell him why I'd cried because he'd be disgusted with me. Who would blame him? I was disgusted with myself.

I had no idea whether James would have had a chance to get over his hurt, but he hadn't canceled. At least Vince would be there to be a buffer between us. I buried my face in my hands. But Vince wouldn't be much easier to be around because of his feelings. Maybe I should have stayed home.

"Oh, please."

Sadie's strident voice cut through my thoughts.

"You've been dating James. You're beyond shame, so don't pretend."

One of these days she might tell me exactly what she had against James, but it was pointless to argue with her.

The tires squealed as Sadie turned into the mall complex. After dropping me off, she was going to her martial arts class a few blocks farther on. The proximity of her class to the mall was the only way Evelyn convinced her to give me a ride. I should have let Vince pick me up, but Hatchet always had a fit when Vince came around.

Pulling up in front of Dillard's, Sadie grabbed my arm. "Find your own way home. I'm not coming back for you."

My jaw set. Being around Sadie was a constant battle in biting my tongue.

When I hopped out of the car, I found Vince pacing by the entrance, hands shoved in his pockets and shoulders hunched forward. I bit my lower lip. He hunched like that when he was either freezing or upset, and it wasn't cold. James wasn't waiting for me.

I hesitated. Vince hadn't seen me yet, so maybe I should slip away. I didn't want to learn James had blown us off because of last night.

My shoulders slumped. As much as I didn't want to face the boys today, it would be worse if I waited to see them for the first time on Monday at school. I took a deep breath, smoothed my hair behind my back, and walked toward Vince.

Why did it feel like I was walking the last mile? Vince was my friend.

As I approached, Vince looked up and gave me a halfhearted wave. "Hey, Melody." He flipped his bangs out of his eyes, then shifted from one foot to the other.

Had he changed his mind about being my friend? I couldn't take that after everything else. I swallowed the lump in my throat and put a hand on his shoulder. "What's wrong?"

His brown eyes took on such a sad expression, my heart broke.

"Um … why don't we go to the food court and get something to eat? We can talk then."

It must be bad for him to not tell me straight out. "Shouldn't we wait for James?"

Vince turned away. "He's here. He went inside already."

His words felt like a punch to the gut. I bit the inside of my lip to keep it from trembling.

Vince navigated around the shoppers until we left the store and hit the main mall thruway. It was packed today. The conversations from passersby washed over me as Vince gently led me toward the food court at the opposite end of the concourse. Neither of us tried to make small talk.

As we passed the stores, I focused on the window displays, desperately trying to keep my mind from imagining all the terrible things Vince would tell me once we stopped. But then I saw the back of James's head. He stood outside the vape shop with a group of his friends. My steps slowed to a halt.

Vince tugged my arm. "Come on, Melody, let's go talk first."

"No." If James was breaking up with me, I wanted to hear it from him. I wasn't going to let him use Vince to do his dirty work. "You stay here."

I marched to the group of guys and touched James on the arm.

He turned toward me with a smile that faded when his eyes met mine. "What are you doing here?"

My worst fears were confirmed, but I had to hear it from him. "We had plans to hang out today."

His eyes took on the quality of hard blue marbles—cold and unfeeling. "That was before you proved you were too much of a baby to be my girlfriend."

His buddies nudged one another and chuckled.

I had to try to explain … but what could I say? "You don't understand—"

"Ha!" James cut me off. "You're right. I don't understand." His nose wrinkled as anger etched grooves into his face. "One minute everything is fine, we're having fun, and the next minute you stiffen up and it's like fucking a mannequin."

His buddies broke into laughter.

The redhead's eyes bulged. "Dude, you did an ice maiden?"

Flames of embarrassment heated my face. What had happened to the James I thought I knew? Yeah, he could be a jerk sometimes, but when we were alone, he had a softer side.

James turned away from me. "Too many girls are willing to put out to waste time with someone so frigid."

My eyes burned as they filled with tears.

James had high-fived two of the guys in the circle when Vince grabbed his arm and spun him around.

"Vince!" I didn't want him to get involved.

James's eyes barely had a chance to widen before Vince punched him in the jaw.

James reeled back a few steps before he righted himself. "What the hell, Vince?"

His buddies formed a wall behind James.

"Apologize, asshole." Vince clenched both fists.

James cocked his arm back. "Like hell. She had no business coming here after you told her it was over."

So I had been right. James had wanted Vince to do his dirty work.

Vince snapped his head to the left to avoid James's fist. "She didn't know."

James's jaw slackened and he faced me, his face a bright red. "Look Mel, you were different, and we had a lot of fun together."

For a moment, the James I knew peeked out from softened eyes.

He stared at the ground. "I … I just can't …"

I had to get away from him. If I started crying, I wouldn't be able to stop.

Rushing past the group, I ran pell-mell through the crowd, brushing against shoppers.

"Melody!"

Vince caught up with me by the planter in the center of the mall. He took me into his arms and held me tight. I burst into tears.

He stroked my hair. "Shhhh … You're gonna be okay." He pulled me to the planter, and we sat on the marble seat.

I buried my head on his shoulder and sobbed.

When the tears finally subsided, I sat up and Vince used his handkerchief to wipe my face.

"I know it hurts right now, Melody. But you'll see, you're better off without him."

I knew Vince meant well, but he didn't understand. My tears were about more than James. The loss of a boyfriend would hurt, but I had lost so much more. The time I spent with James was the only time I could forget about Hatchet.

Shudders cascaded through me at the thought of Hatchet and I couldn't stop shaking.

Vince rubbed my back. "Don't. He's not worth all this."

I gripped the seat edge and rocked. If I told Vince the shaking had nothing to do with James, I didn't think I'd be able to stop from spilling everything.

White dints appeared on either side of Vince's nose as he frowned. "Did he really mean that much to you? Why?"

The hurt in Vince's eyes pierced through me. "It's not what you think."

"You don't know what I think." His lips formed a thin line. "Do you even care?"

"Yes." The word came out in the barest whisper. This couldn't be happening.

"I thought I could do this, but I don't think I can." Tears filled his eyes. "Do you know how hard it is to console you because some jerk broke things off after you slept with him?" He sniffed. "My heart is breaking to see you torn up over someone who doesn't care about you when I've loved you—"

The words hung between us, dividing us like an ever-widening gap.

"Vince—"

"Don't." He held up his hand. "Don't tell me how you've never felt the same way about me." His jaw pulsed. "I want to be your friend. I'm not sure I can."

"Please don't say that. I don't know how I'm going to survive without you." My lip trembled. "You're my sanity." If I didn't tell him something, I'd lose him.

"It's shredding me … and all over someone who doesn't deserve you."

I took his hands in mine and gazed into his big brown eyes. "I can't tell you everything, but this isn't about James … not all of it." I closed my eyes to gather courage—mistake. Hatchet's face rose in my mind, along with the threatening knife he had used to keep me silent. I had to get out. I couldn't go back to the Hatchets' ever again. And other than running away, which wouldn't solve anything, there was only one way out.

I had to do it before I lost my resolve. "I'll tell you one day, and I hope you won't be ashamed of me, but I have to do something first. Can I borrow your phone?"

"Sure." He handed it to me.

"Thanks." I walked a few feet away so he couldn't overhear my conversation. I dialed the number and listened to the line ring. *Please pick up.*

"Hello?"

I took a deep breath. "Miss Prescott, it's Melody. I'm in trouble and need to talk."

CHAPTER FORTY-ONE

Spring 2015 – Melody, age 16

Melody poured the hot water over the tea leaves and put the lid on the teapot. Rebecca sat at the table with stacks of manila folders surrounding her. She had been working nonstop since they'd come home. Periodically, she'd grab a new folder off the stack, run her hands through her red hair and sigh.

While the tea steeped, Melody pulled Rebecca's TARDIS mug out of the cupboard, poured in some hot water, and swirled it around to warm the cup. The TARDIS cup always made Melody smile because it was such a whimsical thing for the no-nonsense caseworker she knew. And it was huge. She strained the tea and poured it into the mugs.

"You're tuckered, Rebecca." Melody set the TARDIS cup next to Rebecca's right hand and took a seat. "Break time."

Rebecca's reading glasses slid to the tip of her nose when she grasped the mug. "Bless you. You don't know how badly I need this." She took off the lid and raised the steaming cup to her lips. With the first sip, she threw her head back and exhaled. "Perfect."

After taking her glasses off, she laid them on the folder in front of her. "I've been so buried with updating my case files, I feel like I've been neglecting you. So tell me about your day."

Melody gripped her mug. "You don't have to worry about me. I'm—"

Rebecca interrupted her. "Hush. You are important to me, and I want to hear what you have to say."

The urge to fall silent overwhelmed her and Melody struggled to unglue her tongue. She had become comfortable talking with Rebecca, but every once in a while, she'd have a moment like this one. Fortunately, Rebecca never pressured her about speaking and would wait until the moment passed.

"Not much to say. Another day of school. Another day of Roger asking me to try talking to someone." Melody plucked at her napkin. "I feel like I'm disappointing him. He says he's proud of how much I've accomplished in a short time, but I know he really wants me to talk."

Rebecca patted her hand. "When you're ready, you'll say something." She smiled. "Then you'll turn back into Quatie's whippoorwill, or at least I hope so."

"I still miss Quatie so much."

"So do I, sweetie." Rebecca took another sip from her mug. "The other day I was trying to remember the special name she used to call you."

"*Atsila*?" Melody couldn't keep the surprise out of her voice. She hadn't known Rebecca knew Quatie had called her a special name.

"That's it." She propped her cheek on her fist. "What does it mean?"

Melody's lips twitched. "Mustard."

Rebecca's brows rose. "Mustard? Knowing Quatie, there is definitely significance behind the name, but what?"

"Do you want the long or the short version?"

Rebecca laughed. "Definitely the long version, but not tonight. I want to have more than two brain cells to hear this one."

"Okay, the short version is you can plant mustard almost anywhere and it will take root and grow. And she thought the mustard fields were beautiful." She'd have to save the story about singing the weasel calm for another day.

Rebecca studied her for a moment. "You do have a certain resiliency. And you've been through the wringer and have still managed to find good things to hang on to. And you are beautiful—inside and out."

Melody's cheeks grew warm. "I don't know 'bout that." She sipped her tea to hide her embarrassment.

Rebecca arched an eyebrow. "I do. All I have to do is look at you to know you're beautiful on the outside. And as for inside, I've never known you to deliberately hurt a person or creature."

Melody snorted. "Some of the kids I go to school with might disagree with you. Have you forgotten I'm being prosecuted for stabbing Troy?"

Rebecca tilted her head. "No. I happen to believe when you are finally able to talk about what happened, we'll hear a different story than the one he's telling. I have faith you acted out of necessity." She grabbed Melody's hand. "Have the kids at school made things difficult for you over Troy?"

She shook her head. "Some started to, but Kelly came to my rescue and shut them up."

"Kelly has been a good friend."

If she spoke to anyone at school, it would be Kelly. He had been there for her from the first day. "But I don't understand why. I don't ever say anything to him. Even I wouldn't want me for a friend. Who wants to hang out with someone who never says or does anything?"

"You don't give yourself enough credit. You're smart and beautiful. And maybe he knows one day you will speak, and it will be something worth hearing."

"I think he became my friend because he hates Troy Alexander."

Rebecca narrowed her eyes. "Is Kelly the first friend you've had since—"

Melody cut her off because she didn't want to talk about Hatchet or Sadie. Or even Evelyn. "Vince." But somehow, mentioning Vince hurt. He probably never wanted to see her again.

Rebecca leaned back in her chair. "You just shut completely down. It was like watching the gates of a kingdom clanging shut. What happened between you and Vince?"

Playing for time, Melody took a sip of tea. When she put down her cup, she had to say something, but what? "Have you ever done something you'd give anything in the world to take back?"

"We've all done things we regret."

"But what if you did it to the one person in the world you never wanted to hurt? How can you ever go back to the way things were?"

Rebecca frowned. "I'm not going to lie to you, sometimes you don't. Sometimes you have to make whatever amends you can and move on."

Moving on was one thing … forgiving herself was completely another.

"I can't imagine you've done anything to hurt someone so much you wouldn't be able to repair the relationship."

"I can't talk about it." Her hands shook at the thought.

"If you ever need to talk, I listen well."

CHAPTER FORTY-TWO

April 8, 2013 – Melody, age 14

When the bell signaling the end of school finally rang, I sighed and waited for my classmates to leave the room. They were all excited to be done with Monday and to hurry home or hang out with their friends. I had to wait for another placement, so a group home of strangers awaited, and after the weekend I no longer had any friends.

James and I had avoided each other all day. When I saw Vince across the quad, he froze, then went the other direction. I'd hoped … but I had to stop hoping. Hoping never brought any good in my life. Hoping only set me up to fall. So I had to stop or I'd fall again.

Five minutes later, I slid the books off the desktop and stood. What had I done so wrong to have nothing to look forward to in life? I shuffled through the double doors to exit the building and headed toward the parking lot. Most of the students had already left the campus, but there were still a few stragglers like me.

A boy behind me shouted to his friends to wait up and ran past so close he almost knocked me over. I kinda felt like that all the time. Like life rushed by knocking me over in the process. I fished my music player and headphones out of my pocket.

Getting away from Hatchet was a good thing, but I worried about how Evelyn would take it. Sadie hadn't been at school so I couldn't ask her. Not that she would tell me anyway.

I put the buds in my ears and turned the player on. Music always helped me cope. No matter what happened, there was a song to tell my story. Something I took great comfort in. I couldn't be the only one going through tough times. Misery loves company. Or was it something deeper of shared experiences?

Someone grabbed my hair and yanked it as I passed the narrow alleyway behind the apartment complex closest to the school. I staggered backward to release the pressure and they kept pulling. I tugged the buds out of my ears and accidentally dropped the headphones. Once I had been pulled into the alley about ten feet, a hand grabbed my shoulder and roughly spun me around.

I faced an angry Sadie. Her dark eyes the merest slit; her dark lips curved in a grimace.

"You couldn't leave us alone, could you?" She spat the words at me.

I clutched my books to my chest. I had seen her angry before, but never to this degree.

"What?" She shoved me with both hands. "Don't have anything to say now?"

Stumbling backward, I ran up against the wall.

Sadie poked my chest. "You had no trouble telling everyone about Hatchet, so don't go quiet now."

I tried to say something, but my voice wouldn't come out.

She knocked my books to the ground. "Do you *know* what the past twenty-four hours have been like?" She shoved me against the wall. "Do you?"

I shook my head, afraid to break eye contact with her.

"They took him away in cuffs. And Evelyn collapsed." The harsh words puffed against my lips.

"She's in the hospital. She was never supposed to know." The hatred in her eyes scorched mine. "Never!"

Sadie had known? I searched her eyes. Then a monstrous idea hit. "Did Hatchet …? You—"

Sadie punched me in the stomach and I doubled over.

"You had no right." She delivered another slug to the gut.

I coughed and gagged. Swallowing the bile rising in my throat, I straightened and tried to breathe. It hurt. "Sadie …" What could I possibly say?

"No." Tears welled in her eyes. "You don't get to talk."

She turned away and hammered her fist against the opposite wall. Her head hung and she clung to the surface, shoulders shaking.

I leaned over to pick up my books. Papers had scattered when the books hit the ground. One of the books had landed next to an overflowing trash can. The stench of soured milk assaulted my nose.

While I stretched to grab a stray paper, Sadie rushed toward me. Before I could right myself, she reared back on one leg and kicked my thigh. I crashed to the ground and rolled against the trash can.

"Don't even think about going anywhere."

Her black boots filled my vision. Pulling my feet under me, I tried to tackle her at the knees.

She skipped backward and I landed on the ground with a thud. She kicked me in the midsection.

Vomit spewed from my mouth. On shaking arms, I pushed up.

Sadie paced in front of me, muttering. Tears streamed down her face; black tears—hatred leaking from her eyes.

"Evelyn was never supposed to know. Hatchet made me promise." She spoke to herself as if she had forgotten me. "He trusted me. I never said a word."

I crawled to my feet, using the wall for support. "Hatchet had no right to so much as touch you, let alone—"

"Shut up!" Sadie whipped around, her fist driving straight toward my face.

I couldn't duck fast enough. Her fist plowed into my jaw. As my head slammed into the wall, white-hot stars flared against black. I slid down the wall, knees buckling.

Halfway down, I pushed against the wall to stop my slide. The blackness faded. Tears streamed down my cheeks from the pain.

My heart pounded. I couldn't feel the tears on one side of my face. I raised a hand to my cheek … and couldn't feel the brush of my fingers.

Sadie shook her hand and flecks of blood flew from the scrapes on her knuckles. Hands on hips, she raised her eyes to the sky. Her lips moved in silent prayer.

I straightened, using the wall for support. My breath caught when I accidentally breathed too deep. It felt like someone had run me through with a sword and twisted it. Sweat beaded my forehead.

She finished her prayer, made the sign of the cross, and raised her crucifix necklace to her lips. Her head drooped.

For a moment I thought the anger had left her. Then her spine stiffened and she turned, her face made demonic by the black streaks. Shivers sliced through me.

She had prayed to God, but the devil took her soul.

Her fist slammed into my ribcage before I had a chance to send out a prayer. I raised my arms to ward off her blows, but it didn't matter. Punch after punch assaulted my body as I crumpled. When I doubled over, she shoved me back and my head hit the wall.

The fiery stars and blackness returned. Then I saw her.

Mama reaching toward me, as beautiful as ever. I gripped my treble and bass clef charm and felt her warmth.

"No one hurts Evelyn and walks away. Hatchet family credo." Sadie delivered a final kick to my midsection.

Mama faded.

White.

White so bright it hurt. My eyes barely opened to slits. Everything hurt. A turn of my head sent a shockwave of pain throughout my body. A scream formed in my throat, but I couldn't release it.

Footsteps mingled with beeps coming from somewhere behind me. Several moments after a click, blackness swallowed the white.

This time I recognized the white. Overhead fluorescent lights. This wasn't my room. Why did I have something attached to my hand? My whole body still hurt, but the ache was more controlled.

I didn't like the thing on my hand. I reached across to pull the tubes.

"Melody. No."

Vince? What was he doing here? I turned my head toward his voice. Eddies of pain made me feel less woozy.

Flashes from the day sped across my mind. Sadie and the alley. Her anger over Evelyn knowing what Hatchet had done.

Vince held my hand. "I've been so worried about you." His thumb stroked my skin. "When I saw you in the alley, I thought my heart was going to stop."

A big drop splashed on the back of my hand. I opened my eyes to mere slits. Vince had tears flowing down his cheeks. My best friend.

"I called 9-1-1 when I couldn't get you to respond and I couldn't stop praying."

The memory of Mama reaching for me flashed. Had Vince kept her from taking me with her? I didn't want this life anymore. Every move made things worse. I could have joined Mama and Daddy.

Someone passed in the hall and Vince nearly jumped out of the chair.

"I'm not supposed to be here. The police were asking me questions like I did this to you." He sniffed. "Like I could ever hurt you."

A moment from the day filled my mind. Vince making eye contact with me across the quad and turning away. *He would never hurt me?* That moment had crushed me, and I couldn't let it show. I had to act as if everything was normal.

I had needed his friendship more than ever, and he abandoned me. Speaking out had cost me my best friend. He'd never look at me the same again. How could he?

No matter how hard I tried to do things the right way, people either hurt me or I hurt them and they left me. I had no one left. The words I spoke cost me every time.

I slipped my hand from his and turned on my side … away from him.

My music player lay on the table next to the bed. I ignored the pain as I reached for it. Music was the only thing I could trust. It didn't hurt and it wouldn't leave me.

I slipped the earbuds in. No more friends. They hurt worse than the haters did.

CHAPTER FORTY-THREE

Spring 2015 – Melody, age 16

Kelly picked her up outside her last class before lunch. He shoved his hands in his pockets and his shoulders hunched forward, guitar strapped on his back. He strode toward the athletic field, staring at the ground with a frown.

Melody nudged his elbow and raised her eyebrows when he glanced at her.

"Sorry, not feeling talkative today."

When they arrived at the bleachers, he climbed a couple of steps, then opened his guitar case. He ran through some notes in a minor progression and tuned the guitar while the breeze ruffled his bangs.

She'd never seen him upset over anything before. He took everything in stride and turned it into a joke. She climbed the bleachers and sat next to him and gave him a one-armed hug because he looked like he could use one.

He slapped the side of the guitar. "My dad and I had a blowout this morning. He's pushing for me to go into the Marines and use the GI bill to go to college to be an engineer. He said the Marines will make a man outta me. Can you imagine me at boot camp? I'll die." He gripped her hand. "And can you think of anything less like a musician than an engineer? But he says, once I graduate, I'm outta the house, so I'd better figure out what I'm doin'." He buried his face in his hands. "What am I gonna do?"

He was her friend and had been there for her. She didn't want to have regrets this time. Melody hesitated then took a deep breath. "Follow your dream."

His head popped up and he raised one eyebrow. "Did Melody Fisher speak?" He pulled back and put a hand over his mouth. "I don't believe it. Alert the press."

Before she had a chance to be embarrassed, Kelly pulled her into a big bear hug.

He whispered in her ear. "You don't know how much it means that you spoke to me. Those words especially." His voice shook.

They clung together like two lost souls. He wept and she trembled. She had spoken at school. The very thing Roger had been waiting for. Her life was about to change, and Melody would have to face the past to have a shot at the future.

What had she done?

After a few minutes, Kelly's sobs subsided, and he released her.

"I'm sorry, Mel. I didn't mean to have a meltdown on you. But you're the first person who believes in my dream. And if you were brave enough to talk, then I can stand firm against my dad." He wiped the tears off his face. "I'm so touched you chose to speak to me, I can't even say."

"I—I couldn't watch you hurting."

He gave her another quick squeeze. "Thank you." He put his guitar back in the case. "Lunch is gonna be over, so we'd best get to class."

Melody stopped and stared at the parking lot. Rebecca waited for her in the usual spot. She wasn't ready for what would happen next. She shuffled to the car, opened the door, and dropped her book bag in the back. Her head drooped forward as dread crawled up her spine.

"What's the matter?"

She closed her eyes as if somehow things would be easier if she couldn't see. According to Hatchet, nothing that happened in the dark counted in the light. He was so wrong. "I spoke to Kelly Garland today."

"Oh."

Melody had expected Rebecca to be excited, but she knew what it meant as well. The demons of the past would be unleashed.

Rebecca took Melody's hand in hers. "Everything is going to be okay. You're going to do fine."

She couldn't know for sure. Things could go wrong, and she could spend years behind bars. But Rebecca believed in her, though she had never told her what had happened. She never wanted to face it again, but she'd have to.

Rebecca pulled into a parking space and shut off the engine. "Do you want me to wait inside for you?"

Melody looked her straight in the eyes. "I want you to come in with me. Please."

She nodded. "If Dr. Kane says okay, then I won't leave you."

Her chest tightened and her breathing became shallow. "I'm scared."

"I know. We're going to get through this together. Never forget how strong you are."

"I'm not strong. I'm weak."

Rebecca smiled. "You are one of the strongest people I know. You've survived more in a few years than most people have in a lifetime. You are a survivor and you'll get through this, too." She opened her door. "Are you ready?"

Melody closed her eyes again and heard Daddy's words. *Soar like a hawk.* "Let's do this."

Lily's eyebrows rose when Rebecca ushered her into the office.

Roger jumped up as soon as they walked through the door. "Miss Prescott, so nice to see you. Good afternoon, Melody."

"I want Rebecca to stay today."

"Fine with me. Let me grab my tablet."

Melody went to her usual spot on the couch and Rebecca sat next to her and held her hand.

Roger sat in his chair and tapped the stylus against his leg. "So, why are we having such a special session?"

She bit the inside of her lip. Rebecca squeezed her hand.

"I spoke to my friend Kelly today." The words felt weird as she said them. Almost like someone else was talking, but making her lips and tongue move.

"Not special. Momentous." Roger's hand stilled. "I am so proud of you, Melody."

She couldn't contain the shakes any longer; her knee bounced and arms trembled. She gripped Rebecca's hand so tight it had to have hurt, but she couldn't let go.

"Close your eyes and lean back. Relax."

Melody did as Roger said … or tried. She pulled out the music player but put it on the coffee table.

"Take a deep breath. Hold it … now release."

He took her through the breathing exercise until she finally got her emotions under control.

"Okay, now that you've calmed down, let's talk about today." Roger leaned forward, elbows on knees. "Why did you speak to your friend?"

She thought for a moment on how to put her feelings into words. "He was upset and needed encouragement. I couldn't let him down."

Roger gazed intently into her eyes. "And how did you feel?"

A whirlwind of emotions blew through her. The ticking of Roger's watch filled the silence while she sorted through how she'd felt. "At first embarrassed, but then it felt good because I helped my friend." The sensation of Kelly's wet cheek pressed against hers flooded back. "And it was easier to talk the next time."

She pulled her gaze away from his. "Then I was afraid."

"I'm not going to tell you there is nothing to be afraid of, Melody. But I will tell you I have complete faith in you. If I wasn't certain you were capable of telling your side of the story to the judge, I'd say so."

Her heart hitched. She wasn't ready to talk. Not about Troy.

"Don't get riled. I'm going to take care of you through the process."

Rebecca let go of her hand and stroked her hair. "It's going to be fine, sweetie. Dr. Kane and I will be with you all the way."

Roger fiddled with his tablet. "Here's the plan. First, you'll tell me what happened on that day and we get you as comfortable as possible with it. Next, I set up an appointment with the judge and you, Miss Prescott, and I will meet with him and have a chat."

A sliver of fear slid into her gut.

Roger held up his hand. "Not about what happened, but to give you a chance to get comfortable speaking with him."

Her racing pulse calmed.

"This way when we're in court, you can focus on speaking to the judge, or if it makes things easier, you can simply tell me the story again because I will be right in front of you making sure you're okay." He leaned back. "It isn't going to be easy, but you have already come so far, I think you're ready."

Rebecca gathered Melody in her arms. "I'm going to be there the whole time with you, too. You're going to get through this. We'll do it together."

The inner shakes had come back. She didn't want to face what lay ahead. But she had no choice. The time had come to put Troy in the past and leave him there.

Roger picked up her music player, connected the speakers, and hit play on "Four Seasons". "I figured some calming music might help. So what happened that day with Troy Alexander?"

Soar like a hawk.

CHAPTER FORTY-FOUR

Spring 2015 – Melody, age 16

The bailiff called the court to order once Judge Grainger had been seated. Melody couldn't stop her knee from bouncing. Her mouth dried and her tongue glued itself to the roof when Troy Alexander took his seat on the right side of the courtroom. He'd brought a buddy with him, but she couldn't tell who it was. Troy's big, beefy body blocked his friend's. Troy sat and leaned against the chair back, legs splayed, and elbows resting on the chair backs on either side. He was relaxed with an arrogant self-confidence. His friend filed into the row behind Troy.

The sight of Troy twisted her stomach into knots. She avoided looking in his direction. What if she wasn't ready to face him? Would the judge postpone the hearing? Or would he get tired of waiting on her and base his decision on Troy's statement alone and put her in jail to await trial?

Rebecca patted her arm. "Remember the tricks Dr. Kane has taught you to help you relax."

She had been trying. Judge Grainger had been nice when she and Roger had met with him, but she feared he would turn into an ogre when she took the stand.

People trickled into their courtroom and took seats behind them. Every new sound caused her nerves to burn. Melody wanted to use her music player to block the noise.

Dr. Kane pulled at his collar to loosen his tie a bit. He caught her looking and winked. He leaned over to whisper in her ear, "Walk in the park, Melody. All you have to do is tell your story the way you told me, and the judge is going to rule in your favor."

They had different ideas about the meaning of a *walk in the park.* She'd rather be walking on the green outside his office and watching the squirrel and the crow fight over hidden seeds. Talking was overrated. Especially when speaking out could cost your life. She had been lucky with Sadie.

"Dr. Roger Kane, please take the stand."

Roger hopped up and tugged his suit coat into place. The bailiff ushered him to the witness stand.

After the bailiff swore Roger in, the judge cleared his throat. "Dr. Kane, please confirm you have been seeing the accused in a professional manner."

Accused. It sounded like she was already considered guilty.

"Yes. I started seeing Melody Fisher in a professional capacity when she was referred to me by this court during the last session on this case. She has faithfully kept her appointment every weekday since that time."

The judge made a note on the paper in front of him. "And in your opinion, not breaching patient confidentiality, is the accused competent to both stand trial and provide testimony here today?"

"Yes, Your Honor, it is my considered opinion that Melody Fisher is not only competent, but has a great deal of mental fortitude."

Troy gave a derisive snort and turned it into a cough.

"Thank you, Dr. Kane. You are dismissed."

Roger bounded back to his seat.

"Melody Fisher, please take the stand."

She rose and her knees trembled. Rebecca patted her back as she sidled past Roger. The witness stand seemed far away. Her heart raced and the pulse throbbed in her temples. Fortunately, she got to the stand before her knees buckled. When she took her seat, she looked into the gallery and her eyes met Troy's.

Troy leered at her with a smirk.

Her stomach heaved. He didn't believe she'd talk. Anger ignited. She wasn't going to let the arrogant son of a bitch get away with it.

Her resolve lasted until the judge spoke.

"Melody Fisher, you heard Dr. Kane's testimony that you are competent to speak on your own behalf. Your testimony will be taken down and become a record of your statement. Do you understand?"

Her throat closed, so she nodded.

"Please state your answer for the record."

Swallowing hard, she took in a deep breath. "Yes."

Troy's jaw dropped. Fear replaced the smug expression in his eyes. He turned around and his buddy hunched forward. Troy whispered in his ear.

"Thank you. For the record, please state the events leading up to the stabbing from December twenty-first last year."

The shakes came back with a vengeance. She took a few deep, slow breaths as she and Roger had practiced.

"Take your time."

The worried look on Rebecca's face was enough to give her back some control. Rebecca was there for her and Melody couldn't let her down. Folding her hands, she put them in her lap.

"On Sundays, I helped with the children's Sunday school classes. The teacher handled all the talking and I would help the children with their artwork and usually stayed after church to clean the classroom and ready the things for the following week."

These words were easy. The harder ones were coming up too soon.

"On that Sunday, one of the kids had stuffed toilet paper into the toilet and it overflowed. The janitor got grouchy when the kids made mistakes, and this particular kid had been going through a lot, so I promised I'd clean it up and not tell the janitor."

Her throat was so dry, her voice cracked.

"The mess was huge and it took quite a while to get it all cleaned up, so I didn't make it back to the classroom until everyone else had finished and gone home."

December 21, 2014 – Melody, age 15

The cold, wet hem of my dress slapped against my knees as I trudged back to the classroom. God bless, but Kylie was getting to be a handful. She had pressed her damp, still-grubby hands against the side of my head to tell me she had overflowed the toilet. Her hands trembled as she cried about the trouble she'd be in.

Poor little thing. I felt so bad for her because she was so young and going through some of the same hell I had been through. Funny. We were at church where the preacher spewed about hellfire and brimstone in the afterlife. The two of us were going through it in the here and now and no one cared. At least I'd had love and family for twelve years before being cast into the inferno of social services. But Kylie had hit the system too young and people wondered why she couldn't control her behavior at five.

A few weeks ago, Kylie had come to me during playtime and pulled me away from everyone to tell me what was happening at home because I was *safe*. I wouldn't tell anyone because I didn't talk.

I stopped at the doorway to the classroom and sighed. Today had been fun because we had made glittery star ornaments for all the kids to put on the tree at home, but Lord Almighty, the room was a mess. I'd better get started on cleaning up the disaster or I'd be here until next Sunday.

I stood in the middle of the room, overwhelmed. Glitter was everywhere and I didn't know where to start.

The only way to eat an elephant is one bite at a time. I smiled. I almost heard Quatie's voice because it was her go-to phrase every time I didn't know how to tackle a project.

Tables first, then the floor. If I started with the floor, then did the tables, I'd have to do the floors again. Besides, the glue on the tables would dry if I didn't get to it quickly. I squatted to pull the cleaning solution out of the bottom cupboard.

"Hello, there."

The deep voice startled me. My heart jumped and I spun and stood. Troy Alexander leaned against the doorway, an arm stretched overhead to prop him up. Because of the hour, I hadn't thought anyone else was around, except the cleaning crew.

He smiled when our eyes met. "I didn't mean to startle you." He took a step into the room. "What are you doing here so late? I thought you'd've been long gone by now."

My eyes flicked toward the carpet sweeper, then back to Troy.

He took another step forward and shoved a hand in his front jeans pocket.

Clad in his letterman's jacket, sweater, jeans, and boots, he'd had time to go home and change. Why had he come back?

Keeping his eyes on me, he took another step forward. "You know, I've been trying to get a chance to spend some time with you, but it seems like every time I come close, you run away." A lock of hair curled on his forehead as he came closer. "Doesn't look like you have anywhere else to be today."

The way he looked at me made my heart race. I couldn't catch my breath. He continued taking one deliberate step after the other. I felt like the little sparrow I had once rescued. Its heart had beat so rapidly, I'd seen its chest thump. Paralyzed from fear, it had watched as I approached, the thumps the only thing giving its agitation away.

Troy had always made me uncomfortable. The biggest guy at school, tall and broad, he used his size to intimidate others. Since Troy was the star of the football team, the entire school thought he was great, except those he picked on and me. I didn't want anything to do with him.

He had the same look in his eye that Hatchet had when he came for his late night visits. I searched the room for a way to escape. My back was pressed against the cabinets behind me and ahead, there wasn't enough room to get around Troy. His arms were too long and he'd catch me with ease. I slid to the side, not wanting to be cornered.

He shifted his approach to keep coming straight toward me. "I'm a friend of James Davenport's. We went to football camp together. He told me about your night at the cabin."

Confused, I stopped moving halfway along the art counter. Why would James have told anyone about what happened at the cabin?

Troy seized his opportunity, took a few swift strides, and stopped directly in front of me. He leaned in, placing his hands to either side of my head.

Trapped.

CHAPTER FORTY-FIVE

Spring 2015 – Melody, age 16

Her voice gave out and her breathing became rapid and shallow. Black spots dotted the periphery of her vision.

"Melody. Focus on my voice."

Roger. The black spots merged and grew.

"Close your eyes."

She did as instructed, and his dress shoes clicked across the tiles as he approached.

"You're doing great. But let's take a moment to relax." He kept his voice low.

Relaxation was the furthest thing from her mind.

The tippity-tap of Rebecca's heels sounded and a moment later, Rebecca gripped her hand.

Roger cleared his throat. "Pretend we're back in my office, with the squirrel and the crow outside the window and it's just the two of us. Then take a deep breath in, hold it for a count of three, and exhale."

She followed along with his words. Thinking about the squirrel's antics helped ease the tightness in her chest. He walked her through a few more deep breaths. The tension released its stranglehold.

"Now open your eyes."

He stood in front of her so she couldn't see anyone else. She gazed directly into his blue eyes. Rebecca kept hold of her hand.

"Better?"

She nodded.

"Good. Are you ready to continue?" He raised both eyebrows.

Her stomach tightened again. "I think so."

Rebecca patted her arm. "Take things slow. We're here for you when it gets tough."

They went back to their seats.

Judge Grainger faced her. "Are you ready to continue your statement, Miss Fisher?"

The real answer was no, but more than anything, she wanted to get this over with. "Yes, Your Honor."

She took one more deep breath and faced the gallery. Mistake. Her eyes met Troy's and the shakes immediately returned. She couldn't remember where she had left off. Her mouth opened and closed a few times, but no words formed. Judge Grainger was going to lose patience with her if she couldn't continue. She closed her eyes to block the sight of Troy.

"He placed his hands on the cupboards behind me, trapping me." The shaking intensified. She wanted to look at Rebecca and Roger for support. She turned her head so she wouldn't see Troy again and opened her eyes.

Rebecca nodded.

Reassured, she continued, "I couldn't move without coming into contact with him. I—I …" She faltered and came to a stop. Not even focusing on Rebecca was helping. She couldn't breathe.

A mist formed behind Rebecca. Melody blinked. The mist cleared and Quatie Raincrow stood with her hand on Rebecca's shoulder. Tears filled Melody's eyes. Quatie had a glow to her, and she smiled. The constriction in her chest lessened.

Another mist cloud formed behind Roger, much bigger than the one before. She couldn't see anyone through the cloud. The mist was opaque like heavy fog.

"Wait, Atsila."

Quatie's voice sounded in her head while the vision moved its lips.

Wait for what?

The mist cleared to reveal Mama and Daddy. Tears spilled over. She had wanted to see them again for so long. She had prayed to God so many times in the past, but God had abandoned her to her fate. They had the same glow as Quatie.

"I love you, Melody."

Mama's beautiful voice sounded in her head, just as she remembered it.

"We're here for you, sweetheart. You are strong like the hawk."

As always, Daddy calmed her fears from one heartbeat to the next. She dared not blink for fear they would disappear on her. And she couldn't tell anyone what she saw, or they'd think she was crazy.

Mama held a hand out toward her. "We've always been here for you, but you haven't been able to see us."

Though the ghost Mama didn't touch her, she felt Mama's arms surrounding her, giving her a hug. After taking a shuddery breath, she continued her testimony. Having her family there supporting her made all the difference.

December 21, 2014 – Melody, age 15

I attempted to duck under Troy's arms, but he caught me in a strong grip. I grimaced. His grip hurt.

He scowled. "You're not going anywhere this time. No more running away from me."

With his other hand, he cupped my face.

I turned away from his touch.

He gripped my jaw and turned my head back toward him. "Knock it off."

This couldn't be happening. We were in church. How could God allow this in his house? Knowing the futility of my prayer, I prayed anyway. *Please God, don't let this happen to me. Not again.*

Troy dipped his face to mine and kissed me, forcing his tongue in my mouth.

I gagged.

He smacked my face and knocked me against the counter. "Will you relax? We're just gonna have a little fun. I've wanted you for a long time."

As he kissed me, I found myself falling back into the old habit of Hatchet. If this was going to happen and I couldn't help it, then going along with it was the way to get it over with the fastest.

Except I couldn't do it anymore. Self-loathing overwhelmed me. I'd sworn when I told Miss Prescott about what Hatchet had done to me, I'd never let another man touch me without my consent.

Troy rubbed my breasts and slid his hand inside my dress. His fumbling touch ignited a fire in my belly. He wasn't going to do this to me.

While he groped and stroked me, I ran my hand along the countertop, hoping to come into contact with something to hurt him with.

I shuddered as he pressed against me and his hardness dug into my thigh.

Spring 2015 – Melody, age 16

Melody stopped and buried her face in her hands. She couldn't relive what happened next. Not one more time. No one should have to live through it once, let alone multiple times.

"I appreciate this is difficult for you, Miss Fisher. Please take a moment to collect yourself."

At least Judge Grainger sounded sympathetic. But Melody couldn't find her voice. She felt like she had in the hospital … like she may never talk again.

"Your Honor, may I approach?"

"Please."

When Roger reached her, he handed her a tissue. She hadn't realized she was crying. Mopping her face, she tried to stem the flow.

Roger leaned in and whispered. "Have you lost your voice?"

She nodded. It had happened a few times when Roger had taken her through her statement.

"You're going to get through this. I know you can do it. You've done a great job so far. I'm proud of you."

She wanted to smile, but her face twisted at the thought of continuing.

"Can you sing it?"

Sing? Melody shook her head, but a song welled up in her heart. A prayer to help her get through this moment. She nodded.

"You've got this, Melody." Roger returned to his seat.

She smoothed her hair back. Would she really be able to sing?

"Sing the song of your heart." Daddy smiled across the gallery at her.

She took a deep breath, closed her eyes, and lifted her voice in song.

In Your name Lord
In Your name I pray
In faith and love
I come to You today
May this not be
My final breath of air
In Your name I pray
The rattlesnake prayer

Down on my knees
You humble me
As the venom spreads
I will soon be free
Nothing for You
I cannot bear
In Your name I pray
The rattlesnake prayer

Not of this world

Do I want to be
With the devil wrapped
All around me
In You I'm strong
No worry no care
In Your name I pray
The rattlesnake prayer

December 21, 2014 – Melody, age 15

He grunted and ran his hands up under my dress. When he touched my panties, I gripped his arms to try and stop him.

He smacked my hand away. "What did I tell you about that?"

He slid his hands back under my dress and tugged on my underwear.

I crossed my legs.

"You wanna be that way? Fine." He stopped trying to pull them down and ripped them off my body. "We can either do this easy or hard, it's up to you."

When he moved in closer, I tried to knee him in the nuts.

He turned and took the blow on his thigh. His hand closed around my throat, cutting off my air supply.

I grabbed his wrist with both hands and tugged, but he squeezed tighter. My lungs felt like they'd burst if I didn't get air soon. Darkness descended and he loosened his grip.

While I gagged and coughed, taking in gasps of sweet air, Troy unzipped his fly and dropped his pants. He grabbed my shoulders, pulled me upright, and pressed me back against the counter.

He spread my legs and entered me with a forceful thrust.

I disconnected and escaped into music.

Stole my spirit … but not my soul
In faith and strength … I'm in control

Thought I'd never … get up again
Now I'm stronger … than I've ever been

No! Not again. Not ever again.

Troy grunted as he pumped away.

My hands scrabbled on the counter and my fingers finally touched something metal and cold. Scissors. I gripped them, brought them over my head and plunged them as hard as I could into his back.

Spring 2015 – Melody, age 16

Troy jumped to his feet. "That's a goddamn lie. Are you going to sit there and listen to her lies?"

Mama, Daddy, and Quatie Raincrow dissolved and reappeared, standing before me in a protective shield.

Mama's voice sounded musically in my head. *"Don't worry, baby. We will stay with you."*

"Bastard!" James stood and punched Troy on the arm. "You raped her?"

James? He was Troy's buddy? Melody felt like she was going to throw up.

"She came on to me." Troy's face twisted into a snarl.

"No." James pushed him. "She would never have come on to you."

"Order in the court." Judge Grainger banged his gavel. "Gentlemen, please take your seats or you will be found in contempt of court."

James had stuck up for her? Why was he here?

They took their seats, though James still glared at Troy with something like hatred.

Judge Grainger smoothed his hair and faced her. "Miss Fisher, what did you do after you stabbed Mr. Alexander with the scissors?"

She had to finish her statement. "He let go of me when I stabbed him, so I ran out of the classroom and straight to the main church building. I raced to the kitchen and crawled into the cupboard under the sink, hoping he'd never look for me there."

"Did he find you?"

"No, Your Honor. He didn't come after me." She had stayed under the cupboard for about fifteen minutes. When he hadn't shown up, she had crawled out and meant to go straight home.

"What happened next, Miss Fisher?"

"After I came out of the cupboard, I went back to the classroom and Troy had collapsed on the floor. I went into the church office and placed an anonymous 9-1-1 call. Left the phone off the hook and ran home."

Judge Grainger finished making some notes. "Why did you call for help?"

Troy stood, but the judge glared at him and he sank back into his seat.

"I called because I didn't want to be responsible for taking a human life. Even his."

"Do you have anything to add to your statement, Miss Fisher?"

"No, Your Honor."

He gave a nod. "Thank you. Please take your seat."

When she rose, her eyes met Vince's. He sat next to Kelly. He raised his hand in a half wave. She choked back tears. She had missed her friend so much.

When she took her seat, Rebecca hugged her. "I'm so proud of you."

CHAPTER FORTY-SIX

Spring 2015 – Melody, age 16

Judge Grainger studied his notes for a moment. "Troy Alexander, please take the stand."

Troy rose and slowly made his way to the witness stand.

When he had re-sworn to tell the truth, he sat.

"I'd like to clarify a few points of your statement before I make a decision to send this case to trial."

Troy remained silent but looked uncomfortable.

"You stated you had returned to the church because you had left your phone and went to retrieve it."

He faced the judge. "Yes, Your Honor. I wanted to call a buddy of mine and realized my phone was missing, so I went back to church."

The judge flipped through some papers. "Then how do you explain the fact that your phone was used multiple times both during and after church and prior to the 9-1-1 call?"

Troy squirmed in the chair. "Melody Fisher must have used it. She had it and the reason I went into the classroom was she told me she had my phone."

Judge Grainger straightened. "How did she let you know she had your phone? She spoke to you?"

"Yeah. She taunted me with having it. Told me she wasn't gonna give it back."

Judge Grainger held up his hand. "Wait a moment." He shuffled his papers. "Dr. Kane, no need to come up here, but in your professional opinion, is it remotely possible for Miss Fisher to have spoken on December 21, 2014, when she had not spoken to anyone for any reason since April 8, 2013?"

Roger stood. "Your Honor, based on my sessions with her, in my professional opinion, it would have been impossible for Melody Fisher to have spoken in such a capricious manner."

"Impossible or improbable?"

"Impossible, Your Honor. Miss Fisher could not have taunted anyone over an electrical device. She had been highly traumatized over a successive period of time and the probability of her speaking to anyone, let alone a random classmate, is so astronomically improbable, it trends into the realm of impossible."

"Thank you, Dr. Kane."

Judge Grainger peered over his glasses at Troy. "You've heard what Dr. Kane had to say. If she would have been unable to taunt you over the phone, the statistical improbability renders the idea of her using the phone ludicrous."

"She didn't have to talk to use the phone. They were text messages." Troy puffed out his chest.

"Young man, I knew they were texts, but since your phone had been surrendered for evidence at the scene, and you have not had it in your possession since that time, you could not have known unless you were the sender of the text messages." Judge Grainger permitted himself a small smile. "And you might want to remember we know what those messages stated and who the recipients were."

"She wanted it. The part about me forcing her is a lie."

Judge Grainger raised an eyebrow. "Mr. Alexander, at no time during your statement had you mentioned having sex with the accused. I think we're done here." Judge Grainger looked at her. "Miss Fisher, the court thanks you for your testimony. We appreciate the hard work you have put in to make your statement possible. I am dropping the charges against you." He raised his hand to summon the bailiff. "Please escort Mr. Alexander to processing. I presume Miss Fisher will be pressing charges against him."

Melody slumped against her seat, tears of relief flowing down her cheeks. She raised her face toward the glowing images of her loved ones. They smiled as they turned to mist and disappeared. Had she imagined them because she needed them so much?

Rebecca engulfed her in a hug. "We'll go home in a few moments. I have a few things to discuss with Dr. Kane and I'll join you outside."

Melody exited the courtroom and leaned against the wall in the hallway.

Kelly burst out of the courtroom and raised his arms in victory. Then he swooped forward and hugged her. "I always knew you had a reason for stabbing the prick." He kissed her cheek. "I have to run, but I had to be here to support you. I'll see you at school."

"Thank you, Kelly."

Vince came out next and hung back as if unsure whether to approach her.

Melody opened her mouth, but her throat seized up. *Not now.* She needed to make things right with Vince.

Vince reached her in two steps. "It's okay. You don't have to say anything."

He must have seen her panic.

He took her hand. "I need to apologize to you and hope you can forgive me for not being a better friend."

Same here. But her tongue kept her mute.

He stared at the ground. "At school after everything happened at the mall, I avoided you because I was embarrassed I had been such a bad friend."

My tongue finally loosened. "Don't … you were the best friend I've ever had, and I thought you were disgusted with me." She held up a hand to stop him from protesting. "I was disgusted with myself and thought everyone else was, too."

"Hey, Mel." James stood about ten feet away shifting his weight from one foot to the other.

When her gaze met his blue eyes, James took a step forward. "I'm sorry.

For everything. I didn't understand. I didn't know what you were going through at home. Sadie told me after Troy—" He stopped.

"I know. I couldn't find the words to tell you."

Vince shook his head and crossed the hallway.

James stared at the floor. "I'm sorry for what I put you through when I broke things off. I was an asshole." He glanced into her eyes. "I swear I never told Troy about the cabin. He heard about it from one of the guys." He looked away. "Maybe one day you'll find it in your heart to forgive me."

Over James's shoulder, Vince's face fell. He shouldn't worry so much. She was done spending time with guys who didn't care for her when a friend who did stood so near.

"I forgive you now, James." She hugged him. "If you hadn't been so harsh, I may not have put a stop to what Hatchet was doing to me. Not then anyway. So, in a way, thank you."

"I came today because the things Troy said didn't match the girl I knew." He squeezed her tight and whispered in her ear. "You always meant more to me than the other girls. When you froze up, it hurt me, and I turned into a gigantic ass to cover my hurt. Thank you." He kissed her on the cheek, then released her.

Vince kicked the ground, then turned and walked down the long hallway.

Melody broke out of James's embrace. Vince's slouched shoulders and shuffling stride broke her heart.

James put his hand on her shoulder. "If you care for him so much, don't let him go."

Vince reached the door before she could get the words out. "Vince, wait."

He stopped and faced her.

James smiled. "You can't let the good one get away. Thanks again, Mel." He shoved his hands in his pockets and strode off.

How could she tell Vince how much he meant to her? The emotions overwhelmed her and she lost control of her words again. Something in her brain clicked and she knew what Roger would tell her. Sing. "In Love With an Angel" had all the words she wanted to say.

He stood by me
When he shouldn't have
Lifted me up
When life was bad
Around every corner
His smile I'd see
No matter what
He was there for me

What I thought I wanted
Wasn't worth a damn
The lie who kissed me
And held my hand
But the truth was there
Picked me up when I fell
I'm in love with an angel
He saved me from hell

Vince walked slowly toward her, then picked up his pace and ran.

When his eyes spoke to mine
Nothing I couldn't do
Said our bond is forever
And I'll support you
Turned away from him
And I don't know why
But life makes a fool
Who falls for the lie

When he reached her, he scooped her up and swung her around. "I have loved you for a long time and I'll prove I can be your best friend."

What I thought I wanted
Wasn't worth a damn
The lie who kissed me
And held my hand
But the truth was there
Picked me up when I fell
I'm in love with an angel
He saved me from hell

As they clung together in the middle of the hallway, she sang the last verse with all her heart. Happy at last.

Never judged me
For all I'd been thru
Told me every day
I love you
Not realizing what I felt
Was with me all along
The guy in the shadows
Is where I belong

A Note from the Author

Dear Reader,

I always felt my characters come to me with their stories to tell, and I am the mere journalist whose job is to breathe life into them on the page. That could not be any truer than in the case of *Speak No Evil.* This was Melody's story from the outset, and my responsibility was to document it in the most compelling way and share it with the world.

I have always believed it important to write stories such as this. Women are more empowered to speak up today than ever before, but far too many remain silent—for good reason. Speaking up about abuse is not always met with support. Too often victims are met with ridicule and judgement, blame and shame.

I, along with many women, have personal experience with this. I chose to go to the police, though felt nothing would be done. I spoke up so the next victim might be believed. I spoke out because he took liberties with my body that he had no right to. I wasn't about to let him take one ounce of my self-worth. I did not *ask for it,* it was not my fault, and *no one* would say otherwise.

Not everyone has a Miss Prescott and Dr. Kane … I was fortunate to have a strong support network. For those who don't, for those who remain silent, it is not your fault. You are not to blame. My greatest wish is that one day you will find your voice and, with it, peace.

Liana Gardner

RESOURCES

If you are being abused or have been abused but have remained silent, please consider reaching out to one of the organizations below. There is help available and you don't have to feel like you are going through this alone. Organizations exist to help you without judgement, who have the knowledge and resources to get you the help you need, and will help you navigate through what can be done about your situation.

If you are not the victim or survivor of abuse, but suspect a friend or loved one is being or has been abused, please reach out to one of the organizations below to find out what you can do to help.

- RAINN (Rape, Abuse, & Incest National Network – National Sexual Assault Hotline – 800.656.HOPE (4673)
- RAINN Online Chat – https://hotline.rainn.org/online/
- RAINN Directory of Local Sexual Assault Centers https://centers.rainn.org/
- National Child Abuse Hotline – 800.422.4453

ACKNOWLEDGEMENTS

The act of writing may be a solitary endeavor, but it takes a village to breathe life into a book and bring it to publication. *Speak No Evil* is no exception. The idea came like a lightning bolt and hit me on my way to work on a clear, sunny morning several years ago. To be honest, the thought of tackling this book in the way it had to be written frightened me because I'd have to delve into things I'd rather not face. But above all, this particular book required something special; something I was not capable of writing. I am referring to the lyrics. It was so important to get those right, and I am not a lyricist.

To Lucas Astor—a HUGE thank you, for writing all of the original lyrics for the story. I hear each song clearly in my head, and they all brought tears to my eyes with how perfect they were for the moment. I am still amazed how you created those songs based on the limited information I provided. Without those lyrics, this book would not be the same, and hopefully one day we can bring those songs to life.

To Italia Gandolfo—my eternal thanks for seeing my readiness to write the story when I couldn't see it myself. Without you, Melody would still be locked inside my head. You have been incredibly patient and perceptive, and your belief in me allowed me to stretch beyond my abilities to put this story on the page.

To my mother—thank you for giving me the empathy to feel the stories I write.

About the Author

Liana Gardner is the multi-award-winning author of 7th Grade Revolution and The Journal of Angela Ashby. The daughter of a rocket scientist and an artist, Liana combines the traits of both into a quirky yet pragmatic writer and in everything sees the story lurking beneath the surface.

Liana volunteers with high school students through EXP (expfuture.org). EXP unites business people and educators to prepare students for a meaningful place in the world of tomorrow. Working in partnership with industry and educators, EXP helps young people EXPerience, EXPand, and EXPlore.

Engaged in a battle against leukemia and lymphoma, Liana spends much of her time at home, but her imagination takes her wherever she wants to go.

www.LianaGardner.com
www.SpeakNoEvilNovel.com